the
BOOKWORM
box

Helping the community, one book at a time

JACK & SADIE

JB SALSBURY

To my Fighting Girls

PROLOGUE

High School Graduation

JACK

Tonight is the night we've been counting down to for the last four years. The culmination of our adolescence, the big send-off into adulthood.

High school graduation.

As much as I've looked forward to my last days at Las Vegas High, these last few months, I've found myself wishing time would slow and the end would drag out a little longer. All because of one girl.

My girl.

Sadie Slade.

Our parents being best friends, we were practically raised together. I can't remember a single day when I haven't been in love with her. Even when she was an obnoxious little brat who would dress my Transformers in Barbie clothes, I loved her. And when she went through the awkward stage in middle school— braces, bad haircuts, and long, lanky legs—I loved her still.

As I watch her across her parents' backyard, her hair wet from the pool and hanging over her conservative one-piece bathing suit—yeah, you got it. I still fucking love her.

"Here." My best friend, Tanner, drops onto the poolside barstool next to me.

The guy is a doppelganger for Archie from *Riverdale*, but with brown hair instead of red. We've been friends since elementary school and are headed to the same college. The only difference is I got in on merit and he was grandfathered in—literally. His grandfather wrote a hefty check.

He hands me a blue Gatorade that's more vodka than electrolytes. "You'll need more of this if you're going to make it through this horrible playlist."

I take the drink and suck back a few gulps, unable to take my eyes off Sadie as she talks to our high school's quarterback as if he's actually saying something of substance for once. *She's a fucking angel.* "My girl loves her eighties music."

Sadie's parents had agreed to host the graduating class's after party. They had it catered by the school's favorite pizza place. There's a dance floor, frosty beverages in every flavor, and a DJ who spins all of Sadie's antiquated requests.

"You know, if you're not creeping *her* out by staring at her all night, you sure as shit are creeping *me* out."

I down another few gulps, feeling the burn as liquor warms my stomach. "Can't help it." I hand him back the bottle. "Look at her."

Sadie Slade is an amusement park for the senses—the way she moves, the way she laughs, the little shifts in her expression as she talks.

He chuckles. "Dude. You are so whipped. How do you expect to survive without her for four years?"

Those words deliver a blow to my chest so devastating it takes away the heat of my buzz and replaces it with that all-too-familiar ache. I snag the bottle back and chug it. "Don't talk about it."

Her ears must be burning because her eyes find me through the sea of graduated seniors. Her makeup-free face seems to glow under the strings of lights above her head, and right on cue, the piano opens to *our* song. "Can't Fight this Feeling" by REO Speedwagon pours from the speakers. She smiles, and I shake my head slowly, a big-ass goofy grin pulling my lips so hard I can feel the air hit my molars.

"God, you two are like a cheesy teen movie," Tanner mumbles.

I ignore his dumb ass. He's jealous. I'm used to guys envying me because they all wish they had Sadie, but she's only ever had eyes for me. How the fuck did I get so lucky?

With a slight jerk of my head, I ask her silently to come to me. Her answering smile is bashful and gets my blood pumping. She excuses herself from the conversation and slips away. Her long, lean body seems to float as she walks toward me.

I always thought she moved as though her feet never touched the ground and figured she'd be an excellent dancer. I was wrong. She hates being the center of attention and prefers hours alone in front of a canvas or with her head buried in a sketchbook.

As she makes her way through the crowd, she's hugged by girls and gawked at by boys. Despite her introverted approach toward life, she's loved by everyone who knows her. I suppose it should bother me, but it never has because of one simple and well-known fact.

Sadie has always been mine.

She stops at arm's length and eyes Tanner. "What's in the bottle?" Her gorgeous blue-green eyes come to me. "And why are you guys being anti-social?"

I snag her hand and tug her between my knees. She smells like coconut with a hint of chlorine. "It's only vodka, and we're not being anti-social. I'm ready for this party to thin out so I can spend some time alone with you." Even though her parents could be watching from any of the dozens of windows at the back of the house, I pull her tightly between my thighs and slide my hands around her waist. "Did you play this song for us?"

Don't grab her ass. I fist my hands at her spine. I want to be respectful. If I'm not, my mom and dad will kick my ass. That is, if Sadie's parents don't get to me first. But we're both eighteen, and we've been an official couple since Sadie's seventeenth birthday. So I keep my hands where anyone who's looking can see them, and she does the same. But as soon as we're alone—

"Of course I did. It's our song." She ducks her chin, and even in the low light, I pick up on her reddening cheeks. "Stop looking at me like that."

Loose from alcohol and feeling a little dangerous, I pull her closer and smirk. "How am I looking at you?"

Tanner huffs out a laugh. "Same way you've been looking at her all night, dude. It's embarrassing."

I don't take my eyes off Sadie and point at my face. "This? Is this the look?"

She grins. "Yes."

"Ahh, well. You should get used to it then. This is me looking at you and thinking about how much I love you—"

"Whipped," Tanner coughs.

"And I'm staring to get my fill so when I leave—"

She presses two fingers to my lips. "Shush! We're not talking about that, remember?"

I smile against her fingertips and kiss them before she drops them from my mouth. "I'm sorry."

"We have time. Five weeks before you leave, right?"

Four and a half, but I don't correct her. "Yep. Plenty of time."

Even though she's smiling, her eyes cloud over with sadness and I regret bringing it up. But I really do have an internal clock running on our time left together, and it's ticking louder and louder every day. If she felt half the urgency I do, she'd call this night quits and send everyone home so we could finally be alone.

She frowns, and I hug her close, sensing she needs it. I always tell her there's nothing she can hide from me. Side effect of growing up together, I know her better than anyone and can read her moods before she's even aware of them. Which is why I need to be strong for her. I'll keep it together and do whatever it takes to keep us together.

Sadie is mine.

She always has been and she always will be.

Nothing will change that.

I won't let it.

SADIE

At midnight, I changed out of my bathing suit and into shorts and a tank top to say goodbye to my graduating class. Needing time to wind down, Jack and I curled up on a cabana to look at the stars. I've never been the most social person, but I can fake it when I need to, and tonight is one of those nights. Socializing is exhausting when it doesn't come naturally.

The boy sitting next to me strumming his guitar? He was born with the gift of gab. He's never met a stranger because he falls into easy conversation with everyone and they become insta-friends. He's on a first-name basis with everyone from the Starbucks barista to our school's principal. It's by mimicking him that I've been able to fake it as long as I have.

Soon he'll be gone, and I'll be alone to forge awkward interactions without him there to swoop in and save me.

No longer in his swim trunks—pity, because the view was so nice—he's wearing jeans and a T-shirt. He turns to me with a warm smile. "Do you have a request?"

Snuggled together with only the stars and moon for light, I rest my cheek on his arm, relaxed and a little drowsy as he strums and plucks soft, soothing music. "What you're playing is perfect."

He kisses the top of my head. "Don't fall asleep." He peers toward the back of the house. "You think your parents are asleep yet?"

"Probably." My dad had his face glued to the window until the party shut down. I look up at Jack. "We can try to sneak up now."

He grins in that crooked way he gets from his dad—charm,

good looks, and people skills for days. I'm the luckiest girl alive. "Yeah?"

"We have to be really quiet, and you need to be gone before the sun comes up."

"You're willing to risk getting caught?"

"I am if you are." I heft myself off the lounger and he follows. We walk toward the house, side by side with our arms wrapped around each other. "You're the one who would catch hell from my dad, not me. To be safe—because I really don't want my dad to murder you—we shouldn't make out, but we can cuddle."

"We can make out a little."

I laugh.

"Your dad will kill me, but..." He presses a kiss to the top of my head. "It would be totally worth it."

Tiptoeing upstairs, we sneak by my brother's room and my parents' room, and we dart into mine. He leans his guitar by the door slowly as to not make any noise.

"I have to take a shower," I whisper as I creep toward the en-suite bathroom.

"You know," he says, following me but pausing in the doorway, his muscular arms braced above his head on the doorframe. "I could use a shower too."

As nice as that sounds, I give his chest a little shove. My parents catching us sleeping would be bad enough. Naked in the shower? That would most definitely get Jack killed. "You can take one after me."

Jack groans, and I laugh as I close myself inside alone.

One day we'll live in our own place and be able to satisfy every urge for each other whenever and wherever we want.

I think back to our first time together. We lost our virginity to each other on our one-year anniversary. Jack's parents were out of town, so we ordered a pizza and swam in his pool under the stars. We hadn't planned to go all the way that night, but one thing led to another. Making love to Jack was everything I'd imagined it would be. He was thoughtful, gentle, and aware, and every time since that has been equally as sweet.

Life with Jack is beautiful.

Which is why these next four years are going to be our first real challenge. The first significant obstacle to our life-long romance.

I step into the shower, and now that I'm alone, I give myself permission to think about him leaving. I try to avoid the topic whenever we're together because he'll read me and know how much I'm hurting from the thought of being without him. Keeping him in Vegas was never an option. He's ridiculously smart and driven. He's played every sport and he graduated at the top of our class. And so...

Jack is going to NYU.

I'll be stuck in Vegas, going to Valley Community College.

...Yay.

I dry off, wrap myself in a robe, and brush my teeth. When I walk back into my bedroom, I find Jack in his boxers and T-shirt, on top of my white eyelet comforter. He looks up from his phone, and his eyes light up when they fix on me.

I shake my head. "I wish I could see what you see when you look at me."

His expression grows serious. "I wish you could too."

I turn away before he can see the emotion bubbling up to the surface. "Shower's free."

His feet shuffle on the carpet to the bathroom, and the door softly closes behind him.

See, here's the thing. I have struggled with self-esteem since I flunked the color brown in preschool. Seriously, who flunks a color? I was diagnosed with dyslexia in third grade and attention-deficit disorder in fifth. From middle school through high school, I had tutors and worked with specialists and still only managed a 2.4 GPA.

No matter how pretty a girl is on the outside, she'll never be pretty enough to make up for what she lacks on the inside. And for me, I've always felt stupid. Never smart enough, always five steps behind my peers. Things that come so easily to others may as well be Sanskrit to me.

I slip on pajama pants and a tank top, then slide between the soft sheets. I must have been dozing off, because Jack wakes me as he crawls in behind me. His big arm comes around my middle and his nose goes to my hair.

I weave my fingers into his at my waist and squeeze them tightly. "I'm going to miss you so much."

"I'll miss you too." He kisses my head. "It's only four years."

"Four years is a long time."

"We've been inseparable for eighteen. Four years ain't got nothing on that. Besides, I'll be back every holiday and every summer."

I nod, not trusting my voice, and close my eyes to hold back the tears.

"Sadie." He pulls me closer so that everything from my butt to my shoulders is fixed to his front. "There is nothing in this world that will ever be as important to me as you are. As soon as I get college out of the way so I can get a decent job, my only goal will be starting the life we always talked about. Three bedrooms on a quiet street with an art studio for you to paint, a dog, and some kids."

"What if you meet someone else and—"

"Not happening." He slips his muscular thigh between my legs. "We were made to be together. No one will ever take your place, not in my heart or in my life."

"I feel the same about you."

"I know you do." He yawns and sinks deeper into our shared pillow. "What we have is the forever kind of love. Never forget that."

I fall asleep to him softly singing the lyrics to "Can't Fight this Feeling," and all is right with the world.

CHAPTER ONE

Five Years Later

JACK

"I'll tell you what." I stir my Bloody Mary and take a sip. "Being hungover in San Diego beats being hungover in New York any day." I tilt my face toward the sky. Even with my eyes closed behind my sunglasses, my brain registers the sting of sunlight, but the heat on my skin soothes the ache.

"It's the beach. Something about the salt air and sunshine," Tanner says. "Why do you think I agreed to fly all the way across the country to get married?"

We're sitting on the beachfront patio of a restaurant at a swanky resort and spa in Del Mar, one of the glitziest cities in San Diego county.

Our server approaches us, the epitome of a California girl with her sun-bleached hair, suntanned skin, and bright blue eyes. "Are you guys ready to order breakfast?"

"We're waiting on two more." Tanner checks his phone. "They're finishing up at the spa."

I hold up my nearly empty glass. "Bailey, if you could keep these coming, I'd love you forever."

She smiles bashfully, and I grin back. "Sure thing, Mr. Daniels."

"Call me Jackson." I watch her walk away, and once she's gone, Tanner shakes his head. "What?"

He shrugs. "I don't know how you do it. Chicks can't hold a conversation with you without turning bright red."

"It's because I'm nice. You should try it sometime."

"It's a shock you've managed to stay single as long as you have." He pulls a big green olive from his drink and pops it in his mouth. "I mean..." He chews and swallows. "Even Maribeth loves you, and she doesn't even like me."

I squint through my sunglasses. "You're saying your *fiancée* doesn't like you?"

"No. She loves my money."

I lift my brows.

"Not that I'm complaining. I love my money too. Most low-maintenance relationship I've ever been in. If I want to become an executive director by the time I'm thirty, I don't have the time to invest in a relationship based on emotions."

"Recipe for a successful marriage," I say sarcastically.

"If it ain't broke, don't fix it."

I hold up my glass, and he clinks his to mine. "Whatever works."

"That's right." He leans to peer behind me, searching the restaurant. "Where the fuck are they? I'm starving."

"Hey, isn't it bad luck to see the bride before the wedding?"

"Please." He leans over the table. "I make my own luck."

"Your humility is inspiring," I say dryly.

We drain the rest of our drinks as Bailey brings our next round. The sound of the waves crashing on the beach, combined with the cool breeze and squawking seagulls, puts me into a state of relaxation I haven't felt in years.

The last five years of my life have been a fucking rat race. I'd heard life in New York moves at full speed, but I had no idea how true it was until it became my life. In college, competition was everything. I was up against some of the smartest business minds in the country, fighting for the best internships and the highest grades. In New York, no excuse is acceptable, and if you miss an opportunity there are no second chances.

I busted my ass to land my position as account manager for Riot Advertising. The scramble to the top didn't stop there. I fight hard to secure the best clients with the fear that at any moment my position could be given to someone with better numbers. The struggle is real and it's never-ending. I suck in two lungfuls of air and slowly blow it out, hard-pressed to remember the last time I actually did that. Ya know, breathed a voluntary breath.

How fucked up is that.

"No, honey. I said *guava* mimosa. With *guava* juice."

I turn toward the sound of Maribeth's voice as she and Anaya make their way to our table. They look like Kardashians, almost identical with their sleek black hair, big lips, and breast implants.

I catch Maribeth's eye roll before she drops her sunglasses to her nose and takes the seat next to Tanner. "There are some incompetent people working in this hotel."

I have to laugh because it's ridiculous for anyone to call this place simply a hotel. Resort, maybe. Luxury destination would be more accurate.

"I said guava mimosa. Didn't I, Anaya?" Maribeth waits for her friend, who takes the seat closest to me, to back her up.

"That's what I heard." Anaya flashes her manufactured smirk, and I give a small smile back.

She's a nice enough girl, but for some reason, Maribeth thought she could push her friend at me over this wedding weekend. Everywhere we go, it's as if we're on a double date with the soon-to-be newlyweds.

"Exactly." Maribeth purses her lips. "This chick was like, '*Huh? Mimosa?*'"

"Babe," Tanner says, "it's not a big deal. She didn't hear you, so she asked to clarify. You don't need to crawl up her ass."

Maribeth gets pouty. "West Coast people are so lazy. In the spa, the masseuse..."

I tune out her bitching. No matter how much money Tanner spends, how nice the restaurant, hotel, or airline, she always finds something to be miserable about. I notice I'm breathing shallowly again, so I close my eyes and deliberately suck in air. Since when did I forget how to breathe?

"Better not screw up our wedding tonight."

Bailey returns with the guava mimosas, and Maribeth doesn't even look at her, much less say thank you.

"Thank you, Bailey," I say for Maribeth and Anaya, who ignore her to sip their drinks.

It's pretty fucking easy to be the nice guy when you're surrounded by assholes.

———

"Tell Simpson we need the proposal sent over no later than five p.m. Eastern time. No exceptions," I say as I pull the laces on my running shoes tighter.

My assistant Andrea's irritated huff comes through my AirPods loud and clear. "Jackson, it's Saturday."

The sun is high behind me and the glassy Pacific Ocean kisses my beachfront hotel room patio. "It is."

"Tanner's wedding day."

The corner of my mouth ticks up. Andrea isn't all that much older than me, but she lectures me as though she's eighty years old to my twenty-three years.

"Would you let me enjoy a weekend with my boss out of town? Please."

"Yes. After the proposal—"

"That isn't due until Monday."

She's right, but it's all about competition, being the best of the best, and nothing says our ad firm is better than the rest like getting our proposal in early.

"I want this account."

"I know you do, and you'll get it. I'll check in with the art department and see if..."

There's a knock on my door.

From the spic and span state of my room, it can't be house-keeping.

I open it only to have Tanner push his way inside. "Fuck, dude. Come on in."

"Thanks," he says, going straight for the minibar.

"Tell Tanner good luck tonight," Andrea says. "I still can't believe he's marrying that bitch."

I chuckle because it's true. Everyone in our office has had a front row seat to their tumultuous relationship, and when he announced they were getting married, the bets were made with two-to-one odds they'd never make it to the altar.

"Let me know the status of the proposal. I'll talk to you soon." I hang up and step close to my bed, where Tanner sits propped up against the headboard with a beer in hand. "What are you doing here?"

"Maribeth kicked me out for her bridesmaids." He looks around the room. "Got any food?"

"I'm going for a jog."

"You fuck Anaya yet?"

I lean back against the dresser. "You're kidding."

He throws me a slanted stare. "You couldn't seal the deal or what?"

"You're an idiot."

"Oh yeah? Well, those AirPods make it look like you've got two tampons stuck in your ears."

"Says the guy who still wears a bluetooth device that looks like a big dildo smashed against your cheek." I pull the Apple tampons from my ears and tuck them back in their case. "And I am not interested in Anaya."

"So what? You're on vacation. Why not have some fun, blow off some..." He motions indirectly to my dick. "Tension."

"I'm not tense."

"Sexual tension."

"I'm not sexually tense either."

"Is that why you're wearing your running gear and barking at your assistant on a Saturday during vacation? Because you're *so* relaxed and not at all tense?"

So maybe I'm a little tense. Work is my life. Even the part of my life that looks like a social life is mostly professional networking. Okay, not mostly. It's all professional networking. But I didn't get to where I am today by partying and blowing off *tension*. I got here by letting the tension build and feed my drive for success. I got here by working.

Not all of us have family connections like Tanner does. His grandfather started our ad firm and put in a good word for Tanner, who was accepted with zero accomplishments. I fought like hell and earned my spot as the youngest account manager in the company's history.

I snag my room key and phone, tuck them into my pocket, then grab my Universal Fighting League hat off the dresser and slide it on. "I'm going for a jog. It's my last day here and I'm not going to waste it indoors. Want to come?"

"Nah, man." He picks up the phone and hits a button. "I'm ordering food—yes, hello. I'd like to order room service." His eyes come to me and he grins. "Yes, charge it to my room."

"Asshole." I head for the door as Tanner places an order for a bottle of the hotel's finest champagne. I laugh as the door slams closed behind me.

Fucking Tanner.

SADIE

Running thirty minutes late, I pull into the underground parking garage of Perle de la Mer Resort and Spa, my red Honda Accord jerking to a stop. Driving from Hillcrest to Del Mar in afternoon traffic can stretch the thirty-minute commute to over an hour. I meant to leave earlier but got caught up in what I was doing and lost track of time.

"Always set an alarm!" I scold myself while I snag my purse, my black tie, and my apron, and slam the car door before racing to the employee entrance.

I punch in and groan, knowing I'm going to catch hell from my supervisor. I manage to slick my hair into a low ponytail as I race through the industrial catering kitchen to the staff lockers.

"Yo, Van Gogh!"

I wave to Jorge as I pass him in the kitchen. "I'm late."

"No shit. Garden room!" he yells at my back.

"Thank you!"

I throw my bag into my locker, and then I fix my tie as I race up two floors to the outdoor ballroom. The tables are out, linens on, and the bars are being stocked with booze and glassware. I search until I spot Ricky's bronzey-gold, stylish hair. I tie on my apron as I scurry toward him.

"Late again?" he asks with a smile. "Bernie is going to fire your ass if you don't start getting here on time."

I grab wine glasses from the rack and stack them behind the bar. "The traffic was really bad."

"The only time you're not late is when we're on the same schedule and we carpool." He lifts one sun-bleached brow.

Finally catching my breath, I level him with a glare. "You don't have to rub it in. You're always on time. I'm not. But I can't help it if there're a million other cars on the road holding me up."

He polishes glasses, but his icy blue eyes study my face. "Traffic. Right." He cups my jaw and swipes his thumb below my bottom lip. He shows me the blue flake he wiped from my skin. "You want to change your story, Pinocchio?"

I flick his well-defined pec, and even through his white button-up and undershirt, I nail his right nipple.

"Ouch." He rubs his wound, but he's smiling.

"Fine, okay." I grab a napkin and scrub my chin. "You want to hear me say it? I was working on a piece and I lost track of time—"

"Like you always do."

I sigh. "Okay. Like I always do."

"Which is why I got you the alarm for your studio."

I scrunch up one eye. "Are you *trying* to sound like my mom, or does this mothering thing come naturally?"

He grins, all straight white teeth and perfect lips. Ricky could be the poster boy for the Southern California Dream Boat. His golden-brown hair is the result of way too much sun, a tan for the same reason. He's dangerously handsome, smart, and he genuinely cares for people. When the cards were dealt in the game of life, Ricky got a Royal Flush. Me? I'm more of a three of a kind girl.

"Rick," our manager, Bernadette, says as she steps up to us. "You're on bar tonight." When her eyes come to me, they tighten. "Sadie, you'll be serving champagne until dinner service."

"Okay." *Please don't notice I was late.*

She scribbles something on her clipboard. "Set the tables."

I drop what I'm doing and nod. "Okay."

When she walks away, I blow out a relieved breath.

"Oh, and Ms. Slade? You'll be closing, ya know, since you were the last one here."

Crap.

Before I can say okay, she stomps off.

———

I've worked a ton of weddings in this hotel over the last two years, and all of them have been extravagant. The resort's six-hundred-dollar-a-night room rate attracts only the richest guests, and tonight's wedding speaks to that.

Not that I'm complaining.

The wedding is being held outdoors on the manicured lawn that overlooks the ocean, and the reception is in our most intimate rental room with glass walls and one hundred and eighty degree views. As if those things alone don't make any wedding a five-star event, this particular wedding takes pretention to a whole new level.

"How much do you think that cost?" I mumble to Ricky, who's dressing the tables with me.

He follows my gaze to the ceiling, where the over-the-top crystal chandelier is currently surrounded by a gigantic hanging garden of exotic, pale pink flowers I've never seen before. "Best guess? Way too much."

"They look like some kind of hibiscus-wisteria hybrid."

He shakes his head. "No clue what that would even look like."

"What kind of person spends money to decorate a ceiling?" I rub my tickling nose. "I can't even look at it for long without getting a pinch in my neck."

Ricky bumps me with his hip to get me to move to the next table. He leans in and whispers, "Waste of money if you ask me."

We go to work on the next table set for eight. "If this is how they dress the ceiling, can you imagine what the centerpieces will look like?" I run my hand along the silk tablecloth while Ricky checks its placement.

"A monstrosity no doubt." He winks at me, and we share a secret laugh as hotel staff, lighting specialists, and decorators scurry about the space. "You're saying, if all this"—he twirls his finger around—"was offered to you, you wouldn't take it?"

"I'd rather keep the money and go on vacation or buy a house." I snag the next table linen from its hanger. "Not that all this would ever be an option for me. I can't imagine a person who has access to this kind of money is a nice person."

The space fills with Ricky's warm laughter. "That's funny coming from you, little rich girl."

"I'm not rich." I sniff and take another swipe at my nose.

"No, but your parents are."

I shrug. "It's not the same. My mom was dirt poor her entire life until she met my dad, and sure he has money, but only because he worked his butt off for it."

"You assume the person who could afford all this didn't work his ass off for it." He lifts a brow. "Is that fair?"

I take one more look around the space, the hanging garden above our heads, the custom flooring brought in to make everything white, and the seven-tier cake covered in gold flowers. "Maybe not, but it's accurate. People who work hard for their money see the value in it and don't throw it away on things like this."

He shrugs, and we move on to the next table. "I see your point. At least it seems they're keeping it small. Only eighty people."

"True." We drape the table linen over the eight-top round. "Which makes me think the bride and groom aren't local."

"Why do you say that?"

"They'd be forced to invite everyone they know, ya know, keeping up appearances and all."

"See? You *are* smart."

I scratch the corner of my eye. "Street smart."

Ricky knows about my learning disabilities, but that never stops him from reminding me that school smarts aren't everything.

There's a commotion across the room as a team of twenty florists trail inside carrying centerpieces that have to be close to four feet tall. It takes three people to set each one on the table.

I grab one of the table napkins and dab my watery eye.

"Oh shit," Ricky mumbles.

I rub the end of my nose. "What?"

His brows are high. "I think I know what kind of flowers those are."

I'm about to ask him what he means when I register the burn in my eyes.

"Lilies," he says with a low grumble.

I turn my head in time to shoulder a fierce sneeze. "Great."

CHAPTER TWO

JACK

Tanner and Maribeth's ceremony went as well as could be expected. I stood to Tanner's left while he repeated the vows and gave her a diamond big enough to take her straight to the bottom if she falls in the ocean. The sunset kissed the horizon as they were pronounced husband and wife.

I couldn't wait to get to the reception and get a drink. My tuxedo is designer and well made, but it's still black. I was ready for some AC and an ice-cold beverage.

After wedding photos that lasted forever, Tanner's brother Nick, golfing buddy Jerome, cousin George, and I were announced at the reception with our respective bridesmaids. Now, finally, I am mostly free of my best man obligations. At least until it's time for the speech.

I find a spot at the bar and order a whiskey and Coke while Tanner and Maribeth make their rounds. The room looks like something out of a fairytale dream world, which doesn't surprise me. Members of New York's upper elite have two rules they live by: success is mandatory and appearance is everything.

"Hey, stranger." Anaya steps close to me, pushing her chest

into my personal space. Her black hair is curled and hangs loose
around slender shoulders. Her face is so made up that she actually looks different. Not necessarily in a bad way, but in a plastic
way. "What does a person have to do to get a drink around
here?"

I open my mouth to tell her all she has to do is tell the man
behind the bar what she wants, but that seems dickish. "What
can I get for you?"

"Champagne, please."

At least she said please.

I turn to the bartender and order for her while she's standing
three inches from me. Why do some women do this? Make
themselves appear helpless when they're not?

I hand her the glass, and she presses it to her glossy lips. I
look away, not wanting her to get the wrong idea. If there's one
thing I've learned about Anaya, she takes even the slightest kindness to mean more than it does.

"Did you see Maribeth's mom's dress?" she says close to my
ear. "She bought it from Sears." She snickers in the most unat-
tractive way. "You know Maribeth doesn't come from money,
right?"

I ignore her last question because it's fucking gross. "She
looks fine to me."

In an attempt to put some distance between us, I turn
around and lean my elbows on the bar, giving her my back and
hoping she takes the hint.

She doesn't. She only moves closer. "You're a guy. You don't
get it. Wearing a dress like that to a wedding of this caliber is
trashy."

"It's a wedding, not New York fashion week." I roll my eyes.

The bartender clears his throat, or maybe chuckles. All I
know is when I look up, it seems as if he's holding back a smile.

"Maribeth is so embarrassed about it," she says from behind
her champagne glass.

I drop my chin and groan only to have my attention called to my drink as the bartender tops it off with another shot of whiskey. "Thanks, man."

He lifts a brow toward Anaya, who's studying the guests for her next fashion victim. "No problem. Looks like you're gonna need it."

I laugh and shake my head. "No shit."

"Oh my *gawd*, Tanner's aunt is wearing white shoes—"

"I'm going to go say hi to... someone." I grab my drink. "I'll be back." No I won't.

"But—"

I lift my chin to the bartender and mouth *Good luck,* and he grins and shakes his head. I actually feel sorry for him. Good-looking guy like that stuck behind an open bar with Anaya? She'll have her claws in him before dinner is served.

I'm grabbed by Tanner's grandmother, who looks in desperate need of an interruption. When I see who she's talking to, I understand why. Pete McMillan from our advertising firm loves the sound of his own voice.

"Jackson, it's lovely to see you." Her eyes are wide in a *save me* way.

"Mrs. Haute, it's nice to see you too." I hook her hand around my elbow before addressing Pete. "If you don't mind, I need to steal the grandmother of the groom for a bit."

I don't wait for him to okay it before I guide her to the table where Tanner's family will be seated.

"Thank you," she says under her breath. "I love my grandson, but I can't stand these uppity rich people."

That makes me laugh. Tanner's family has money, but after his mom died of cancer, his grandmother moved to Vegas to help out. His dad threw his grief into work, moved to New York, and only saw Tan on holidays. Even though Tanner's grandmother had plenty of money, she still shopped at Walmart and Target and clipped coupons. I always respected her for that.

"I'm with you." Except I'm working to become one of those rich people, minus the uppity part.

"How are your parents?"

"Good. Still working together at the UFL. My dad's training fighters and my mom basically runs the place. Happy as always."

"Send them my love when you see them."

"I will." I frown, trying to remember the last time I saw them. I've been meaning to get home but haven't been able to take the time to do it.

"And your sister?"

"Axelle's good. She and Killian have three kids. He's still with the UFL, and she does her massage therapy stuff."

"Oh, that's wonderful." Her gaze slides around to take in the room's abundance and settles on the garden hanging from the ceiling. "This is... over the top."

"That's Tanner for you."

Her warm gaze settles on mine. "And how about you? Any wedding bells in your future?"

I sip my drink and chuckle. "Nope. Not unless it's possible to marry your job."

"Nonsense." She squeezes my forearm. "Life is way too short. Don't be like Tanner's grandfather looking back at seventy and realizing he forgot to live."

I do that thing where I take an intentional breath and realize Mrs. Haute is right. I don't want to be that guy, but I'm only twenty-three years old. I've got plenty of time to live *after* I make my millions.

The image of one particular brunette shoots through my mind without permission, but then, she always does when I think about any kind of future that involves marriage and kids. Because she was the last woman I loved and the only woman I swore to love forever.

Funny how time changes everything.

SADIE

I pull the Kleenex out of my nose and toss it into the employee bathroom trash before checking my reflection one more time. My eyes are still glassy and the skin around them puffy. My nose is red, but at least I can breathe and my headache has dulled a little.

I finished setting up the reception hall as the lilies waged a take-no-prisoners war that left me a snotty, sneezing, puffy-faced mess. Ricky insisted I go to the gift shop for some allergy meds and told me to hang out until they kicked in because "the last thing we need is you dressing the salads in your snot." He had a point.

Thirty-eight minutes later, I smooth my ponytail and make my way back to the party. I cinch my apron tighter and straighten the cuffs of my button-down. My bow tie is centered, and when I push through to the reception hall, the place is filled. I head to the bar where I left Ricky. He's listening to a woman talk—one of the bridesmaids, I assume, judging by her dusty rose dress that matches the room's accent décor.

Ricky's eyes catch mine and he excuses himself from the conversation. "Hey, you feeling better?"

"Much." I grab a tray and load it with champagne glasses before filling them each carefully. "Let's just hope the meds hold. How many of those death flowers do you think are in this place?"

"Besides the ones dripping from the ceiling, I counted thirty at each table, so three hundred."

My nose twitches at their mention. "I'm going to dose up again in a couple hours." I hoist the drinks on one hand to take them around and offer them to guests. "If I don't forget."

Ricky winks and uncorks a bottle of red wine. "I won't let you forget."

I head off to the right and make my way around the edge of the room. I'm a little late with the champagne—most people already have a drink in hand—but this crowd seems to be the partying type. Most everyone takes a glass of champagne anyway.

I spot an older lady sitting at a table alone and without a drink. I head over to offer her champagne before I realize she's not alone. A man standing nearby is talking with her, seeming to block her from the rest of the party with his tall body and broad shoulders.

I scoot around to her opposite side. "Can I offer you a glass of champagne?"

She smiles at me and there's something familiar about her face. I just can't put my finger on—

"Sadie?"

My posture stiffens. She didn't say my name, but the voice that did makes my skin tingle, leaving no question as to who he is. My heart pounds a little harder, my stomach flutters, and my palms sweat.

The older woman's gaze narrows on me. "Sadie Slade, is that you?"

I stand to my full height, some part of my higher reasoning taking over and telling me that yes, indeed, I have crashed head-first into my past and there is no way to avoid it. So I tilt my head and smile. "Hey, Jack. It's been a long time." Why is my voice so high?

Jack steps close as he puts his hand on the older woman's shoulder. "Sadie. I can't believe it. I haven't seen you since..." His smile falls a little.

He's only gotten more beautiful with age. The angles of his face are more defined, what was once a boyish twinkle in his eye is now a seductive glint, and that smile. Well, he mastered the crooked, cocky smile in kindergarten, and it seems he's been perfecting it ever since.

My hand holding the tray shakes, so I set it on the table and clear my throat. "Christmas. Over a year ago."

He flinches, and his eyes narrow. "Really? That long ago, huh?"

Nice to see our last in-person interaction left an impression. I ball my fists and my teeth grind together as I bite back a shitty response.

"I'm Debbie Haute," the older woman interrupts, as if sensing the tension. "I'm Tanner's grandmother." She offers her hand.

I take it to be polite, though I want to run like hell. "I thought you looked familiar."

"Tanner stopped having people over to the house once he got to high school, but I remember you came to his thirteenth birthday party."

"I did. Yeah."

Debbie's gaze jumps between Jack and me as an uncomfortable silence builds.

"I better get—"

"You work here?"

There's nothing wrong with the way Jack asks the question, but I can't help but hear condescension drip from the words.

"No, I like dressing in shirt-and-tie to crash fancy weddings." My eyes wander the room, searching for an out, anything to get me away. "Call it a hobby."

He frowns. "How did I not know you work here?"

Last he knew I lived in San Diego and worked cleaning brushes in the art department at my community college. He'd never expect to see someone like me in a place as upper-class as Perle de la Mer in Del Mar. Clearly he's never even asked about me or my parents would've told him.

I shrug. "How would you know?"

The better question is how did I not know this was Tanner Haute's wedding? I gather my tray back into my arms, handing a glass of champagne to Debbie then Jack. He takes the glass and our fingers brush, leaving a tingling that makes me want to wipe them on my apron.

"Dinner service is starting soon."

"Wait!" Jack scampers around me so my choices are to stop walking or smack my forehead on his chest. He has a drink in each hand, but doesn't seem to notice or care as his green eyes refuse to let go of mine.

I'm grateful when someone walks by so I can pull my eyes away and smile. After all, I'm the one working. I'm just doing my job.

"Are you upset? Your eyes. Have you been crying?" His eyes travel around my face, and I imagine what he must be seeing.

He's forgotten. I guess I can't expect him to remember tiny details like my allergies since we broke up. "Of course not. I'm fine."

"Are you upset with me?"

"What? No." My sinuses burn. My chest aches. "I have to get back to work."

"We should get together, you know, to catch up?" He acts casual, unaffected, but I see a flicker of hope in his green eyes.

No. We shouldn't. I have zero desire to take a stroll down memory lane. "I'm pretty busy this week."

"It would have to be tonight. I leave for New York in the morning."

"Oh, you're still in New York?" Yep, totally knew that, but he doesn't need to know that. "I'm working until late. I don't think—"

The band announces it's time for the guests to take their seats for dinner service.

"What time do you get off?"

Dammit. "I'm usually done at three."

That's a lie. We shut things down at midnight.

"I'll wait up. Where can we meet? In the lobby? Or you could come to my room and—"

"Jack." I'm already shaking my head. "I'm not going to come to your room, and I'll be exhausted."

"Fine, tell me where you'll be and I'll meet you there."

"I—"

"Sadie, please." He steps closer, and I get the feeling if he didn't have a drink in each hand, he would try to touch me. "Even if only to walk you to your car."

A flicker of anger stirs in my gut, chasing away any excitement or nervousness I felt when I first saw him. "We haven't spoken in over a year. Now you decide you want to talk to me and it has to be tonight?" Everything has always been about Jack on Jack's terms. Well, not anymore. I'm not the same girl he once knew. "No. I'm sorry."

The woman I recognize from Ricky's bar pushes up next to Jack, linking her arm in his and plucking the glass of champagne from his hand. "Jackson, if I didn't know better, I'd think you were trying to get me drunk." She leans into him, lustful eyes on his lips.

He blinks, his shoulders straighten, and he clears his throat as if replacing the mask he'd let slip unknowingly. "Anaya—"

"I'm not that easy." She winks and slips her hand into his, interlacing their fingers. "Come on, let's go grab our seats."

I always wondered what kind of woman Jack would move on to after we broke up. What kind of woman would attract him? I thought he'd go for a blonde—

"Hello, do you speak English?" She snaps her fingers in my face. "Can you please bring Jackson another whiskey and Coke?" She mouths each word like if I wasn't an English speaker, her slow speech would help me understand.

I glare at Jack as he leans toward her and mumbles, "It's okay, Anaya. I'm good."

"No, you're not. You need another drink." She lifts a brow at me as if to ask which part of her demand I did not understand.

Jack looks at me apologetically.

I storm off and leave him to his female barnacle.

God, she's beautiful. Probably graduated with some fancy degree from some even fancier college. I'm sure her and *Jackson* sit around talking about microeconomics and rocket science and... other academic shit. I'm not even smart enough to come up with legitimate hypothetical smart stuff!

Stupid Sadie.

I head toward the back and grab plates for the first of five courses.

It's going to be a long night.

JACK

"This food cost a fortune and you'd rather drink your dinner?" Tanner drops his fork on his plate and glares at mine, which hasn't been touched.

"I'm not hungry."

"Dude. You're always fucking hungry."

I don't want to eat because that would mean I'd have to lower my eyes to my plate rather than watch Sadie as she moves around the room. I had forgotten how much I loved watching her. It sounds creepy, I know. But watching Sadie move and interact with people is like watching waves roll to shore or the dancing flames of a fire. Relaxing. Mesmerizing. Her fluid movements and genuine smile always managed to soothe my frayed edges. I keep thinking she'll eventually look up, catch me watching, and we'll share a moment that'll end in me calling her over. She'll grin and blush and when she—

"Holy shit, I thought I recognized that look on your face. Is that Sadie Slade?"

Sadie is clearing plates and laughing with guests.

"She hasn't changed much," Tanner says.

That's a lie. She has changed. The angles of her cheekbones and delicate jaw are more prominent. Even pulled back in a ponytail, I can tell her hair is shorter than I remember. Tanner wouldn't notice the most obvious difference—that the bright innocence I always saw in her eyes when she looked at me is gone and replaced by a guarded skepticism.

"Did you talk to her yet?" he asks.

"Yes."

"And how did that go over?"

She darts through a door with two armfuls of dirty dishes. I was hoping she'd be serving our table so I could talk to her, get a closer look at her, be near her, but she's stayed to the farthest side of the room.

I sip my drink and shake my head. "Not as good as I'd hoped."

"What did you expect?" He laughs and gulps his wine. "You promised the girl the world, then left and never looked back."

I glare at him. "That's not true. I looked back. A lot."

"Did you?"

I stare at the door, waiting for her to come back out and thinking about the last time we spoke. "I did. Until the day I looked back and she was gone."

———

The reception is coming to an end. The guests are drunk and swaying off beat to the music, and dirty cake plates have been cleared from the tables. I know this because it was the last time I saw Sadie.

With my back to the bar and a whisky—minus the Coke—in hand, I continue to peruse the room. Did she leave? My pulse pounds at the idea that I missed my opportunity to see her again tonight. I tug on my open collar and check my watch. It's been over thirty minutes since I watched her disappear behind the *Staff Only* door.

"We're about to do last call," the bartender says behind me.

I turn around and face him. "Then make it a double."

He grins and fills a fresh glass with ice. "You got it."

"Can I ask you a question?" My speech is lazy, and my tongue feels as if it weighs ten pounds.

He doesn't seem to notice or care that I'm buzzed as he hands me the glass. "Sure."

"You know Sadie?"

His eyes narrow and the friendly expression he wore disappears. "Yeah. I do." His answers seem clipped, or maybe I'm imagining it.

"What can you tell me about her?"

He crosses his arms and tilts his head as if he's sizing me up. "Nothing."

I'm confused. "But you said—"

"I know what I said."

"How long have you known her for?"

"None of your business."

Protective. Interesting.

"Ah. Okay." I feel sick to my stomach. "So you and her... you two are a... like, a thing." Of course they are. Sadie probably spends a lot of time with him at work, and I've seen the way his bar has been surrounded by women all night.

Fuck.

He doesn't answer, but his shoulders coil with tension and his jaw gets hard.

I hold up my hands. "Easy. I'm an old friend."

I frown as soon as the word leaves my lips. Friend? We were so much more than that. We were soul mates, destined to be together forever. From the moment I remember having life, she was in it. Sadie was my first love. My first *everything*. She was mine, and I was hers.

"Oh yeah? Old friend from where?"

I do not like this guy's tone, not one fucking bit. "We grew up together."

"Huh... what's your name?"

Does this guy think he's Sadie's dad? Shit. "Jackson. Daniels."

He's already shaking his head. "She's never mentioned you."

"You're obviously not that close to her then." God, please, let him not be too close to her.

The dude smirks.

What the fuck does that mean?

"Jackson!" Anaya throws her drunken self against me, her arms dropping heavily over my shoulders. "Take me to bed." She bites her lip, I'm sure in an attempt to be seductive, but it does absolutely nothing for me. "Get me out of this dress."

I lock eyes with the bartender, who's staring at me with a generous load of judgment. And maybe a bit of satisfaction. He pours out my untouched drink.

"Have a good night," he says, but he doesn't say it as though he means it. It feels more like he is telling me to go fuck myself.

"Whatever," I mumble, and I steer Anaya toward another bridesmaid who is dancing by herself. I drop Anaya off with her. "Make sure she gets back to her room safely."

I pull my tie loose from my neck and head out in search of the employee exit.

CHAPTER THREE

SADIE

"Whoa, what are you doing?"

I startle at the sound of Ricky's voice and turn to find him standing at the top of the stairs to my loft bedroom/studio, his eyes wide on the canvas in front of me.

He takes a few steps toward it. "Why are you painting over it?"

After avoiding Jack at the wedding last night, I managed to finish my shift in the kitchen, buried safely in the hotel basement, where he'd never find me. But seeing him sent my mind back to all those years ago, when life was much less complicated. Emotions were cut-and-dry and I could trust everything I felt.

I look at the canvas that was once a mix of blues, blacks, and reds, now mostly covered in white Gesso. "I woke up this morning and decided I didn't love it."

"But you've been working on that one for days."

I'd lain in bed and dwelled on the moment that things changed between Jack and me, the boy I'd always considered to be the other side of my heart. When I woke up and looked at the painting I had been working on all week, I hated it. I hated it for the part of me it represented.

I shrug. "I know, but... I didn't love it."

He blows out a breath. "Is it even possible to love these?"

The concern in his voice makes me want to scream, but I don't. "I think so."

His gaze travels around the room, taking in all the canvases covered in sheets. "How many will there be?"

"As many as it takes."

He looks at me as if he can't decide whether to say what he's thinking or drop the conversation all together. It doesn't really matter—he's not nearly as disturbed by my project as I am. I just hide it better.

I clear my throat and give him my most genuine forced smile. "Stop looking at me like that. I'm fine. I woke up feeling a little distracted, that's all." I swipe the Gesso on the canvas.

"This wouldn't have anything to do with the handsome executive type asking about you at the wedding last night, would it?"

The brush stills on the canvas. "Maybe."

His face comes into view, his gaze knowing. "You haven't talked about him in a while."

I continue brushing. "I know."

"He seemed really interested in reconnecting—"

"He's not. He lives in New York. He's moved on and so have I." The words rush from my lips and I suck in a shaky breath.

"I have to hand it to him, he's persistent. Which reminds me, we need to go pick up your car. I've never had to smuggle you out of the parking garage lying on the floorboards before."

"I didn't expect him to be there waiting." God, he'd looked so pathetic and beautiful at the same time, slouched against a wall in his tux, open collar, jacket balled in his lap, and sound asleep. "It's for the best things didn't work out between us back then. Trust me."

I feel his gaze narrow on me, and I refuse to look even as my cheeks grow hot.

"Whatever you say." Ricky heads over to the only window in my room and cranks it open. "You're killing brain cells with the fumes." He runs a hand over the surfboard propped against the wall, collecting dust. "We missed you this morning. The waves were so clean. You would've loved it. Might be time to give it another shot."

I stare at Ricky until he can't hold my gaze any longer and he looks away. "Maybe after my show..."

"Yeah."

"I'll try to get back out there."

"And dating?"

I hide behind my canvas so he can't see me, and I close my eyes with a shudder. "Yeah, that too."

"Mm-hm." He doesn't believe me.

I don't believe me either.

JACK

Facebook. Nothing.

Instagram. Not even a hashtag.

Twitter. Snapchat. Fucking Linkedin.

Not a single whisper of Sadie Slade.

If not for the subtle ache and emptiness I've felt in my chest since seeing her two days ago, I'd question if she even existed at all.

I punch in her name again, searching Google for any kind of social media site related to Sadie, and come up with absolutely nothing. How is that possible?

I slam my laptop closed and lean back in my desk chair, rubbing my eyes. I'm so damn tired. I left the parking garage the morning after Tanner's wedding with barely enough time to shower, grab my stuff, and get to the airport.

Needing to hear her voice and find out where she's disappeared to, I'd called her old number—only to be met with an automated voice telling me the number was no longer in service.

So I called my mom the second my plane landed and asked her for Sadie's number. She gave me the only number she had, which also happened to be the number I had that was disconnected.

I stayed up all night, searching for her online. Dragging my ass out of bed this morning to get to the office on time was torture, but here I am, half asleep, running on caffeine fumes, and totally confused.

There's a knock on my door. "Meeting with the myBubble people in twenty."

My eyes dart up to see Tanner standing in my doorway, looking nothing like a man who just got married in his suit, tie, and Ferragamos. "Shouldn't you be on your honeymoon?"

"Money first." He winks.

I'd laugh at how idiotic he sounds if I didn't feel so bad for him. What happens if he loses his job or becomes sick and can't work? All his self-worth is tied up in his ability to make money. A sluggish whisper in my brain suggests I may be like Tanner, but I push the voice away and call it a liar.

"Is it possible for a person to leave no cyber footprint? To just disappear?"

"People don't disappear." He drops into the wingback in my office. "Why?"

"I've searched for Sadie everywhere and she doesn't exist."

"So she's not a social media person. There are people who are like that, ya know."

"She was all over it when we were in college."

"People go offline all the time." His eyes narrow. "You cyber-stalking her?"

The collar of my dress shirt seems to tighten like a noose. "Something feels off. She avoided me at your wedding. She's closed all her social media accounts. I tried her number and it's disconnected. Her new number isn't listed anywhere."

"Call her parents and get her new number. Her parents love you."

I lift a brow.

He rolls his eyes. "Okay, her mom loves you."

"I don't want to seem too obvious."

He seems exhausted by the conversation. "What other choice do you have?"

He's right. The sooner I can get a hold of Sadie and put all my concerns to rest, the sooner I can get back to focusing on work.

I grab my desk phone. Having dialed Sadie's parents' phone number my entire life, the digits come back easily. Her mom picks up on the second ring.

"Mrs. Slade, hi, it's Jackson."

"Who?"

"Oh, um, Jack, Blake and Layla's—"

"Jack! Hey, how are you? And why are you calling me Mrs. Slade?" She laughs, and it's warm and familiar.

Sadie's mom, Raven, was our high school's MILF. Not only was she smokin' hot, but she could also replace a transmission and rebuild an engine. She always had grease stains on her tank tops. I could see the appeal, but I never lusted for Sadie's mom because I had my own personal version. I had Sadie.

We shoot the shit and exchange small talk, most of which is inconveniently free of Sadie's name.

The clock is ticking—I have a meeting—so I get to the point. "Hey, I've been trying to get ahold of Sadie, but must've lost her new number."

She rattles off the number and I scribble it on a legal pad, excitement billowing in my chest. That was easier than I thought.

We say our goodbyes and my hand quakes when I punch in the numbers. It rings as Tanner watches, eagerly thumping his fingers on his thigh. I want to hear her voice. After too many rings, her voicemail picks up, and it's not her voice. It's the automated outgoing message followed by a beep.

What the hell!

I hang up and try again.

And again.

And one more time.

No answer.

I try for a fifth time and decide to leave a message.

"Sadie, it's Jackson. I, uh... I missed you after the wedding. I hope it's okay I got your new number from your mom. I mean..." I chuckle. "I'm sure you're cool with it, right? It's not like you got your number changed to avoid me."

Tanner's face scrunches up as if he's in pain listening me to fumble.

"If you get some free time, give me a call. I'd really like to talk to you. Okay. Call me." I scare myself as the words "I love you" want to roll off my tongue. Old habit.

I hang up before I embarrass myself further and grab my files for our meeting. "I can see you laughing at me."

Tanner laughs out loud as we head down the hallway toward the conference room. "It's been a long time since I've seen you so shaken."

"I'm not shaken."

"Dude. You are."

CHAPTER FOUR

SADIE

"Are you going to get that?"

The vibration of my phone from my purse fills the quiet art studio at Southern Cal Community College for the thousandth time today, and Paula, a fellow student, has reached her limit.

"I'm sorry." I grab my phone and the caller ID makes my heart thunder. Again. New York area code. My phone has been blowing up since Jack left San Diego, and it's no mystery why. My mom told me he called, asking for my number. She was surprised he didn't already have it.

That's because she doesn't know the truth about why I changed it. She doesn't know the truth about a lot of things. If I told her, my parents would wrap me in bubble wrap, drag me back to Las Vegas, and lock me in my old bedroom. I love my parents more than anything, but they're stupid overprotective.

I hit Decline on Jack's call and don't even have my phone shoved back into my purse yet when it vibrates in my hand. This time, I turn it off and get back to my painting.

If only I could silence my brain as easily as I can my phone, build a permanent dam to keep the memories from flooding in.

Because every good memory of Jack reminds me of all we lost, and my mind spirals from there, bringing me back to that night on the beach.

Mr. Tull, my professor, makes his way around the room and I hold my breath as he stops behind my left shoulder.

"What an interesting... concept?"

"Thank you," I say, even though I can tell by the way his voice went up an octave that he's totally disturbed by the subject matter.

"The blood is very realistic."

"Thanks."

"Will you be attending the L'Atru gallery opening this week-end? I think you'll find a kinship in Steve Winnow's work. It's very provocative."

I set down my brush and shrug. "I don't know."

"I suggest you come." He moseys on over to Paula's painting of a fruit bowl.

A night out. Alone. No Ricky.

Am I ready for that?

JACK

One week has passed since I saw Sadie. An entire week of her avoiding my calls.

I did a thorough job of stalking her online, digging at every nugget of information only to slam face-first into dead end after dead end. Then I remembered she used to talk about her room-mate, Dawn Arroyo. I never would've remembered the name except we went to school with a kid named Duane Arroyo and used to joke about them being related. After hunting down Dawn's page, the most I could find on Sadie were old photos from years ago.

From what I gather, Dawn lived with Sadie for a little over a year before she fell in love, got married, and moved to Florida.

After she moved, there's no photographic evidence that they'd seen each other or spoken again.

I memorized—and okay, fine, maybe I saved—a few (all) of the photos of Sadie from Dawn's page, mostly selfies of them at various places—coffee shops, the beach, sushi dates. My favorite was Sadie holding a surfboard. It had been taken when we were still technically together. How did I never know my girl surfed?

Ex-girl.

Fuck you, brain!

She's wearing a rash guard and blue bikini bottoms, her smile brighter than the sun that brings out the freckles on her perfect nose. God, she's so fucking beautiful it hurts to look at her.

"How long?" Tanner's voice comes from behind me.

I slam my laptop closed. "I'm finished with the proposal for the myBubble campaign—"

"Don't change the subject, you fucking creeper." He walks around my desk, grinning like he caught me with monkey porn, and drops into a seat. "Have you been stalking Sadie all week?"

I don't answer because he obviously already knows.

He shakes his head.

I reopen my laptop, no use hiding it. "She's avoiding me." I shift in my desk chair, feeling uncomfortable. I'm too hot and my suit pants feel too tight. "I hate that she won't talk to me. I'm frustrated and... itchy."

"That's called jock itch," my assistant, Andrea, says as she breezes into the room with file folders clutched to her chest. "They make ointment for that."

"You're hilarious," I say as I take the offered documents.

"Girl problems?" She nods toward the open laptop with the photo of Sadie and her surfboard.

"Is nothing sacred?" I stare between my best friend and assistant, who look at me as if I'm speaking a new language. I roll my eyes. "Yes, okay. Maybe."

Andrea props a hip on my desk. "One-night stand gone wrong?"

"No."

"Ol' Jackson here ran into his ex in San Diego," Tanner explains. "He's looking to reconnect, but she won't answer his calls."

Andrea sucks air through her teeth. "Ouch. Bruised ego then."

"No. It's not that." Maybe it is a little. "I'm curious what she's been up to, that's all. If she had social media, I could get all caught up on her life and move on. I don't understand why she won't talk to me."

"Why'd you guys break up?" Andrea's eyes tighten to little slits. "You didn't cheat on her, did you?"

I'm already shaking my head. "It was nothing like that. Long distance relationship became too much. I guess we grew apart."

"You guess?" Tanner laughs.

Andrea squeezes my shoulder. "Give her some time. Women are complicated. She'll either come around eventually or she won't." She straightens and gathers her files.

"That's not helpful," I mumble while fixating on Sadie's photo.

"You have a conference call at three," Andrea says as she walks from my office, closing the door.

"You know..." Tanner leans over my desk and tosses the myBubble proposal in front of me. "Sadie might be interested in a smaller, more exclusive social media app."

The myBubble people had explained that their biggest selling point was the app's exclusivity keeping out people their users don't want in.

"If she won't accept my calls, she won't accept a myBubble request from me."

He shrugs. "Maybe not from *you*."

"You're saying I should pretend to be some other guy?"

He sighs. "Try to keep up. Lesson one? Chicks don't trust men to be their friends. They know we all secretly jerk off to fantasies of them naked."

I open my mouth then slam it shut. "You were friends with Sadie in high school."

"If you're asking me if I ever rubbed one out to thoughts of Sadie naked, the answer is *hell yes*. And so did every other dude who knew her."

I cup my head in my hands. "Please, stop talking."

"Wake the fuck up." He throws a stack of Post-its at me. "If you want her to open up, you'll have to friend her as someone she can trust." He nods toward my computer. "Are you understanding me now?"

"You're suggesting I catfish Dawn to connect with Sadie?"

"Yes, dumbass! Get in her head, find out how she feels about you, figure out what the fuck happened that made her hate you. Once you have all the info, you'll have a better chance at coming up with the proper ammunition to launch your attack—"

"I don't want to attack her, I want to..." What do I want? "I want to know her again."

"Exactly." He points at the file folder. "And there's your in. So what are you waiting for?"

SADIE

"Have you ever heard of myBubble?" I grab my purse from my locker at work while Ricky bundles his tie and apron, waiting for me.

We had a small dinner to work tonight, only twenty-five people, and they weren't big drinkers, so we managed to get off before nine o'clock.

"I thought you weren't on social media anymore?"

I shrug, and we walk together through the kitchen to the garage where Ricky's truck is parked. "I'm not, but I got a text from an app called myBubble saying Dawn wants to reconnect. Must be new. I've never heard of it."

"Dawn Duckface?"

"Yep, selfie-queen of So Cal CC."

He chuckles. "Whatever happened to that girl?"

"She moved to Florida, remember?"

He doesn't answer.

"You went to her going away party."

"I remember the party, just not where she moved." He hits the key fob to unlock the doors and we climb inside.

I put on my seat belt and pull up the text message with the myBubble logo. "I haven't talked to her since I deleted all my accounts. This myBubble thing says it's small, more secure, and private."

"If she wants to catch up, why doesn't she text or call you?" He pulls out of the parking garage onto Highway 1, which leads down the coastline.

I look from my phone to his face then back. "Good question. I guess I'll have to accept the request to find out."

"How did she get your new number?"

"Probably the same way Jack did." I would call my parents and ask them to stop giving my number to anyone who asked, but that'd open up too many questions. Because it wouldn't make sense that I don't want Jack or Dawn to call me.

"Are you thinking of downloading the app? If you're asking my opinion, I say go for it. It's a safe step to getting you back into the whole social thing."

I glare at my best friend. "You hate social media."

"I do, but I didn't say social media, I said social. You remember what that is, right? Talking and spending time with people who share your likes and dislikes." He smirks, but it's not teasing. He's gentler than that. "Come on, Sadie. Give it a shot. You don't need to hide from the world forever."

"I know that," I mumble to the window as I watch the great black abyss of the sea stretched out before me. "I'm afraid of my own judgment when it comes to meeting new people."

"Dawn's not new people. Give it a shot, use a different screen name, and if you hate it, then delete it and be done."

I look at him. "You must get so sick of me."

I cut everyone except Ricky out of my life a long time ago, and he's the only person I've been able to talk to. I should accept the app request for his sake. Give him a break from being my only source to vent to.

"Never." He winks and turns up the radio. Duran Duran's "Rio" comes pouring through the speakers.

One of the many things Ricky and I have in common is our love of eighties rock. My parents introduced me to all kinds of music growing up, but my love of old rock came from Jack's mom, Layla. She was always blasting Metallica, Queen, and Guns N' Roses.

I sing along with Simon Le Bon while following the instructions on downloading the myBubble app. "I need a name."

"That's easy." Ricky's fingers are thumping out a rhythm on the steering wheel. "Van Gogh."

CHAPTER FIVE

JACK

My couch sucks.

Usually I'm only home to sleep, so I've never spent this much time on the piece of furniture that cost more than my first car. After adjusting my position for the millionth time, I discover what I have is more of a padded bench than a couch. The low to the ground, clean, modern look seemed to fit well in my tiny apartment—another thing that costs a fortune and doesn't seem worth it.

At midnight on a Sunday night—or, I guess, it's Monday morning—I should be sleeping. Instead, I stare at the screen of my television with the remote in one hand and my phone in the other.

Sadie received a myBubble request from Dawn hours ago. Seven hours ago to be exact. She still hasn't responded.

I check my phone again in case I may have been so zoned out I didn't feel the vibration of a text ping.

Nope. Still nothing.

I've gone over all the reasons why Sadie could've disappeared from social media and can't come up with any logical explanation other than she's too good for public consumption. Which she is. She's never been overly obsessed with herself or even all that comfortable talking about herself. And that's all social media is, right? Self-promotion.

As much as I wish she was still reachable through one of the big four social media outlets, I respect her for not participating. Hopefully she'll find myBubble non-threatening enough to join.

My eyelids get heavy, and when I'm about to either crash on the couch or drag my ass to bed, my phone vibrates and pings. I say a quick prayer it's not Tanner, then slowly open my eyes to find the message I've been waiting for.

Your myBubble request has been accepted. Click here to chat with VanGogh.

My fingers move so fast they're practically a blur. I punch out a quick message and hit Send.

Sadie, it's been a long time.

Hi Dawn. I know. How did you know it was me?

Oops. I didn't think that through. I stare at my television, searching for an answer.

You're the only person I sent a request to. How are you?

As she types her response, my stomach clenches with excitement. I'm talking to Sadie. *My* Sadie. I'm finally going to get some answers.

Good. You?

Good? That's it? "Shit, this is going to take longer than I thought."

Still married in Florida. How about you? Why aren't you on social media anymore? In a relationship with anyone special? Are you married?

I bite my lips, waiting for her answer. Seconds pass. Both my knees bounce in time with my rapidly beating heart. Text bubbles come and go. Then finally an answer.

Nope. You know me. Haha.

"What the fuck does that mean?" No, she's not married, or no, there's no one special? And I know her, all her life I've known her better than anyone, but now? I know nothing.

I type my response and hit Send.

What does that mean?

———

"What do you think that means?" I ask Tanner in the break

room as we huddle around the coffee pot. "She never responded. I did what you suggested and it's not working."

He flicks his finger onto the screen, scrolling, reading. "I think it's pretty obvious." He slides my phone across the counter to me. "You suck at being a chick."

"I don't even know how to respond to that."

He huffs annoyingly. "You're talking to her like you're a guy talking to another guy, going straight for the important information."

"That's the whole point of this. To get information. To get in her head and find out why she's ghosting me. And I talk like a guy because *I am a guy*."

"No. You're Dawn. Female conversations are a marathon, not a sprint."

I slump against the nearest wall. "I don't know if I can do this."

"You can." He stirs his coffee and tilts his head. "Don't you ever listen to girls when they talk to each other?"

"Honestly? Not really." I'm not surprised that Tanner would eavesdrop on conversations between women, probably hoping to hear his name.

"What are conversations like between your sister and your mom? Think about the way they talk to each other about their lives. Have you ever had a conversation with your mom or sister that lasted less than thirty minutes?" When I don't respond, he calls to a female employee passing by. "Mikaela? Can you come here for a minute?"

She comes in, iPad in hand, pushing her glasses up her nose.

"Have a seat." Tanner nods to the nearest table and we all sit.

She seems a little put out but does what he asks. She looks between us. "What's up?"

"Did you have a good weekend?" Tanner asks.

"Yes," she answers suspiciously. "Did you?"

"I tried that new restaurant on Fifth."

"Oh, the Moroccan one?" She relaxes a little. "How was it?"

"Really fucking good. Best bastilla I've ever had."

"Is it as good as Uncle Ali's?"

"I'd say it's better. And that gelato place right across the street? So good."

"My friend Janice lives for Moroccan food. I'll have to tell her about the bastilla. We tried Kitchen25 Friday night and the food was meh."

"They have a great bar though."

She shrugs. "It's all right. It's a scene. Everyone who wants to be seen was there."

I watch their back and forth as if I'm watching a tennis match.

"That can be so annoying after a long week," Tanner says with more empathy than I've ever heard from the guy.

"Right?" Mikaela's expression morphs from guarded to open and animated. "This guy kept buying us drinks, but it was so obvious he only wanted to show off in front of his friends. I hate that."

"What a douche. Bet it felt great to blow him off."

Her cheeks flush. "Oh, I didn't. I brought him home anyway."

"Women have needs," Tanner says and high-fives her. "No judgment."

They laugh together as if I'm not even here. Tanner swivels his head around and smirks.

After her laughter calms, she checks her watch. "Shit, I have to get back to work." Her eyes warm on Tanner—not in a sexual way but with a genuine look of appreciation. "It was really great talking to you."

"You too. And let me know what you think of the Moroccan place." As soon as she's gone, Tanner clears his throat. "And *that*, my friend, is how it's done."

"How did you do that?"

"With women, you have to build up to the big stuff. Start off small, non-threatening, totally irrelevant, then you do what's called spider-webbing. That's hopping from one subject to another—in this case, Moroccan food to a dirty but no doubt thrilling one-night stand."

"That sounds really confusing."

"Look, Dawn and Sadie haven't seen each other in years. You can't just hit her with direct personal questions. You have to warm up to that. It's like foreplay."

I stare at my best friend. "Every single part of me is saying I shouldn't listen to a word you say."

He throws his hands up and slumps back in his chair with a satisfied grin. "You can't ignore the result. You could keep blowing up Sadie's phone until you've pissed her off so much she blocks your shit." He leans forward, elbows on his table. "Face the facts, brother. You're great with authentic relationships, but I'm great at manipulation. If you want information on Sadie, my advice is your only option."

CHAPTER SIX

SADIE

As I sit at my favorite table on the patio of the best coffee shop in Hillcrest for people watching, I'm aware of all the couples surrounding me. Some pass by on the sidewalk, holding hands. Another bickers in whispers at a nearby table. Some tag-team their coffee experience by one ordering while the other grabs a table.

I wouldn't have noticed them before, but for some reason, today I do. Only because of the twinge of jealousy I feel. And where the hell did that unwanted feeling come from?

It's been over a year since my last attempt to date. Over a year since I last trusted anyone. Over a year since I last trusted myself. And as terrified as I am to try again, to trust again, there's a deep yearning welling up inside me that longs for romantic companionship.

I blame it on my run-in with Jack.

I miss what we had, the ease of our relationship.

They have names for it.

Puppy love.

First love.

High school sweethearts.

Everyone knows those are the most fragile kinds of love. They rarely, if ever, manage to withstand growth and change, and rather than being a dependable kind of love a couple can build a life on, they're the feeble feelings of an untouched life and underdeveloped brain.

I swirl my coffee as a group of three ladies sits at the table next to mine. They're all smiling and laughing as they talk about last night's events, which include alcohol and a house party. Two more things I've cut out of my life—close friends and booze. Neither help with my trust issues.

Except Ricky.

He's the only person who's stuck by my side, putting up with my otherwise irrational fears without making me feel stupid or like a freak. Probably because Ricky was always treated like a freak himself. Nothing grows compassion in a soul quite like suffering.

My phone buzzes, and I see I have a new myBubble message from Dawn. I contemplate ignoring it when it buzzes again.

Dawn left San Diego before my life fell apart. I don't need to worry about her asking a million questions about what happened. With her, I can be the old me.

Remember sushi Sundays? I'd give anything for a salmon roll.

I grin, remembering those nights that had more to do with sake than sushi. I type back.

I thought you hated salmon. You always ordered Cali rolls.

.   .   .

I love it now. Remember the selfie we took in the bathroom? I still laugh about that.

Do I? Yes. The image of you stumbling drunk out of the stall with your pants around your ankles is burned into my memory forever.

We had some good times.

Yeah we did.

I think back to the time I spent with Dawn. That was the beginning of when life got hard for me. Jack was my entire world until he left for New York. I stayed in Las Vegas for two years, until finally, with my parents' blessing, I decided to move to California, go to school, and live outside of waiting for Jack. That's when I met Dawn in Art History. She was a year older and showed me around. The following year, she moved away.

Once I was left on my own, I managed to fuck up everything.

I type back and hit Send.

Remember my twenty-first birthday?

How could I forget?

I chuckle sadly.

. . .

I know. I was a mess.

Alcohol will do that to a person. ;)

I wasn't even that drunk! Thanks to you. I remember you saying drowning a broken heart in liquor won't kill it, it'll only make it hurt more.

Her text bubbles come. Then go. And come and go again. As I wait for her response, my phone rings.

I check the caller ID.

New York area code.

I send the call to voicemail, gather my things, and head home.

JACK

Goddammit, Sadie, answer your phone!

Her twenty-first birthday.

Fuck.

I'd had plans to fly out and spend the weekend with her but ended up cancelling last minute to go to a dinner party with two CEOs of a prestigious ad firm.

I remember telling her I had to cancel and apologizing all over myself. I swore I'd make it up to her. She said it was fine, assured me that she understood, and even said she didn't want to make a big deal over her birthday anyway.

She'd lied to me.

Heartbroken? On her birthday. And I did that!

I drop my phone facedown on my desk, not surprised that she didn't answer. If she'd given me the chance, I would've told her again how sorry I was. I wish I could tell her I made a mistake. I never should've cancelled my trip to spend her birthday with her. It was a dick move, but she should've been honest and told me I was breaking more than just our plans.

I broke her heart.

CHAPTER SEVEN

JACK

Being Dawn is a part-time job. Between scouring her social media pages for things to talk about with Sadie, crafting vaguely worded messages to her, and my usual workload at the firm, I barely have enough time to squeeze in gym hours.

The more I talk to Sadie, the more I realize how much she's changed. She's guarded, secretive, and when I get close to anything personal, she diverts the conversation to a different subject.

Tanner wasn't joking when he said female communication is a marathon. In four days, the most I've been able to get out of Sadie is that she lives in a town called Hillcrest, loves the coffee shop on the corner called the Magic Bean, and is finishing up her fine arts degree with an exhibition in six weeks.

Oh, that's another thing I've spent hours studying. Art. Who knew that Salvador Dali thought he was his dead brother reincarnated or that Edgar Degas was obsessed with painting ballet dancers? We've spent time discussing art, and the passion in her messages comes across so clearly, I can almost hear her voice in her words. Makes me wonder though, how often did I ask Sadie about her passion for art when we were together?

Not as much as I should have.

My phone pings on my desk, and I scramble to check it.

Sorry to do this to you, but do you have a minute?

I type back quickly and hit Send.

I have as much time as you need. What's up?

Which dress do you think looks best on me?

I wait with trembling hands and sweaty palms. My pulse pounds because I'm finally going to get a recent photo of Sadie.

The first image comes in and I'm knocked back in my desk chair. She took a picture of herself in a dressing room mirror, her slender body encased in a red dress that clings to her full breasts and hips, and fuck... her feet are bare. I zoom in. My eyes dance over every inch of her body, my memory so sharp I remember the taste of her neck, the weight of her tits in my palms, the slick heat of her tongue. My muscle memory sparks as it pulls up the feeling of her soft bare thighs straddling my hips, her chest pressed to mine.

The second image comes fast, robbing me of the first, until I realize this dress is more revealing. Shorter, strapless, and the sheer white fabric is so thin I can make out the shape of her nipples. I screenshot both images and save them to my photos for further inspection and personal use. I know it's wrong, and I hate myself for doing it, but I'm a starving man who's been offered a crumb and I'm fucking ravenous.

Did you screenshot those?

"Oh shit." I look around my office as if I'll find a hidden camera. Am I sweating? Um... I type back.

I needed to zoom in to see the details on the skirt part.

I hit Send, panicked and sure I've given myself away. Skirt part? I sound like a man.

Oh, ok. Weird, the app just notified me that you screenshot the images.

I scribble down a quick note to pass my criticism on to the myBubble people. Why the fuck would that be a feature to add? Makes me look like—makes Dawn look like a total freak.

Do you have a favorite? I can't decide.

Right, she's waiting for girl advice. How would a woman respond?

"Andrea! Come here, please! Quick!"

She comes running in. "What?"

I look up from my phone and feel bad when I see the slight panic in my assistant's face. "Sorry. It's... I have a friend who wants my advice on a dress and I told her I'd get a female opinion."

I show her the red one followed by the white.

"Hm... I guess it depends on the occasion. The white one is hot, great for a night out with the girls, but not appropriate for, say, a wedding. The red is sexy but understated enough for a wedding, cocktail party, or—"

"Hold on, slow down..." I do my best to type word for word what Andrea is saying. "Okay, or what?"

"A first date."

My fingers still on the keypad. "A date?"

"Yeah. The red is sexy but doesn't give too much away. Perfect first date dress, gives a hint to what's going on underneath without actually showing it, whereas the white one, well, that's a great dress for an after-sex date. Giving a man a peek at what he's already had his hands on, ya know?" Her brows pinch together. "Jackson?"

"Huh?"

She nods toward my phone. "Why aren't you typing?"

I close the app and turn my phone facedown on my desk. "I need you to book me a round-trip ticket to San Diego leaving tonight."

SADIE

Working in hotel catering, I rarely get a weekend off, which makes today so valuable. Sitting on the patio of my favorite coffee shop with my sketchpad and pencil, I find inspiration in the simplicity of life that buzzes all around me. Even with my messy bun, puffy eyes from little sleep, and my T-shirt and shorts that I slept in, I become an invisible spectator, blending and disappearing in the atmosphere.

My pencil shadows the page as I draw the two men at the table in front of me. They lean toward each other, their body language communicating they're intimate. I keep my eyes on the page, only sneaking the occasional peek to make sure I'm hitting the right angles in my sketch. It's a little voyeuristic, and I wonder if I get caught, will people get upset I drew them without their permission?

A chair scrapes the concrete patio behind me. I startle and slam my sketchbook closed. I peek over my shoulder, hoping the person didn't see my drawing. My pulse pounds in my neck and my face instantly flushes. "Jack?"

His head turns slowly as if he's not sure whether or not he heard his name. I almost wish he wouldn't have, because when he does, his face lights up and his lips curve into that signature Daniels smile I fell in love with as a kid. "Sadie?" His beautiful green eyes narrow. "Is that you?"

"What are you doing here?"

His smile falls and he turns his seat more fully toward me. "I was about to ask you the same thing. Are you stalking me?"

"I live here." I point down the street. "A few blocks down."

"No shit?" He sips his coffee. His big hand wrapped around the cup is a reminder of how familiar they were when he'd absently play with my fingers, or trace patterns on the sensitive underside of my forearm. I was always amazed at how gentle those big hands could be. "I'm in town meeting with a client."

"Here in Hillcrest?"

He brings his coffee to his lips and mumbles, "Mm-hm."

"All the way from New York. Must be an important client." I laugh uncomfortably, feeling jittery and I have an intense need to run. I have been avoiding his phone calls for weeks and he's sure to ask me why. I try to come up with a justifiable reason for ignoring him. I need to leave, but my brain refuses to engage.

"Mind if I join you?" Whatever he sees in my expression makes him frown.

"I guess, but I was getting ready to leave soon..."

He's already pulled out the chair across from me, and his knee brushes against mine as he settles in at the two-top. He's dressed in a T-shirt and jeans, but he's always managed to look like a model even in the most casual clothes. I fidget in my seat and tuck in loose strands of my hair. I must look like such a slob.

"Sadie." He says my name with such care, as if the letters themselves could be broken if spoken too harshly. "You look great."

Flames light my cheeks and I stare at my coffee. "You're lying, but thank you."

Here it comes. He's going to ask why I haven't been taking his calls. He's going to want answers I can't give him and—

"What are you working on?" He thumps my notebook.

"Oh, um, nothing really. I..." I laugh softly. "I'm sorry, this is kind of weird for me."

"It doesn't have to be."

I blow out a breath.

He smiles. "It's just me. Jackson."

I scrunch up my nose. "When did you stop going by Jack?"

He lifts his brows. "It's hard to be taken seriously in the professional world with the name Jack Daniels."

That makes me laugh. "I guess that makes sense."

"Why?" He flashes that gorgeous crooked smile. "You don't like it?"

"I don't know. I mean... you'll always be Jack to me."

JACK

My God, she can kill me with my own name.

I maintain steady breathing, relax my shoulders, and try to act casual when all I want to do is pepper her with a million questions.

Like, why the fuck are you avoiding me?

What the hell happened to you?

What the hell happened to us?

And who the motherfuck are you dressing up for, Sadie girl?

I pat myself on the back when I manage an easy smile and say, "You're still doing art."

The hint of lightness I started to see in her eyes disappears. A scowl pinches her delicate features, and she bites out, "Yeah."

I rewind quickly, try to figure out where I went wrong. She seems to enjoy talking about her art with Dawn.

"That's great." I move forward cautiously. "You always were a fantastic artist."

"Thanks." Her response is a little softer, but now she won't look at me.

I sip my coffee, which tastes like a dog's asshole. Seriously, why is this her favorite coffee shop? I swallow back the bitter brew. "So you're still in school I guess?"

She chuckles, but the sound is harsh and she's still looking everywhere but at me, "Not all of us manage to graduate in four years."

One thing is clear—the time lost between Sadie and me has made it so I can no longer read her like I used to.

"Very few do. I busted my ass to get finished in four years." Mainly because I couldn't wait to get back to Sadie. Whatever happened to that goal?

Her eyes come to me as slits of angry fire. "Oh, and I don't bust my ass?"

I'm shaking my head before she's even finished. "That's not what I meant."

"What did you mean?"

"Nothing. Just having a conversation." Why do I get the feeling that no matter what comes out of my mouth, she's going to twist it and use it as another reason to freeze me out?

Change tactics. Marathon. Think marathon.

"Would you go on a walk with me?"

She blinks and seems to struggle to get her rage back on track.

I pounce. "I'd love to see more of the city, and what better person to show me than a local?"

She looks around the coffee shop, watching people as they pass by. She even seems to search the buildings for an excuse.

Finally she draws those gorgeous blue-green eyes up to meet mine. "I guess I can show you around."

I hop to my feet and hold out my hand. She stares at it and begrudgingly slips her soft, small hand in mine. The second our skin touches, every cell in my being remembers hers and tingles with awareness. Unfortunately, once she's standing, she pulls her hand away and gathers her things.

"Where to first?"

She pushes by me. "Let's just start walking."

"You want to swing by your place so you can drop your things off?" And show me where you live. Hash tag stalker!

"Yeah, okay."

As she walks ahead of me, I do a small air punch of victory, earning a nasty look from a guy wearing cut-off shorts and rainbow socks.

Let him judge. I'm close to Sadie and nothing can bring me down.

CHAPTER EIGHT

JACK

"This is abstract, right?" I'm staring at the five-foot-long canvas hanging above Sadie's couch in her small loft-style apartment. More specifically, I'm staring at a faceless naked man with an elephant-sized dick painted on the five-foot long canvas.

"No," she calls down from the loft. She disappeared up there two minutes ago, telling me to wait here and that she'd be right back.

No? "But the, uh, size is somewhat exaggerated."

The soft pad of her sneakers on the wooden steps as she comes back down the stairs is the only thing that pulls me away from the gigantic cock. Sadie changed from her soft shorts and flip-flops into denim cut-offs and Keds. Her legs have always been long and muscled, but they're more feminine then I remember, curvier.

She settles in next to me, less than a foot away, and I stare at her pretty face. *Stop being weird, dude!*

Thankfully she's looking at the painting and not me. "Not really, no."

My jaw threatens to hit the floor, but I smash my teeth

together to avoid it. "So you pulled this image up in your head from memory, huh?" I rock into her shoulder and chuckle at my joke.

She doesn't smile. "No. I had a live model."

I glance at the painting. Monster dick guy got naked and posed for her? Of course he did. She's gorgeous. Probably hoped by doing it he'd get in her pants, sick fucker. I only wish I could see his face, but in this pose, his head is tilted back so all I can see is his jaw, neck, and Adam's apple. "Who?"

"Me."

I whip around at the sound of a male voice. It's the bartender from the wedding, the guy I liked until he got all bitchy when I asked about Sadie. And he's not wearing a fucking shirt. "*You.*"

"Nice to see you again, *Jack.*" He tightens the towel wrapped around his waist.

My fingers itch to grab Sadie, pull her to my chest, and press her face into my neck to protect her from Moby Dick here.

I fist my hands as she smiles at the fucker. "Hey, you're up late."

He grins, and it's pretty obvious the guy bleaches his teeth. "Long night."

It's on the tip of my tongue to roar, "What the fuck is going on here!" when another guy comes out from the short hallway. He's buttoning his shirt, his hair a mess and his feet bare.

"Ricky, I'm gonna take off. Oh hey, Sadie." The dark-haired guy kisses Sadie on the cheek then looks at me.

"Scott, this is an old friend of mine. Jackson."

Friend? Jackson? She may as well have kicked me in the nuts.

I exchange pleasantries with the guy. Okay, maybe not my usual over-the-top pleasantries because why the shit is Sadie living with two guys who look like they just stepped out of a fucking Armani ad? Guys who have a girl roommate are supposed to be skinny pale nerds, not Magic Mike look-a-likes with jumbo dicks. Scott kisses Ricky.

On the lips.

Pulling the release valve from my chest, I exhale long and hard and find myself smiling. Big. "You're gay."

Ricky's eyes narrow.

I want to laugh with relief. "I'm sorry, but you don't *look* gay."

He tilts his head. "What exactly does gay look like?"

Scott laughs. "That's my cue to leave."

"Oh! I parked behind you when I came home last night." Sadie takes off with Scott trailing behind her.

She lives with a gay guy. I am so okay with that. I can't stop smiling.

Ricky steps to my side, facing the painting of him. "She's talented, isn't she?"

"She really is," I say, trying to fight my grin. "You could've told me at the wedding she was your roommate."

He crosses his arms and shrugs. "Where's the fun in that?"

I laugh, because how could I not? I'd thought this guy was a threat *before* I knew what he was packing beneath his jeans. Such a relief to know he's not interested in Sadie. "I'm a lot more comfortable knowing she's not your type."

"Don't get too comfortable." He grips my shoulder and squeezes. Hard. "I swing both ways."

My smile falls and the fucker laughs his ass off all the way back to his room, where he slams the door behind him.

SADIE

"You did this?"

My heart hitches a little at the pride in Jack's voice as we study the ten-by-ten-foot mural painted on the brick wall of a record shop.

Since we left the loft, we've stuck to safe topics—his work, my art. He asked me which piece I'm most proud of. I couldn't tell him the truth, so instead I brought him to a piece that's in my top five.

"Sadie, this is phenomenal." He runs his hand along the wall. "The color, texture, it looks three-dimensional."

"Thank you." I spent a month sketching, painting, and perfecting the mural depicting a naked girl-bird hybrid with long, elegant wings in a cage. She's not locked inside, the door is open, but she refuses to leave the safety of her own prison. I leave out the part about it being a self-portrait. The girl in the painting might not look exactly like me, but the feeling the image conveys represents my torment. Vulnerable. Insecure. Trapped in a cage of my own fears with an open door I could walk out of if only I were brave enough to do it.

He walks back and forth, studying the image from different angles, and I try hard not to stare at the way his body moves. He's bigger than he was years ago. Not taller, but fuller. More man, less boy. His hair is cut short on the sides with that longish, hip-professional mess on top.

He comes to stand next to me, and his arm brushes against mine. My skin warms where he touched me and I squeeze my elbows in, hoping to avoid it happening again.

"You're so talented. I always knew you were, but this..." He blows out a breath. "Wow."

I brace myself for the delicious shock I'm about to get when I turn to face him. Looking at Jack has always done weird things to my body. I make it quick, turning and asking, "What do you want to see next?"

His eyes meet mine. He doesn't speak. It's as if he's searching for something.

When I can't take the connection for another second, I turn for the door to the record shop. "Let's check out the music." At least then he'll be busy looking at records and not at me.

The door chimes when we walk in. The smell of vinyl and dust swirls in the air, along with Janis Joplin's voice.

"Sadie!" Crab, the manager, waves at me from behind the register. "I haven't seen you in a while."

With Jack at my side, I greet my friend. "Crab, this is an old friend of mine from Las Vegas. Jackson, this is my friend Crab."

They shake hands, and the visual is pretty funny. Jack is New York *GQ* while Crab is a Point Break surfer offspring in a tie-dyed tank and bandanna.

Crab's warm brown eyes seem to smile when he focuses on me. "Where've you been?"

"Mostly working, finishing up my degree, trying to be a responsible adult."

Crab flashes a thumbs-down and makes a fart noise with his mouth. "Bo-ring."

I see the emotion flicker behind his eyes and take my cue to redirect the conversation before it gets started. "We're gonna check out some records."

I start to walk away when he says, "We've been missing you in the water."

I freeze mid step and feel Jack's eyes on me. *Act casual. Don't give anything away.* "I'll be back when school mellows out."

Please take the hint and don't ask more. *Please.*

"I know what happened was—"

"INXS!" I grab the first record I see and shove it into Jack's hands. "Remember my mom listening to INXS until our ears bled?"

"Yeah," Jack says absently, but he's lying too. My mom never listened to INXS.

I put the album back, moving deeper into the shop and away from Crab.

"Everything okay?" Jack asks, his fingers thumbing through records even though his eyes are on me.

"Yeah, great." I pretend to search for a specific album.

"Surfing, huh?"

The back of my neck prickles with unease, but I'm used to faking like I'm okay, so I nod. "Impossible to live in San Diego and not give it a try."

I sound casual enough. I feel his eyes on me, and I dip my chin and hope it hides my face.

"That's cool." Finally he goes back to looking at records. "Maybe you could show me. We could head down to the beach—"

I slam back the stack of records. "Don't you have a meeting to get to?"

His eyebrows squish together and he fidgets with the albums. "I do. Not until this afternoon though."

I check the Pink Floyd wall clock. "It's almost eleven. I should probably get back. I have a... thing."

His eyebrows drop low in suspicion. "Actually, I wanted to ask if I could take you out to dinner tonight."

"I can't. I'm sorry."

"Tomorrow?"

"No, busy."

"Sadie, I'm trying to be patient here. You're blowing me off left and right and I have no idea why."

A slow fire stirs in my gut. He seems genuinely unaware. How could he not know? "I haven't heard from you in almost two years."

"So that's it? We grow apart and now we're broken forever?"

We aren't broken. I am. My bottom lip quakes, but I refuse to let him see me cry. "Goodbye, Jackson."

I run out of the record store, cursing myself for not being stronger. Frustration fuels my steps as I consider the unfairness of life. Things could've been different if only I'd made better choices. If only I hadn't been so desperate to feel loved again.

I am pathetic.

Any more time spent with Jack, he'd eventually see it too.

It's best he can still see me as the girl I used to be.

JACK

Watching *Mission Impossible* in a five-star hotel room on Saturday night was not how I saw this whole spontaneous trip to San Diego thing playing out. I thought for sure that after spending some time together, Sadie would feel all the things I felt when I saw her at Tanner's wedding—the rush of memories, the resurgence of feelings, the regret of too much lost time.

I assumed once we were face to face, I could get her to open up to me. I suppose I should be happy her closed-off, flippant attempts to redirect conversation aren't reserved for only Dawn but me as well.

I may not be able to read her like I used to, but I have killer intuition, and something about Sadie seems wrong. Telling myself it's because we lost touch isn't working anymore. Something is going on with her and I won't give up until I know what it is.

I look at the last myBubble message I sent her.

I had the worst day. My dishwasher broke, I got a flat tire, and I spilled wine on my new couch. Tell me yours was better.

The clock says it's nearly seven o'clock, so whatever her event was tonight must have started already. I grind my teeth, thinking about where she might be in one of those sexy dresses—or who she could be with.

Mister I-swing-both-ways-gigantor-dick Rick didn't exactly leave me with the warm fuzzies after our interaction earlier today. If only she'd talk to Dawn more, really open up and spill her guts.

I get an idea and punch out a new text.

.   .   .

Do you ever feel like no one understands you?

When there isn't an immediate response, I set my phone down and drown my discouragement in a mini bag of pretzels. Tom Cruise is on his seventh escape from near death when the myBubble app pings.

My day was weird. And yes, I constantly feel like an outsider. I'm sorry about your crappy day.

I toss aside the pretzels and stare at her message as if it's a door and my response could be the key that'll open her up. Or my response could add another lock. So I type carefully.

Weird sounds interesting.

I hover over the send button for at least a minute before finally hitting it.

I ran into my ex-boyfriend. Jack. Do you remember him?

I never met Dawn—at least, not that I can remember. Did she ever make a trip to Vegas with Sadie? I know they talked about me. The twenty-first birthday thing is one example of how my name would've come up. I'm struggling over how to respond when her next message comes in.

. . .

He just so happened to be in San Diego this weekend.

She goes on to recap our day together but doesn't add anything about how spending the day with me made her feel. I consider Tanner's advice on female communication and type my response.

Are you going to see him tonight? If so, I vote the white dress.

No, I have no plans to see him again. Thank God.

Ouch.

No more feelings for him, good for you. Moving on to bigger and better.

I gag a little while typing those words, but I press on and ask the question that's been burning a hole in my chest.

What are your plans for the dresses you tried on?

They were for an art gallery opening my art professor suggested. He said the artist's work is similar to mine.

Is it a new studio or one I would know?

New. It's on 4ᵗʰ and Grand. Not sure if I'll make it.

. . .

Why not? More important things to do?

It takes longer than usual for her write back.

No, actually. Maybe I will go.

And that's how I find myself in downtown San Diego, lurking in the shadows across the street from a new art gallery. She wore the red dress, and she uses it to wipe her palms on throughout the night. Still socially awkward, I see. Her body language is stiff and uncomfortable when people brush by her or speak to her, but it does nothing to diminish her loveliness.

If I were there with her I'd keep my hand on her lower back so she could feel my support. I'd start conversations for her and drop back once she found her groove. Like I used to when we were young.

"Why won't you let me in again, Sadie?" My words die in the shadows.

Hidden in the dark, I make myself comfortable and don't go back to my hotel until I see her safely home.

CHAPTER NINE

JACK

"Is it no-shave November?"

I lean back against the wall of the elevator as Tanner hits the button for the forty-eighth floor, where we'll be meeting with the myBubble execs this morning.

"Not that I'm against the whole I-don't-give-a-fuck look you've got going on." He pushes his sunglasses up onto his head. "You look like a coffee shop hipster."

After a weekend of creeping around Sadie, I've managed to learn nothing new about her. Her conversations with Dawn are as surface as her conversations with me, and I'm losing hope that I'll ever find out what's going on in her head. I stayed up all night, staring at photos and racking my brain for ideas on how to approach my next conversation between her and Dawn while mapping out my next move as Jackson. The entire situation is giving me a multiple personality headache.

The elevator doors open, and we head toward the myBubble offices.

"No luck with Sadie in San Diego I'm guessing?" Tanner says from behind his to-go coffee mug.

"I don't want to talk about it." I blew off two networking opportunities this weekend to chase after Sadie, only to fail epically. I don't need Tanner giving me shit about it.

We let the receptionist know we're here for our appointment, and she leads us back to a conference room, explaining that the execs will be with us shortly. I drop into a chair, bend over my knees, and rub my eyes.

"If you need help tracking her down, I've got a great PI on retainer."

I peer up at my friend, convinced I heard wrong. "What do you need a PI on retainer for?"

He shrugs. "He checks in on Maribeth for me from time to time."

"Why?"

"Make sure she's not fucking around on me."

"If you thought she'd fuck around on you, why'd you marry her?" Shit, I need a coffee.

"Welcome to marriage in the twenty-first century, my friend."

"That's just sad."

"Sadder than you going all the way across the country to stalk your high school ex-girlfriend?"

He's got a point. "Thanks, but I don't need help finding her. I found her this weekend."

"And?"

Will he ever let up? I side-eye him and shake my head. "She still wants nothing to do with me."

"That's good, right? You got your answer. Now you can move on." He lowers his voice. "Anaya's been asking about you."

"Hard pass, bro."

Just because I'm not interested in moving on with Anaya doesn't mean Tanner's not right. I do want to move on. Cut the last emotional tie that's tethering me to Sadie so I no longer have to think about her, wonder about her life, dig for answers she refuses to expose. A twinge of irritation builds in my gut when I consider my life up until Tanner's wedding. Free of

Sadie Slade. This renewed fascination I have is her fucking fault.

My obsession with Sadie is like a cancer.

I was in remission for a couple years, but she's back and I'm afraid there's no cure.

The myBubble executives file into the room, greeting us with handshakes before taking their seats around the table. Tanner hands them each a copy of the advertising strategy we came up with.

"Before we get started, I have a question about your app," I say, earning a wide-eyed *what the fuck* look from Tanner. "What is the purpose of the screenshot notification?"

The three of them share a confused look before one of them speaks up. "I'm happy to see you're using the app."

I grunt in response and wait for his explanation.

"All of our app's features are for the purpose of transparency between users. The idea is that you only let those you trust into your myBubble. You'd want to be notified if they kept a personal copy of an image or conversation. It's the same with the location feature."

Oh God... "Location?"

"That's right."

"Can you turn it off?" I blurt.

"Yes, but users will be informed it was turned off."

My pulse pounds in my neck, and I feel Tanner tense beside me as I say, "That's fucked up."

"Excuse me?" The only exec who looks older than us glares at me.

"I agree with Jackson," Tanner says, his voice light as he slaps me on the shoulder and squeezes. "Fuckin' genius. Great way to promote this new social media service that, with our help, will make all other socials irrelevant. If I could direct you gentlemen to the media packets in front of you, I'll explain exactly how we plan to make that happen."

I hold up my hand. "Hang on..."

The myBubble guys share a look.

"What if a woman friends a man and doesn't want him to know where she is at any given time. Ya know—" I cough and clear my throat. "For safety reasons or..." I drink water, my throat suddenly dry.

The younger of the executives' eyes tighten, and I wonder if he sees through me when he answers, "The feature doesn't give an exact location. But I wouldn't think this is important for our purposes today."

With my forearms on the table, I lean in. "What if—"

"All right," Tanner interrupts with a brutal squeeze on my shoulder. "Moving on."

I subtly free myself from his hold and fall back into my seat.

Location. If Sadie wanted to find out where Dawn is, she would see New York and San Diego this weekend and she'd know for sure it was me. If I turned the feature off, she'd see that too and get suspicious.

My plan to get closer to Sadie could go to shit, and rather than getting her to open up, I may end up pushing her further away.

SADIE

"It's been over a year. You sure you don't want to try?"

I usually find it impossible to ignore Ricky's pleading, puppy dog eyes. Not to mention him standing in our kitchen offering me a cup of coffee and wearing nothing but board shorts is a pretty view. But even the suggestion of going back to the beach makes my pulse race, and I break out in a sweat. "I'm not ready."

"How will you know if you don't try?" He offers the mug again for me to take.

I hold my hand up to his eye level and watch his eyes register the quaking of my fingers.

"Shit. I'm sorry." He sets the coffee on the counter next to me. "You sure you don't want to go talk to someone, a therapist or something?"

"I tried that, remember?" With shaky hands, I grab the coffee and take a sip. "I'm better in a lot of ways, but I still can't go to the beach."

"Can't or won't?"

I shrug. Those feel like the same thing to me. "Both, I guess. Besides, my art is the best therapy."

Ricky runs a hand through his bedhead hair. "You know I love you."

"But...?"

"No buts." He presses a kiss to my forehead. "I love you."

"I love you too," I say to his back as he disappears out the door to meet everyone at the beach to surf, something I used to love.

Now I can't feel sand against my skin or hear the rhythmic sound of crashing waves without losing my breath and feeling pain all over. A warm rush of saliva floods my mouth and I make it to the sink in time to spit and breathe deep to fight off the nausea.

"It's over," I whisper. "That happened a long time ago."

My hands are still shaking as I set up my paints for the day. With a fresh canvas in front of me, I lift the mental barrier that blocks the memories.

The fear floods my mind, and I make the first angry slash of color on the canvas. Adrenaline spikes through my system as my lungs seem to compress on their own. I dip into reds, blacks, and blues, dark colors that symbolize pain and panic as my brush paints the picture of humiliation. I don't cry, but I imagine that I am and add them to the image in streaks of shame-soaked color. My arms fight against the feeling of being held down as I make bold strokes from one end to the next, and I feel the cold sand between my toes.

My phone rings, startling me out of my daze. Aftershocks of

where I allowed my mind to go give me a sense of urgency to grab for the lifeline. Without looking, I answer it.

"Hello?"

Silence from the other line until finally... "Sadie?"

I blow out a breath to calm my racing heart and sniff back the lingering emotion. "Jack?"

"Yeah, I uh... I didn't think you'd answer. Are you okay? You sound winded."

"Fine. I just um... ran up the stairs to grab my phone." I roll my eyes but pray he buys it.

I'm met with silence then a stuttered, "I'm sorry, I wasn't expecting you to answer and now I don't know what to say."

Feeling my pulse calm a little, I blow out a breath and drop to the floor, feeling as though I went three rounds with Mike Tyson. "I wouldn't have answered if I knew it was you calling."

He chuckles, and the sound sends a soothing warmth all through my revved up central nervous system. "Thanks for your honesty. I'm glad you were blinded by cardio and picked up. What are you doing on this fine Thursday afternoon?"

"It's morning here." I stare at the canvas on the easel and cringe at the image it bears. "Painting mostly."

"For your exhibition?"

I blink and stare at my paint-splattered feet. How did he know about that? Did I tell him when I ran into him this weekend? His presence made me scatter-brained. I must've mentioned it without thinking. "Yes."

"How's it coming along—*shit*. Sadie, can you hold on for a minute? Don't hang up. Okay? Promise me you won't hang up."

There's a woman's voice in the background, but she doesn't sound intimate or flirtatious. Her tone is all business. His assistant maybe?

"I'll think about it." I'm smiling because it's been a long time since I heard Jack so frantic and I have to admit, I miss having that effect on him.

He groans. "Always keeping me on my toes. Hold on."

He pulls the phone from his mouth, but I hear him running down a list of demands that include words like creative, art department, signing off on proofs, and pushing them through to production and media. She comes back with a series of appropriate follow-ups that Jack answers with a confident yes or no. I'm surprised to feel a swell of pride at how far he has come. He accomplished exactly what he set out to. I still hate that he had to leave me behind to do it.

There's a muffled sound like he's covering the phone with his hand, and he's back. "Sorry about that."

I don't respond.

"Shit. Sadie? Are you there? Goddammit—"

"I'm here." I cover my mouth when a spontaneous wave of laughter claws its way from my chest.

"Enjoy giving me heart attacks?" There's a smile in his voice, and the sound is so familiar, it makes me long for the old days.

But those are long gone.

Along with the girl who lived them.

"What do you want, Jack?"

He clears his throat, all vestige of humor gone. "I'm going to be in town again this weekend and I was wondering if I could take you out to dinner."

"I can't this weekend, I'm sorry."

"How about the following weekend?"

"No, I'm busy.

"The weekend after that?"

"Can't."

"Hmm... why do I get the sense you're lying to me, Sadie girl?"

I suck in a quick breath at the sound of my old nickname and feel my resolve weaken. "And you're being totally honest with me?"

He doesn't answer right away.

"You expect me to believe you'll be in San Diego every weekend for the next three weeks?"

"All right, fine, you got me. I do need to go back for work, but the weekend is flexible, so I'll go back whenever you're free for dinner."

"I work the next two weekends and I'll be out of town the weekend after that."

"Oh yeah?" I expect him to ask where, but he surprises me by not asking. "Breakfast then. This Saturday. I'll pick you up at nine."

"Jack, I don't—"

"Eat? I know you do. I also know you've never been able to turn down French toast."

I sigh because dammit, he's right.

"I'll see you on Saturday. And Sadie?"

"Yeah?"

"Thanks for picking up."

CHAPTER TEN

JACK

"Flowers?"

I look from Sadie's scrunched up face to the two dozen purple tulips wrapped in yellow tissue paper in my hand. "Huh, is that what these are?" I shrug and offer them to her again. "I thought they were Slim Jims."

Exasperated, she tilts her head and props a shoulder on the frame of her front door. "This isn't a date."

"Oh wow, okay. So a guy brings a girl a couple dozen Slim Jims and suddenly it's a date." She doesn't laugh at my lame attempt at a joke. "They're not lilies."

"Ah, so you do remember."

I feel the corner of my mouth pull into a grin. "How could I forget?"

She studies me through narrow eyes. Her gaze bounces between me and the bouquet. "You realize spending money on flowers is pointless, right? They just die."

A woman who doesn't like getting flowers from a man. She always did respond better when I brought her cherry Blow Pops, her favorite candy, but I figured she'd matured beyond sweet treats.

I pull back my offered flowers and find an elderly man walking his dog. "Excuse me!" I jog up to him and hand him the bouquet.

His eyes light up behind thick glasses while his little dog yaps at my ankles. "What's this?"

"It's random act of kindness day," I say and wave goodbye as he walks off with a smile tucked into his flowers. I turn back to Sadie, who's failing to hide her smile. "I hope he likes processed meat products." I flash my empty hands. "There. Can we go to breakfast? I'm starving."

She shakes her head, but she's smiling, so I'll take that as a win. "Come on in, I need to grab my shoes."

I follow her inside, feeling maybe I should've been more specific about this morning's breakfast. I assumed she'd know I was asking her out on a date, but she's dressed in a pair of cut-off shorts and a baggy tank top that shows a lot of bra. Sadly it's not some colorful lacey number, but a plain ol' white sports bra. Her hair is in two braids with small paint spatters scattered throughout. Her feet are bare.

I'm no expert on dating—the few real dates I've been on have been for work events—but I think for most dates, women get dressed up and eagerly answer the door, ready to go. Sadie looks like she wasn't sure I was going to show, so she decided to clean the house instead. And even still, her beauty is staggering.

When she heads upstairs, she doesn't tell me to wait, so I follow her up to the loft. She disappears behind a large easel with a big canvas on it, but I'm unable to see the painting because it's covered by a tarp. I look around the space and see several canvases covered similarly. In the corner, under the small, single window, is a twin mattress with a gray comforter that looks like a Walmart buy. The surfboard I recognize from Dawn's photos is propped against the wall and looks as if it hasn't been used in a while.

"I would've accepted the flowers," she says as she slips on a pair of purple Vans.

I drag my eyes away from her luscious tan legs and make a slow walk around the room. "This is where the magic happens, huh?" I peek under a tarp only to have Sadie knock my hand away.

"They're a secret. No peeking."

"Ouch." I shake out the fake sting from her hit.

She smiles sweetly. "I'm sorry. These are for the exhibition."

"Fair enough." I continue to walk around, taking in her room, but I don't try to touch any more. There are multiple canvases of different sizes leaning against the wall, but all of them are facing in so I can't see what's on them. The space is more like an open attic. No doors to hide her secrets, yet she does it so well.

"Let's go."

I follow her back down the stairs. "Where's your roomie?"

"Out." She snags her keys and phone, and once out the door, she locks it behind us.

"I'm over there." I start toward my rental when I hear Sadie's sneakers stop on the sidewalk. I turn around, and she's staring at the car with her mouth open. "What?"

"A convertible Mercedes?" Her pretty blue-green eyes narrow. "Don't you think that's a little over the top?"

I click the key fob, unarming and unlocking the doors. "I've got people to impress." Specifically, one person to impress. I open the passenger side door and motion for her to climb in.

"I hope it worked on your clients," she says as she climbs inside.

I frown at her implication that it's not working on her. Standing on a quaint Hillcrest sidewalk, I feel like a complete douchebag. Sadie has lived with money her entire life, but has never been impressed by it. I should've shown up in a minivan or a Prius. She would've respected me for either of those.

Circling the car that now feels more like a disgusting dick pic than it does a European automotive masterpiece, I paste on what I hope to be a charming smile and fire up the engine. "I hope you're hungry."

She props a pair of cat-eye sunglasses on her perky nose. "I'm always hungry."

With the roar of wind whipping around our heads, it's difficult to hold a conversation, another thing I'm kicking myself in the ass for. I *had* to get the convertible. Luckily, the horsepower and my eager gas pedal foot get us to La Jolla in record time. I find a parking spot near the restaurant and hurry around the car to open Sadie's door.

She's already out by the time I get there. I try not to pout. She never took issue with me opening doors for her before. Then again, we were together back then. I feel as if she's doing everything she can to ensure I know this outing is *not* a romantic one.

"La Jolla." She tilts her head back and takes in the strip of upper class storefronts. "Fancy."

I open my mouth to defend my choice then slam it shut because goddammit, I did it again!

I shove my hands in my pockets, acting casual. "What? I like it here. And according to Yelp, this place has the best French toast in town."

That's a lie. They have French toast, but I mainly picked the location to impress her.

She sweeps a hand in front of her. "Lead the way."

I head upstairs to a rooftop deck that overlooks the Pacific Ocean and tell the hostess my name. "Reservation for two."

"Of course, Mr. Daniels. Follow me."

SADIE

I glare at our hostess through my sunglasses as she shamelessly flirts with Jack on our walk across the patio to our table. I tell myself I can't be annoyed because, A. this isn't a date, B. Jack is kind of flirting back, and C. the pretty hostess is probably someone who would be impressed by Jack's expensive white linen shirt, Sperry Top siders, overpriced car, and foo-foo breakfast place. Who am I to get in the way of two people who seem to speak the same love language?

I catch myself grinding my teeth and force myself to relax and take in the view. The landscape is breathtaking. The cloudless morning sky gives way to sun that reflects off the choppy sea. The toe of my sneaker catches on a chair leg, earning me a nasty look from a beautiful older woman dripping in diamonds.

"Sorry," I mumble.

Her gaze moves up my paint-splattered legs to my ripped denim shorts, tank top, and finally my two braids. She sneers.

"Your table." The beautiful hostess, who looks like a young Lucy Liu with much bigger boobs, sets down our menus. She speaks directly to Jack as if I'm not here. "Your server will be right with you."

"Gorgeous," Jack says, swinging his gaze from the view to the hostess.

She blushes as if his response had a double meaning.

I chuckle as I take my seat.

"What's so funny?" Jack shakes out his linen napkin and lays it across his lap with that charming smile he was born with smeared across his face.

"Nice place." I take in my surroundings, realizing we got the best seat in the house—right on the corner.

He leans forward, elbows on the table. "You're unhappy."

"I am not." I grab my menu and use it to cover most of my face. "Apple cinnamon, death by chocolate, tres leches? Don't they have regular old French toast?"

Jack clears his throat, shifts in his seat, and studies his menu.

I guess I could order the apple and have them hold the apples. Even the juices are insane—dragon fruit juice? What the hell is that?

The sound of Jack's heavy menu hitting his plate calls my

eyes to his. His grin morphs into laughter, and I watch him dissolve into manly giggles.

"I'm sorry." He takes a few gulps of water in what looks like an attempt to stop laughing.

"What's so funny?"

Another roll of his laughter gets scowls from nearby tables. I don't know why he's laughing, but the sound is contagious and I find myself grinning.

"This." He motions to our surroundings. "I should've known better."

A flicker of anger tweaks behind my ribs. Is he implying that my presence in a place like this is laughable? "Known better what?"

"It's breakfast!" He's still chuckling. "I'm sorry, Sadie. I was trying to impress you. I feel ridiculous."

"Don't." I smile with him and wave off his concerns. "The view is really breathtaking and I'm hungry, so I'll find something on the menu to eat."

The waiter takes our order. I get the appleless French toast and Jack orders a twenty-two-dollar omelet. It's ham and eggs!

"So tell me, what have I missed?"

My eyes dart to his. "What do you mean?"

"What have you been up to since... since we..."

"School mostly. Work."

"What do you do for fun?"

"Same stuff I've always done, I guess."

His brows pinch together. "Like what?"

"To be honest, I haven't had a lot of time for entertainment."

He tilts his head, studying me. "Why'd you stop surfing?"

"Too busy. So what about you? How is New York treating you?" Seamless subject change, thank God.

"Busy." He doesn't take his eyes off mine, and I wonder if he can see through my sunglasses or if he's imagining he can. Either way, I feel his penetrating gaze. "Time slipped away on me. I've been caught up in the rat race."

"Sounds awful."

"Yeah," he says without hesitation.

The busboy breaks the tension by filling our water glasses. The hostess passes by and flashes a not-so-secret smile to Jack. He smiles back, but it's tight and a little awkward.

"She's pretty."

His eyes narrow. "And?"

I lean back in my chair. "I think she could be your type."

He shifts in his seat, scratches his eyebrow, and chuckles. "What makes you think that?" There is no humor in his voice. He even sounds a little irritated.

"You seem like the type of guy who would fall for someone like her."

"Then you don't know me that well. Because I'm the kind of guy who fell for someone like you."

My face heats and we get locked in a staring battle until I concede, look away, and see our plates arrive. A long, rectangular plate is set in front of me with four miniature pieces of toast, swirly syrup and powdered sugar art all around them. Jack's plate isn't much different. There can't be more than one egg in that omelet.

I pick up my fork and stab one square before smearing it in the decorations. The flavor is... typical. Nothing special. I finish after five bites and my stomach hardly registers it's been fed.

Jack pushes his food around the plate as if moving it will reveal its other half. He finishes quickly and sets down his silverware. "That was... pretty good."

"Mine was good." I could've eaten ten more.

He scrunches up his face. "I'm still hungry."

"Me too." I laugh.

He tosses his napkin onto his plate. "I give. I clearly failed miserably. This is your town, so why don't you take us to breakfast, or hell"—he checks his watch—"lunch?"

I should say no. Spending this much time with Jack can't be good for either of us. It took me years to get over him, and it wouldn't be fair to trick my heart into thinking he might be back.

But I am pretty hungry.

"You pick, I buy," he says.

"Can't resist that."

He tosses a few bills on the table and stands. "Let's get out of here."

JACK

"Oh God, I ate too much." Sadie groans and grips her stomach.

"You only ate half a burrito." I ate mine and her other half. Way fucking better than that wimpy omelet.

"Did you see the size of it though?"

I smirk. "That's what she said."

She bursts into laughter and throws a wad of napkins at my chest. "You're turning into your dad."

"Why, thank you." I mock bow as she rolls her eyes. "But yes, I did see the size of it. It was *huge*. I don't know how you fit all that in your mouth." I can't stop smiling.

"You're the worst!" She laughs and throws an extra salsa cup at me.

"And you swallowed!"

She bursts out laughing and throws another salsa at me. "Shut up, you're so gross." She's still laughing. I'm grateful this restaurant is inside because her sunglasses are on her head and I can see her eyes. Maybe it's the breakfast burrito that has lulled her, or maybe it's the low-key surf shack décor, but whatever it is, I'm grateful to see her finally relaxed around me. "Now this is the Jack I remember."

I hold out my hands. "Hey, it's always been me."

"Agree to disagree," she says as she gathers our trash to take to the garbage.

"Is that why you wouldn't answer my calls?" I say to her back as she's shoving dirty napkins and burrito papers into the can.

Her shoulders rise and fall once before she turns around to face me. "I don't have it in me to discuss our history and everything we lost."

"Lost?"

"You know what I mean."

I cross to her and stand closer than I should, but I can't avoid it anymore. I miss her. After being around her all morning, her laughter washing over me, her smile piercing through me, I need to be closer. "I don't. We had plans. Remember? Four years and—"

"You moved on."

"I didn't move on. I may have lost track for a bit, but I never moved on."

She looks everywhere but at me. "I should go. I need to get ready for work."

"Sadie—"

"What do you want? We can't do this, okay? For a million different reasons, we don't work. You live in New York, I'm here. You're twenty-two-dollar omelets and expensive cars and flirty socialites who don't walk around with paint splatter in their hair."

Her words are a sucker punch to the gut—mostly because she's right. Those are some of the things I've become because I could afford to. And I don't have control over who flirts with me. So I latch on to the one thing I can protest. "We weren't on a date. You made that abundantly clear. Why do you care if a hostess flirts with me? Or if I flirt back?"

She crosses her arms, shoves out her chin, and shrugs. Finally, a hint of the old Sadie surfaces, and this one I can read. "I don't care. I was merely proving a point."

I bite my bottom lip to keep from smiling. "Oh, you've proved it all right. You're jealous."

"I am not!" Her face flushes with color—either from anger or embarrassment at getting caught, I'm not sure.

"You are." I step closer, and when she tries to retreat, her ass hits the trash can. I study her slender neck and watch her pulse race beneath her smooth skin. Her chest rises and falls a half second faster. "You still like me."

"I don't." She sounds out of breath, gasping to catch air into her lungs.

"I don't believe you."

"Ask me if I care."

"Oh, Sadie girl, you care." I want to push a messy braid off her shoulder and run my fingertip along her collarbone, but I've finally made a breakthrough and don't want to lose the headway. "I know things seem impossible between us, but I'm going to figure it out, because I've decided I want you back."

Her shoulders stiffen and her lips press together and thin out. "You've decided? You don't even know me anymore. I'm not the little girl you fell for who'll sit around waiting while you run off and live your life."

"Is that what you think I did?"

She slips out from between me and the trash can. "Doesn't matter. I really need to get home."

She storms out the door, and only when it closes behind her do I finally manage the words, "It matters to me."

CHAPTER ELEVEN

SADIE

"Who are you texting?"

I slip my phone into my apron, well hidden behind the cake table at a wedding while a room full of drunk wedding guests scarf down the vanilla crème cake. "Dawn."

Ricky smiles, slices, and places cake on the plate in my hand. "You guys have been talking a lot lately."

"Outside of you, she's my only friend."

"What about Jackson?" He winks.

I try to hide my response to hearing Jack's name because what the fuck? I don't want to have a reaction to hearing his name. I thought my heart was done with him, I thought we had both moved on, but leave it to my traitorous heart to come back to life at the mention of his name. It's infuriating.

"I guess we're friends. I wouldn't say we're close or that we ever will be."

Because I'll make sure he doesn't get close. If he finds out what I've been through, he'll tell my parents, and that's not the worst of it. He'll no longer look at me with hunger in his eyes. He won't see me as the woman I once was, but as a broken, scared, vulnerable, and naïve girl. I can handle his distance, I can even handle him giving up on me, but I can't handle him feeling sorry for me.

One of the main reasons I loved him when we were young was because, despite my learning disabilities, he always treated me like an intellectual equal. He'd even say I was smarter than he was, which is laughable. I'm not the one who got into NYU. It's taken me five years to do what most people do in four, and my grades are shit with my best efforts.

I pull out my phone and read Dawn's reply to my last text.

He showed up in a Benz and took you to a luxury restaurant for breakfast? And you're not in love with him? What's wrong with you?

Money doesn't impress me. He ate one and a half Surfer breakfast burritos right after though. That did impress me.

I got heartburn just reading that. Those burritos are monstrous. What else do you like about him?

I take some time to think about that one. What else do I like about Jack? Before, there wasn't a thing about him I *didn't* like. Now? It's hard to say.

I type my response.

I don't really know him anymore.

He's changed?

. . .

Yes.

How?

He's changed in a lot of ways, but mostly... I chew my lip as I type back and hit send.

The old Jack never would've let me go.

It isn't until late that night when I hear my phone ping with a new message from Dawn.

Maybe he hasn't.

———

Two weeks go by quickly. Between school, working on my paint-ings, and picking up shifts at the resort so that I can get my shifts covered this weekend when I go home, I have zero free time. It's been easy to avoid Jack's calls with the excuse of being busy. The couple times I have answered, I was forced to get off quickly because my shift was starting or I needed to get back to work before the paint on my canvas dried.

Ricky pulls his truck up curbside at the airport. "Are you sure you don't need me to come with you?"

I gather my duffle bag and purse. "I'm sure. I'll be fine. It's only for two nights."

He reaches behind my neck and pulls me in for a kiss to my forehead. "All right, babe. I'll pick you up on Sunday."

"If you're busy, I can take an Uber—"

"Sunday. I'll be right here."

My chest warms. "Thank you, Ricky."

I shut my door and he drives off, merging into airport traffic. It's late on Friday and the airport is crowded with people. Crowds and bodies knocking against mine makes my skin clammy and my pulse pound a little harder.

I manage to get through security and hunt down my gate with thirty minutes to spare, so I grab a coffee and settle in. I play games on my phone, delete spam emails, and finally decide to message Dawn. She doesn't get back to me right away. Maybe she's out having a social life on a Friday, rather than sitting in an airport alone, waiting to go home to see family and answer a million questions about my life and if I'm being safe and making good choices.

Boarding the plane, I put my phone on airplane mode and tuck it into my purse. In one short hour, I'll be back in Las Vegas.

————

"Princess!" My dad's thick arms wrap around my shoulders and the heat of his lips press against the top of my head. "You're home."

"Hey, Daddy," I say and wrap my arms around his massive torso.

The second he releases me my mom smothers me in a hug, pressing kisses all over my face. "We missed you so much. You can't stay away that long anymore."

I force a smile and say okay even though I know I'm going to keep prolonging the time between visits until I'm sure I won't slip up and spill my secrets. "Where's Carey?"

I wouldn't be surprised if my seventeen-year-old brother had more important things to do than pick his sister up from the airport.

"Football practice." My dad takes my luggage and wraps an

arm over my shoulder, and my mom holds my hand as we walk to the garage.

"Assassin!" a male voice calls from across the terminal.

My dad waves, and when he does, he gets the attention of others. The murmurs and shouts from UFL fans get louder and louder, until my dad shifts my mom and I under each arm protectively. At my dad's truck, he tosses my stuff in the bed, then opens the door and helps me inside.

My mom climbs in the passenger side and twirls around to look at me. "You look so good, baby. I missed you. I'm so glad you're home."

I laugh at her excitement.

"Are you hungry?" Dad asks. Leave it to him to always be thinking of food.

"I could eat."

We chat about school, art, and all the go-to subjects that are safe to discuss until we pull up at Nori Pizza and Italian. Because of who my dad is, and because this has been our family's go-to restaurant my entire life, we get seated right away. We don't need to look at the menu before we order, so the three of us sit around staring at each other until Mom breaks the silence.

"So you've been talking to Jack again?"

I don't have to ask how she found out. My mom and Jack's mom, Layla, are good friends, as are our dads. "Thanks for giving him my phone number."

She doesn't pick up the sarcasm and instead squeezes my hand. "You're welcome, honey. How are things between you guys?"

I shrug and pick at a piece of garlic bread. "We're only friends."

My dad swallows a cheekful of garlic bread. "I've heard that before. About three days before I caught you two suckin' face in his car."

I roll my eyes. "Whatever. This time we really are just friends, I promise."

"Good," my dad says as he fishes another piece of bread from the basket. "Never did trust that kid."

"That's only because you think he's exactly like his dad was before he met Layla."

I didn't know Blake then, obviously, but I've heard stories. Jack does have some Daniels blood in him—Blake and his brother, Braeden, are equally as beautiful, but Jack was never a playboy like his dad and uncle. I was always enough for him.

Until he moved to the big city and got a taste of what it's like to be a big shot. I'm sure he's been with a million women since we broke up. My dad might be right—Jack may be as bad as his dad was before he met Layla.

"Are you okay?" My mom presses her palm to my forehead. "Do you have a fever?"

I duck to avoid her hand and assure her I'm fine. "I was thinking I'd hit the mall early tomorrow. I need to find a dress for Dad's thing tomorrow night."

My mom and I both despise shopping. We prefer more practical clothes that can be bought at Walmart or Target over the fancy shit people spend a fortune on at department stores.

"Eve dropped off a few dresses for us. I'm sure there's one that'll fit you."

My auntie Eve has an eye for fashion, thank God. "Lifesaver. That would be great."

"So tell us about what you've been working on," my mom says.

My dad's hazel eyes zero in on me, and I force out the semi-truthful answer I've been practicing all week. "It's an exposé series. Thought-provoking. Relevant."

Exposing.

Humiliating.

Necessary.

CHAPTER TWELVE

SADIE

Apparently this award my dad is accepting is the first of its kind and it's a really big deal. The event is being held at the Las Vegas Waldorf Astoria and everyone who is anyone in the UFL will be in attendance. They're even making my brother wear a tux. I'm grateful three of the five dresses Eve dropped off fit me, and I pick the one I feel the most beautiful in.

I run my fingers through the sheer fabric of the full-length skirt, finding a slit that cuts to mid-thigh. The bodice is formfit-ting to the waist, thank goodness, because the back is crisscross spaghetti straps that tie on the lower back. I'll need the support to go braless. It's sexy and elegant, and, no surprise, it's navy.

Eve always says I look best in blues.

I pull my long hair back in a low twisty bun that looks sloppy because it is sloppy, but with my makeup and the sequins in the gown, it looks intentional. With my feet shoved into a pair of nude patent leather ankle strap heels—again, thank you, Mom— I walk down the long hallway of my parents' house to meet the rest of my family, who is waiting for me in the kitchen. My dad and brother whistle, and my mom smiles with her hand on her chest as if she's trying to slow her heart.

"You look hot, Sade!"

I do a slow twirl for Carey. "Thanks, bro."

"You really do look amazing, honey." My mom presses a kiss to my temple then wipes off the smudge of lipstick that she left behind.

My dad scowls. "That's the dress Eve brought over? She didn't bring something, I don't know, baggier? With a pattern on it, like anchors or something?"

"A bigger dress with anchors? Dad..."

"What?" He tugs absently on his collar. The man has always hated dressing up. Not that I blame him. It takes a lot of seams and starch to wrap that big ol' body. "Nautical's a style."

"Maybe for babies."

He kisses my cheek. "You look incredible. Anyone who looks or speaks or even thinks about you inappropriately tonight is going to get his jaw broken."

"I concur," Carey says while shoving a fistful of grapes in his mouth.

I salute them both and motion to my brother. "When was the last time you fed this kid?"

My mom sighs. "Growth spurt."

"Again?" I motion to his mop of black hair that stands a foot taller than my head. "He's huge."

My dad thumps his chest. "Good genes." He grips Carey's shoulder. "Put the grapes down, son. They'll have food there."

It's a ten-minute drive to the resort where the party is being held. Carey helps me disembark from Dad's lifted truck so I don't fall off my heels, and my dad does the same for my mom. A man in a tux greets us at the door, and we follow him to the banquet room.

The place is crowded already. The guest of honor, it seems, showed up last. The room erupts in cheers and catcalling, hoots and hollers. A big palm comes up from behind my dad, squeezing his shoulder, and when he turns around, Dad reveals Jack's dad, Blake.

"Nice of them to honor you right before you die, old man."

My dad glares at him, but there's a grin on his face. "I'm not that old."

"Old enough." Blake's eyes fix on me, and I see so much of Jack in them. The green is identical, and his smile and bone structure is spot-on. The rest he gets from his mom. "Sadie, what's up, princess?" He wraps me in a firm hug. "Happy you could make it."

"Thanks, Uncle Blake."

Jack's mom, Layla, comes to stand at his side. She's a petite blonde who is dwarfed next to her husband. She's wearing a gorgeous emerald dress, and she wraps me up in a hug. "You're home. I'm so happy to see you."

"Thanks, I wouldn't miss it for the world." Not that my parents gave me much choice.

"This makes a lot more sense now," Layla says under her breath to her husband.

"Yeah, it does," Blake mumbles from behind his beer.

Layla hugs me again and holds on for a beat too long. "Thank you."

"You're welcome?" I laugh uncomfortably. "I'm not exactly sure what I did."

Blake grins that cocky smile that Jack has perfected. "You brought him home."

My stomach bottoms out. My expression falls.

Then, a tall, smiling man in a tux holding two glasses of champagne steps up to us. "Hello, Sadie."

Jack.

His eyes move over my body, this dress so snug over my breasts and ribcage I can hardly take a full breath. Once he ends at my face, he offers me the glass. "You look incredible."

"Thank you." I nod toward the glass. "But I don't drink."

He frowns. "Since when?"

"She has a mild allergy to alcohol." My mom feeds Jack the lie I fed her a year ago. "I'll take that." She snags the offered glass. "Thank you, Jackson."

Jackson? He's even having our families call him by his fancy New York name? Speaking of family, they all seem to disappear into the crowd—except for my brother, who keeps his eye on Jack and me from a safe distance.

I lean close. "What are you doing here?"

"You *acquired* an allergy to booze in the last two years?" His eyes roam my face and squint.

My shoulders back, neck stiff, I nod. "It happens."

He casually sips his champagne. "Whatever you say."

"Why are you here?" I hiss.

"Are you kidding?" His eyes drink me in again. "I wouldn't miss this for anything."

JACK

One would think that the angry flush coloring Sadie's cheeks, the hard line of her mouth as she spits words at me, and the firmness of her jaw as she grinds her molars would make her less attractive. One would be very wrong.

Goddamn, I missed this side of her.

"You're lying. You came here to see me."

I lean in close, smirk, and whisper, "Never said I didn't."

An adorable growl rumbles up from her throat, and I have the irrational urge to feel it against my lips, my neck, feel the sting of her bite on my shoulder—*whoa, Jackson. Reel it in.*

I turn my head and suck in two lungfuls of air that aren't tainted by the clean, floral smell wafting off her body. I noticed during breakfast last weekend that her fragrance has changed, like she switched body wash and shampoo, but underneath the cloying fragrance, I pick up the crisp, dick-hardening essence of my Sadie.

"You're unbelievable."

"Oh, come on. Your dad is as much my family as mine is yours. My parents invited me to come. When you mentioned you'd be here, well..." I shrug because there's really nothing more to say. "You sweetened the deal."

"God, you make me sound like a bonus check." She crosses her arms under her ample cleavage.

I force my eyes to her lips, something I learned to do at an early age in order to hold on to my young life. I saw what happened to boys who got caught ogling Sadie's tits. Even my own dad would temple-thump my friends for checking out Sadie. When Carey was eight, he kneed me in the balls for watching Sadie's ass when she bent over to tie her shoe, so yeah, call me programmed for self-preservation.

"There isn't enough money in the world to pay for what time with you'd be worth," I say.

"What are you doing?"

I sip my champagne, slip a hand in my pocket, and shrug. "What do you mean?"

"Are you flirting with me?"

"Maybe I am."

Anger washes from her features and she looks... tired. "Well don't. You're wasting your time." She gathers the long skirt of her dress in her fists. "I'm going to go find my seat."

Her long, lithe form disappears into the crowd, the gentle sway of her hips—pain erupts at my temple.

"What the fuck, Carey?" I rub my head.

The seventeen-year-old who's my size glares at me while he shoves two puff pastry appetizers into his mouth. "Thath's my thisther."

"No shit, Gigantor. I wasn't being disrespectful. I was making sure she got through the crowd okay."

His glare tightens, and damn, he looks more and more like Jonah every day. "You mean making sure her *ass* gets through the crowd? Because your pervy laser beams were set on the waist down, dickface."

"Jesus, what the hell happened to the cute kid I could bribe with toys and candy?"

He snags a handful of shrimp from a waiter passing by and shoves one in his mouth. "He grew up. You can try to bribe me with hundred-dollar-bills, but I'll still feed you your own testies if you fuck with my sister again."

I grab his elbow to keep him from walking away. "What do you mean *again?*"

He glares at my hand on his arm, but he can chill the fuck out because I'm still older and we're equal in height. "You can't be that stupid."

"Let's pretend I am."

His scrutinizing stare doesn't let up. "Mr. NYU didn't get his degree in common sense."

"Carey, just tell me."

"She can hide it from my parents, but I know my sister and I watched her fall apart. She came home to visit and I caught her crying in her car, her room, and I'm pretty sure she cried during every shower she took, *Jackson*. If you care about her at all, you'll stay away from her."

"She always said she was fine—"

"Ladies and gentlemen, if you could take your seats. Dinner service will begin."

Carey's grin is about as friendly as a great white shark's, all teeth and a lot of threat.

I walk around, searching out my parents and find them—oh, what do you know—at the same table as Jonah's family. My sister, Axelle, and her husband, Killian, are next to my mom and dad. Sadie's smiling at her dad while he tells everyone at the table a story, and when her eyes land on me, she frowns. I hesitate, wondering if I should fake an illness and excuse myself for the night.

"Jackson, you can sit right here next to Sadie," Sadie's mom says. She doesn't seem to notice Carey's glare aimed at me from across the ten-top table.

I lower myself into the seat and feel Sadie tense. Clearly I have something I need to apologize for. I only wish I knew exactly what that was.

———

Three hours into the event, after a video highlighting Jonah's career, and after his acceptance speech brings a room of the toughest fighters in the world to tears, the festivities are winding down.

Clutched to his wife, Jonah moves from table to table, greeting those who came to honor him. I'm feeling the itch to get out of here, but I won't pass up an opportunity to be close to Sadie.

I drum my fingers on the table. "Your dad's journey to the octagon was fascinating. I didn't know he struggled with a learning disability." I'm only trying to make conversation with Sadie, who has pointedly ignored me all night.

"I hate to be a party pooper, but I'm tired," she announces to the table while standing and grabbing one of those hand purses women carry. She looks at Carey. "Tell Mom and Dad I took a cab home."

"I'll take you," I say a little too eagerly.

"No, it's fine," she says without really looking at me. "You stay."

"Yeah, Daniels," Carey says with a frown. "Sit. Stay."

This fucking kid.

"I was leaving anyway. I have a-an early conference call in the morning." I'm already up and fishing keys from my pocket.

"That's good," my dad grumbles. "Make sure she gets home safe. I don't trust people for shit anymore. World's going to hell in a used condom."

"Gross," my sister says, cringing. "Nice visual, Dad."

"He's right." Killian smiles at me. "Such a gentleman, Jack. Gentleman Jack. Get it?"

I roll my eyes. "Funny, bro."

That's exactly why I started going by Jackson in college. I've heard enough Jack Daniels jokes to last me a hundred lifetimes.

"You don't have to do this," Sadie says through a clenched-tooth smile.

"I know. Come on." I ruffle Carey's hair as I pass him. "Good night, Care Bear."

"I hate you," he mumbles.

"No, you don't."

"Drive safely," my mom says.

"Don't fuck around. You've got precious cargo," my dad orders.

I give my old man a thumbs-up and take the opportunity to touch Sadie by guiding her through the tables and clusters of people. The moment my palm touches her bare lower back, she stiffens as if she's got a metal rod running from the back of her head to her sweet ass.

"When our families get together, it feels like we have twenty-five parents," I say close to her ear.

She shivers. "Yeah."

Not in the mood for talking? I smirk. We'll see about that.

I hand over my valet ticket and leave Sadie to her silent brooding. I have a feeling she'll be more likely to open up once we get in the car.

Her eyes do a double-take as the valet returns with the vehicle. "Oh my God, is that...?"

I grin inwardly.

Bingo.

CHAPTER THIRTEEN

SADIE

The valet guy pulls Jack's white 4-Runner to a stop in front of us, and Jack jumps in front of me to open the door.

"I didn't know you still had this," I say as I carefully put my high-heeled foot on the running board and hoist myself inside.

He gently gathers the flowing length of my skirt to make sure it's all safely in the cab before he closes the door, and my heart squeezes with nostalgia. He was always so cautious with me.

While he pays the valet, I run my hands along the worn leather seats and breathe in the familiar scent of high school Jack's cologne—Fierce by Abercrombie. Every time I pass the store in the mall, I'm reminded of Jack. I noticed at our last non-date breakfast that he's switched it up to something more manly, spicy, something that I'm sure costs a small fortune.

He slips off his tuxedo coat and tie and tosses them in the back before climbing behind the wheel. "My parents wanted to sell it, but I wasn't ready to part with it." He punches a couple buttons on the stereo and "Every Breath" by The Police comes on.

"Wow. How many times did we listen to this song in this car?"

He's merging into traffic, checking mirrors and flipping his turn signal, but he couldn't look more relaxed—knees wide, elbow propped in the open window, a little slouched. Such a familiar view, I almost forget I'm not still seventeen and lovesick. "If memory serves, we *did* a lot to this song, both in this car and outside of it."

A furious blush explodes at my chest, crawls up my neck, and sizzles my cheeks. "That too."

He turns the music up, signaling the time for talk is over, and allows me to quietly enjoy this small dip into the good ol' days. The window is down and the warm breeze tosses my hair around my face, pulling strands free of my messy updo while the lyrics remind me of another lifetime.

Visions of his gentle hands on my body, his whispered affirmations that eased my nerves, and his warm lips as he kissed every inch of my exposed skin. Jack had a way of touching me that only ever felt like the purest kind of love. And even when he'd get wound up, pushed beyond what he could control, he would shake with the effort it took to hold back until I gave him permission to unleash his passion for me.

My nerves zap to life beneath my skin. How many times did we end up naked, sweat-soaked, and clutching one another in the backseat of his truck? More than I can count.

I notice belatedly that we didn't take the exit to my parents' house. "Where are we going?"

"You looked so at peace over there"—he looks back and forth between the road and me—"I figured I'd go for a little drive. If that's okay? We don't have to—"

"No, actually." And I'm surprised to hear myself say it. "That sounds nice."

"Africa" by Toto comes on next, and again my body remembers the many places we went together, music masking the sounds we'd make. U2, Queen—the playlist is the soundtrack to our entire relationship. I wonder if Jack planned this on purpose. As if bringing me back to a time when we were good might soften me up to his advances. Judging by the released tension in my shoulders, the heat gathering in my lower belly, and the warmth in my cheeks, his attempt is working. I'm enjoying the trip down memory lane.

The truck slows to a stop, and in the distance, I can barely make out a set of swings. I want to tell him his attempts are pathetic, but knowing Jack, he'd see right through my lie.

"Do you remember this place?"

I pinch the fabric of my dress, needing to give my hands a job in order to keep them from pulling Jack's lips to mine. "How could I forget? We came here on our first date. You told me you were in love with me."

"I was so nervous." He slides his gaze from me to the darkened park. "I wasn't sure you felt the same way I did."

But I had felt the same way. He confessed his feelings and I confessed mine right back. We kissed like two starving people who had been forced to hold back for way too long.

"Do you ever wonder what would've happened if you hadn't moved to New York?"

He nods. "I don't need to wonder, I know. I would've married you the second I was out of high school. I would've worked for the UFL or at Braeden's gym. We'd be living in some..." He blows out a breath. "Run-down, piece-of-shit apartment because it's all I could afford. You'd be pregnant with our fourth kid we couldn't afford and we'd probably be miserable." He grins at me, but when he sees my expression, he frowns.

"How do you know we'd be miserable?"

"Because we'd be poor. And you deserve better."

"Would you have loved me?"

"Of course."

Now it's my turn to stare blankly at the playground. "That would've been enough for me."

"Women say that, but—"

"Do they? What women have said that to you?"

He must hear the accusation in my tone, because he looks at me and scowls. And dammit, that is one attractive scowl. "A few. The irony is all they really cared about was money and the life-style I could give them. What? Stop looking at me like that. You're saying you haven't been with any other guys since we stopped seeing each other?"

"That's what we're calling it? First it was we grew apart and now it's we stopped seeing each other?"

"Don't change the subject."

"Yes, I have been with someone else since you."

He makes a face like he ate something rotten. If he only knew the truth, he'd know I make the same face when I think back on my attempt at moving on from Jack.

He drops his head back on the headrest then turns and looks at me. "I owe you an apology."

"For?"

"This wasn't the plan I had for us. We were forever, ya know."

I shrug. "Distance is hard on a relationship. Things change. People change. It's life."

He stares into the darkened park. "Four years. Then I was supposed to come back and we'd make a life together."

No shit. Nice to see he remembers. I'm not sure I'm relieved by that or if it pisses me off more. Because the truth is, Jack didn't only forget the promises he made when he left. He also forgot me.

He scratches his jaw. "I fucked us up." His gaze fixes on mine. "Didn't I?"

"I don't know. I can't let you take all the responsibility. Maybe we both did."

He frowns, and as silent seconds stretch between us, I'm forced to look away from those pretty green eyes that always managed to captivate me. "I was so nervous the first time I kissed you."

I smile. "I remember."

"Sadie?"

At the pleading sound of his voice, I turn toward him.

"I miss us. I miss you. I really want to kiss you."

My stomach seizes, and I swallow the lump swelling in my throat. If I say no, he'll notice that something's wrong with me. Do I even want to say no? Jack's full, almost pouty lips were always so soft and gentle. I miss what we had too. I miss the Jack who promised me a future with such confidence that I couldn't help but believe him. I miss the days when something as simple as a kiss didn't make me want to crawl out of my skin.

His eyes drop to my lips. "Can I kiss you?"

Not trusting my voice, I nod.

The corner of his mouth tips up, and he adjusts his position to angle his body toward me. He leans over the center console, and even with my heart hammering, I meet him halfway. Our lips hover mere inches apart, and the scent of Jack is so familiar, so calming, that I'm able to close the distance and press my lips to his.

I'm seventeen again.

His eyelids flutter before they close, dark lashes fanning over smooth skin. He moans softly and tilts his head. His fingers slip into my messy hair, and his tongue licks at my upper lip, a polite request for entrance. I part my lips cautiously and he slowly, patiently coaxes my tongue to slide against his.

This isn't a forceful invasion. A selfish pillaging.

Jack's kiss is a humble request ripe with honor and respect.

Oh, how I missed these.

His hand stays in my hair as he allows me to set the pace, the depth, and advancement. His eyes remain closed. I know because mine remain open, even if only as small slits.

Our tongues work together as if they were trained by the other, which they were, and memories of intimacy with Jack come roaring through my body. His hands, strong body, arms bracing his weight above me because he was always so concerned with crushing me. I secretly begged that he would. I wanted to feel his suffocating weight on top of me.

I deepen the kiss as a moan of pleasure glides up my throat. His taste, the feel of his lips, the rough scrape of his five o'clock shadow is a heady combination. My eyes slide closed.

Phantom fingers grip my upper arms. My pulse pounds.

Pressure of a forceful thigh slides between my legs. I squeeze my knees together to prove it's not real. *Not real.*

The hand in my hair makes a fist, tighter, tighter, so tight I yelp.

Jack breaks the kiss, his eyebrows dipped so low they practically touch his lashes. "What's wrong?"

"Nothing." I pat his wrist, the one with the hand in my hair, and find it only loosely holding me. *None of that was real.* "I'm fine."

He picks up my silent request for freedom and slips his hand free. "Your heart is racing."

"Nah…"

He nods toward my neck. "I can see it."

I cover my throat with my hand and feel it shake against my skin. He sees it too and scowls. I look out the window to hide his intrusion into my head.

"Maybe this time it's me who's nervous." I laugh. The sound is shaky, believable.

"I guess I should get you home." I hear a satisfied smile in his voice. He bought it. "Unless you're in the mood for ice cream."

My pulse slows and I plaster on my best fake smile. "You know I'd never turn down ice cream."

CHAPTER FOURTEEN

JACK

I lied to Sadie.

Last night when I took her to our first date spot at the park, I lied about having been with other women. I tried, I really did. But I wasn't lying about what the women I'd met in New York were after—a successful man with a fat bankroll.

In school, I had been devoted to Sadie and my studies. After that, I was on a raceway to the top that I couldn't get off of if I tried. I'd meet attractive ladies in social settings and catch them staring at my watch or trying to peek into my wallet when I paid a bill. Some came right out and asked where I lived and what kind of car I drove. The money symbols flashed in their eyes, and I knew if I invited one into my life—even only to satisfy my most basic needs—they'd never leave.

After kissing Sadie last night, I realize that she's the main reason I never moved on. My heart couldn't allow someone else in. The space had been taken.

Is still taken.

And what the fuck am I supposed to do about that?

Doubled over a plate of scrambled eggs, bacon, fruit, and

whole wheat toast at my parents' kitchen table, I lean back when my mom slides two more strips of pork onto my plate. "Thanks, Mom."

"You're welcome." She winks at me, her face glowing with pride. The woman loves nothing more than to fill my bottomless stomach. "You got home late last night."

Thankfully I have a mouthful of food, so all I can do is nod.

She takes the seat next to me. "How's Sadie?"

I swallow, the mention of her name making my lips curve up. "Great."

"That's it? Great?"

I set down my fork and grab my coffee mug. "What do you want to know?"

She props her elbow on the table, cups her chin, and leans in. "Are you guys back together?"

"No."

She pouts. "Oh."

"Not that I don't want to. I mean..." I picture her in my truck, her lips so close to mine. Visions of us together flood my head and make me dizzy. Her hypnotic blue-green eyes shone in the dim light of my dashboard as she gave me permission to kiss those perfect fucking lips. I refuse to get a hard-on in my parents' kitchen, so I push away those thoughts. "Did you see her last night?"

"I did." Her voice is bubbly, and her grin brings out all her laugh lines. "She keeps getting prettier."

"Right?" I pop a piece of bacon in my mouth. "I've got a few things to figure out—the first being how I'm going to convince her to move to New York. Once I do that, then I'll lay out my proposal and hope it's too good for her to refuse."

My mom wrinkles her nose. "Are you trying to win her heart or get her business? Because it sounds like you're planning an acquisition rather than confessing your love. And why does she have to move to be with you?"

I chuckle. "I appreciate what you're saying, but you haven't seen where she lives. I'm not trying to be a dick here. I'm being realistic. It's logical that we'd live where it makes the most sense financially."

"Hmmm, yeah," she says, her eyes getting all dreamy. "Every girl's dream come true. Logical love that makes sense financially."

"Exactly—*ow!* Why'd you hit me?"

"Because you're being an idiot. Sadie isn't a damsel who needs to be saved and dragged off to your castle to be protected forever. She's her own person, independent, and should have equal say in whatever happens or doesn't happen between you two."

"Listen to your mother," my dad says as he breezes into the kitchen, sweat-soaked from a jog. "She's always right."

"See?" my mom says proudly. "Always right."

My dad shakes up his protein and props his ass against the cupboards. "What are we talking about?"

I roll my eyes. "Mom's being romantic and I'm being realistic."

"Talkin' about Sadie?"

"Yes. Why are you glaring at me?"

He shrugs. "If you go after her again, this time better be forever."

"Okay, I appreciate you being protective over my girl, but you're *my* dad. Shouldn't you be on my side?"

"She hurt you?"

"No."

"She break your heart? Cheat on you?"

I'm already shaking my head. "No."

"You understand when you left for college, you promised her you'd be back and never came back, right?"

"Fuck, Dad, that's not fair."

"A good woman will give you one fuck-up. *One.* Don't waste a second chance you're not ready for, son."

"I'm ready!"

They stare at me with raised eyebrows.

"Oh my God, you guys. I'm ready."

My mom rubs my forearm and squeezes. "Sadie's flight leaves today at noon."

With that, she gets up and leaves me at the table.

My flight leaves at two. "I could get an Uber to take us both to the airport, soak up a few more hours together."

She turns around and looks at me as if to say, "What are you waiting for?"

I hop up, bring my plate to the sink and rinse it as fast as I can, then I speed walk to the shower. I call, "Thanks, Mom!" over my shoulder.

———

When I pull up to Sadie's parents' house shortly after ten o'clock in the morning, her dad is waiting outside. I expected as much after I called and spoke to Sadie's mom, suggesting we carpool to the airport. Jonah's massive, heavyweight-champion arms cross over his equally massive chest, his dark eyebrows dropped low over a glare that would melt a lesser man's face right off.

Lucky for me, I grew up with Jonah. He's always been like a second dad, and as intimidating as he is, he's only looking out for his daughter. We have that in common. I respect it.

I hop out of the backseat of the Uber, feeling like David when he faced off with Goliath. "What's up, Uncle Jonah?" I hop the steps to the front door and stand in front of him, my nose hitting him at shoulder level. "Sadie ready?"

"What are you doing?" he growls.

I smile, mostly unaffected by his intimidation. "Hoping to spend some time with Sadie before her flight—"

"You haven't been home in close to two years." He steps closer, his voice menacing. "Now you're showing up when Sadie's around. She doesn't need you fuckin' with her head again, son."

I find myself... offended. I choose my words wisely. "Jonah, with all due respect, I would never hurt Sadie."

That killer scowl of his morphs into utter shock and his brows rise on his forehead. "You're kidding, right?"

"No, not even a little—"

The front door swings open and Sadie's surprised expression fixes on me. "Jack? Is everything okay?" Her gaze slides between her dad and me. "What are you doing here?"

Now it's my turn to look at Jonah in shock. *You didn't tell her I was coming.* He was hoping to fend me off at the door.

"Hello? Can anyone hear me?" She flashes an awkward smile as if her dad and I have a secret joke that she's not privy to.

Well played, Mr. Slade. Well played.

I give Sadie my most sincere smile, which isn't hard to do because she looks so fresh-faced and full of life and so fucking beautiful. "Mornin', Sadie girl. I heard you needed a ride to the airport and figured since I was heading the same way, I'd swing by and pick you up."

Her gaze darts to her dad. "Really?"

Jonah's jaw pulses. "I'm happy to take you, princess. Say the word."

"Oh, um..." Sadie chews on her lip as if trying to decide.

Her mom walks by, does a double take, scowls, and joins the standoff at the front door. "Jonah?" There's an unspoken *what the fuck is going on* in her voice. "Hi, Jackson. Sadie, you should grab your bag or you're going to be late."

That snaps Sadie out of her confusion. She scoops up her duffle bag and purse. "I guess I'll hitch a ride with Jack since he's here and headed to the airport anyway."

Jonah pulls her into a bear hug, and her tiny frame practically disappears under his gigantic biceps. He doesn't take his eyes off me, his laser beams making it clear that if I hurt his daughter, he'll kill me in a slow and painful way.

They say their goodbyes and tell her not to stay away so long next time. I wonder why they don't mention seeing her this weekend at her art exhibition. Knowing Sadie's parents, the only reason they wouldn't attend is if they weren't invited.

SADIE

I'm seventeen years old again.

As my dad's arms grow tighter around me, I don't need eyes in the back of my head to know he's scowling at Jack over my shoulder or that Jack is meeting that glare with a charming smile. He always was so great with putting up with and handling my dad's overprotective nature.

"Dad..." I pat his broad back that's solid steel. "You're crushing my ribcage."

"Oh, shit." He releases me. "Sorry, princess."

"I think three hugs is enough to send me off."

Jack's been standing at the back door of the Uber since my dad placed my bag in the trunk before wrapping me in one last embrace.

"Don't stay away so long next time," my dad says.

I push up on my toes and he lowers his cheek—from his six-foot-five height—so I can place a kiss there. "Love you, Dad."

My mom waves from the front door. "Have a safe flight!"

I wave back then duck into the car all the while pretending not to notice how good Jack looks. And smells! Seriously, what cologne is that? And why does the scent on a man take him from simply good-looking to dreamy sexy? As he shakes my dad's hand and waves goodbye to my mom, I crack my window in preparation of being locked inside a car with him.

After last night's mind-scrambling kiss, Jack is currently dressed in a white T-shirt, perfectly worn jeans, and black boots. So he's got the James Dean thing going on and looking at him makes me stupid.

I'm hit with his heavenly scent seconds before his door shuts, and the car lurches forward to take us to the airport. I tilt my head back and allow the dry desert air to wash straight up my nostrils, hoping it'll clear my head of Jack.

"Are you excited about your exhibition?"

There's one way to kill my buzz. I'm happy he brought it up though. It's for the best. I busy myself in my purse, making sure I have my ID, phone, gum, and lip balm. "Excited to get it over with."

"I bet. I remember before I graduated, I spent seventy-two hours awake, studying for finals and perfecting my final project."

"It won't be that bad. It's not a big deal."

His eyes narrow, and I turn away to look out my window. "It's your senior exhibition. The final product of all your hard work. That's a huge deal."

I stare out the window, fearing he might see something in my eyes that gives me away. "It's a small school. They don't make a big deal out of it."

"I'd love to come—"

"No!" I'm looking at him now. His eyebrows raise high on his forehead, eyes wide, lips parted in shock. I chuckle, infuse light-heartedness into my voice, and plaster on a smile. "Don't come. If I knew you were there, it would make me nervous."

He doesn't seem to be buying it.

"I'm not proud of this series, ya know, not as proud as I am of the mural and the pieces I've already shown you." Sounds convincing.

"Well, whatever it is, I'm sure it'll be amazing." He seems to let it go, and I exhale in relief. "You've always been a gifted artist."

Growing up, people said I was good at art, but it always sounded like a backhanded insult. Like when people say a girl has a great personality, implying she isn't that pretty. Stupid, slow Sadie, but at least she's good at art. With Jack, his appreciation for my talents has only ever come across as just that.

"Thank you," I say, and leave it at that. Because this partic-ular exhibition will be like nothing anyone has ever seen from me. The impact will have reverberations that last a very long time. That is, if all goes to plan.

The rest of the ride to the airport, Jack entices me into conversation until we're forced out of the car and to our respective gates.

"You have an hour before you board," Jack says as we head to the security checkpoint. "Would you have a cup of coffee with me?"

"Sir," the TSA guard checking Jack's ID says, "you're First Class and get expedited security check in that lane over there." He points from the roped-off coil of people stacked ten lines deep to the empty ropes with the yawning security guard. "This line is for coach only."

Jack's cheeks take on a little color. "It's all right. I'm fine in this line."

"Really?" the guard says.

He nods.

"Suit yourself." The security guard waves us through to the long line.

"You don't have to do this for me, Jack. That's stupid." And kind of embarrassing.

"No, what's stupid is breezing through when all these older people and moms traveling with babies are standing in the long line. I'm able-bodied. Just because my company can afford a faster check-in doesn't mean I'm comfortable taking it."

"Jack Daniels, always so self-sacrificing."

I realize my tone the second Jack glares. "What does that mean?"

"Nothing."

"Okay, I was going to wait to ask this, but I'm getting a little sick of everyone making it seem like I'm some big bad asshole who broke you."

"Everyone?"

"You, your brother, your dad—*fuck*, even my own damn parents."

The line moves forward, so we shuffle along with it. I peek around to see how much attention Jack's burst of frustration is attracting. Thankfully, only a few casual glances from those closest to us.

"Don't worry about it, that's old news."

"Is it? Because I feel like I'm being punished for something I didn't realize I had done eighteen months ago when *we* decided to break up."

I whip my head around to face him. "*We?* Which part of our break up involved me?"

His eyes grow wider and he scoffs. "Tell me you're kidding."

We're facing off and our voices are rising, attracting a small audience. "Can we please talk about this later when we have some privacy?"

He blinks, looks around, and smiles tightly at the onlookers. "Fine. But we will talk about this before you get on that plane."

The line moves along slowly, one X-ray machine closing down for technical problems. Jack and I scoot along in uncomfortable silence. In the cramped space, sandwiched by people nervous about missing their flights, we accidently brush up against each other and that stupid tingling only Jack can incite is left behind on my skin.

Time drags on. He checks his watch impatiently as the hour we had before my flight is quickly eaten up. Shoes off, phone out, and my bag on the conveyer belt, I finally manage to squeeze through security ten minutes before my flight is supposed to take off.

I slip on my shoes and sling my bag over my shoulder as Jack grabs his from the bucket. "Sorry, our talk will have to wait. I need to go or I'll miss my flight."

He nods, but the disappointment is evident on his face. "Promise me you'll answer my calls from now on?"

"Yeah, of course." I back away. "Bye, Jack."

He smiles sadly. "Bye, Sadie."

I speed walk to my gate and hand the attendant my ticket.

Her eyes go round seconds before I feel strong arms wrap around me from behind and warm lips at my ear.

"I'm sorry, okay? For whatever I did to hurt you, I'm so fucking sorry. And I'm sorry for chasing you down and attacking you, but I-I needed to hold you for one more second before you leave for your side of the country and I leave for mine." His arms constrict tightly for a few seconds before he releases me, and I suck in a full breath.

The flight attendant scanning my boarding pass smiles tearfully. "That was so sweet."

Jack runs a nervous hand through his hair and steps back. "Have a safe flight."

"You too."

And with that, I race to claim my seat on the plane. My heart is pounding so hard I fear the glue holding it together is bound to give.

Damn him for being sweet and beautiful. Damn him for making me wish things were different between us.

CHAPTER FIFTEEN

JACK

Sadie's plane landed ten minutes ago. I'm sitting in the airport bar having my second—no, third—whiskey on the rocks. Is it too early to call and talk? My plane already started boarding, but I have another thirty minutes until I need to make my way to my gate.

Probably not the best idea to have this talk when I'm pressed for time and not so sober. Our heart-to-heart will have to wait. I'll sleep off my buzz on the flight home and call her when I land. It'll be midnight her time, but maybe she'll be up.

A group of women walk into the bar and sit next to me. They're loud, and it's clear they've been hitting the Vegas pools all day, as they smell of suntan lotion and are loud and slurring. I'm not eavesdropping, but it's impossible not to hear them, and I pick up quickly that they're having some kind of divorce party.

"Men suck!" they all cheer in unison.

"*All* men can't possibly suck," I mumble into my drink.

"We're better off without them. Seriously," one of them says, and the others back her up. "Unless we borrow one for recreational use."

Yikes. I shift my body, angling away from the group of man-haters.

"This was the best weekend of my life, you guys," the divorcee says. "I didn't realize how badly I needed to vent!" She laughs and holds up her drink to cheers again. "To good listeners!"

I hold up my drink and secretly cheers with them, feeling like I've earned it. I mean, I'm being forced to listen to her too.

"Josh always loved his job more than me."

"Yeah, well, I bet his job doesn't give good head," one of them says, and they all burst into laughter.

"Right?" the drunk divorcee says. "He's going to regret letting me go. I sucked his balls!"

I laugh into my drink. I have to agree with her—jobs aren't good bed buddies. I should know.

"He'll be back," another one slurs. "One weekend without you and he'll get lonely. Then he'll be back when he realizes his job doesn't welcome him home like you did."

"Guy sounds like an idiot," I say to myself.

I drain my drink before tossing a few bills on the bar and grabbing my duffle bag. I smile as I pass the group, but they mostly glare. My balls crawl up into my body to hide from the hate vibes they're giving off.

As I'm weaving through the crowd toward my gate, I get a brilliant idea. I pull out my phone and open the myBubble app. I hit Sadie's contact and type.

Men suck!

I hand over my boarding pass and head to my first-class seat. I stow my bag, fasten my seat belt, and accept a glass of ice-cold whiskey before checking Sadie's response.

. . .

Most do, that's true. But not all.

Interesting response. I type back.

Prove it.

The flight attendant goes through the speech about safety precautions and I anxiously wait for Sadie's response.

I spent the weekend with one of the best men I've ever known.

My heart leaps and my fingers work quickly to respond.

Who?

The lights dim in the cabin and the plane taxis. I stare at the screen of my phone, waiting to see my name appear. The text bubbles go on for what feels like forever until finally—

My dad.

Her *dad?* After our kiss last night and my impulsive goodbye where I laid myself bare for her? And she says her dad?

I shut off my phone and drop it into my cup holder, and then I close my eyes and fall asleep.

———

"You've got to be kidding me." Sadie's sleepy voice meets my ear and I shoot up in bed.

"You answered!"

"Didn't have much of a choice. You called eight times in a row."

"Shit, sorry about that." I think it was more like ten times.

She sighs, quick and hard. "What do you want?"

"How was work?"

There's a rustling of bed sheets, and I wonder if she still sleeps in a T-shirt and underwear or if she's matured to something sexier. Not that there's anything in the world that could look sexier than her wearing one of my shirts. "You're calling to know how my shift was? Um, well, it was okay. Kind of slow and we were overstaffed, so it was hard to stay busy. I ended up getting cut at nine."

"That's... too bad."

"Can I go back to sleep now?"

"No! I mean—*fuck*." I run a hand through my hair. "I shouldn't have called, it's just." I take a deep breath and blurt, "Ever since I ran into you at Tanner's wedding, I've sensed you were upset with me."

"Jack—"

"Please, hear me out and I promise I'll leave you alone."

When she doesn't respond and I don't hear the click of a disconnected line, I take that as permission to continue.

"After this weekend, I realized our breakup was more one-sided than I thought. See, the thing is, you always seemed okay when I missed visits home or trips out to see you. I didn't realize I had broken your heart. And a group of women tonight at the airport bar helped me see where I may have gone wrong." I take another deep, intentional breath. "I've always been driven to succeed because I wanted to be the best possible husband and provider for you and our future family. Then somewhere along the way, I got addicted to the drive and the straight A's and the accolades. I think—no, *I know,* at some point, it wasn't us that was driving me anymore. It was my pride at being the best. And here I am, married to my job and jobs don't give blow jobs—"

"What?"

"No, that's not what I meant."

"Please, explain what you did mean."

"I miss you. I want you back. I want us back. Kissing you the other night, I can't explain what that meant to me. I need you back in my life, and if you're willing to hear me out, I think I might know how we can make it work."

"I'm listening," she says softly.

She's listening! That's... something!

"Okay, if you come to New York, I can support us financially so that you can work on your art. There are so many art dealers out here. We could find you an agent and you could focus solely on your dream."

"My dream is painting?"

I open my mouth to answer, but then I register the snarky tone in her voice. "Why do I get the feeling there isn't a right answer to that question?"

"Jack. You were my first love."

"I know! And you're mine. The only woman I've ever loved—"

"Can I finish?"

I clear my throat and demand my racing heart chill out. "Go on."

"When you moved to New York, we made promises to each other as eighteen-year-old kids. There's no way we could've expected things to work out the way we'd planned. We both had some growing up to do."

"I made a promise to you, and I broke it."

"Yes, you said you'd be back in four years and we'd pick up our lives together. But guess what? If you'd come back four years later, I wouldn't have been there. I moved to California. So then what?"

"I guess I would've expected you to move back to Vegas or I would've come to you, I don't know."

"We can't make life decisions based on what could happen. We have to live for ourselves, with only ourselves in mind."

"Sadie—"

"That's all you did. You looked out for you, as you should have. I was heartbroken, sure, but only because I had to mourn the loss of a dream and I was afraid of a future without you in it because you were all I ever knew."

"I don't want a future without you. I want to get back together. I want the future we promised each other as kids. I guess the real question is, do you want that too?"

She huffs out a breath. "So much has changed. I'm not the same girl I was at eighteen."

"I don't believe that, but if that's true, give me a chance to get to know you again."

"You may not like what you see."

I laugh, because really, that's fucking laughable. "I doubt that."

She's not laughing. Is she even breathing?

"Are you saying you'll give me a chance to do that? You'll start answering your phone and sharing parts of your life with me?"

"I don't know if I can," she whispers.

"What are you so afraid of me seeing? That you dated other guys? Okay, I got that. I don't like it, but I get it. I don't want to dwell on who you were with before. I want to move on and make you forget every man you've ever been with, including a young and selfish Jack Daniels."

She clears her throat. "What if you can't do that? What if one of those men has changed me forever? What if you have to live in the constant shadow of someone else?"

My stomach rolls over on itself and I feel as if I might be

sick, but I have to know. "Are you saying... are you in love with him? With one of your ex-boyfriends?"

She doesn't answer.

Yep, I'm going to be sick. "Your non-answer says it all."

"We can never be what we were. If you're open to being something new, then yeah, I'll give you that chance to see inside me. And I won't even be mad at you when what you see makes you change your mind."

"That's not happening." Because whoever Sadie thinks she loves, I'll love her harder. I'll love her so much, I'll squash every memory of every other man from her soul until all she's filled with is us and the plans for our future together.

"You're so confident."

"I believe in us. Since we were little and you'd play tea party with all my Dino Trucks, I knew you were it for me. I got off course and fucked things up, but I'm back on track and I'm coming for you, Sadie Slade."

"We'll see."

I hear a smile in her voice. But it's far from happy.

CHAPTER SIXTEEN

SADIE

"You sure you want to do this?" Ricky holds up the black velvet envelope with the blood-red ribbon.

I stare at the gold embossed lettering. "I *have* to do this. If I don't, I'm afraid I'll never be able to move on."

He frowns at me from across our small kitchen table. "I hate that it has to be this way."

"It's not like I was given much of a choice. There has to be some kind of justice or..." I shrug. "Or I don't know what. I only know I need to do this. For me."

His warm brown eyes soften. "For what it's worth, I'm proud of you."

I grab his hand and squeeze. "I never would've had the strength to do this if you hadn't been there for me."

"I don't believe that. You're stronger than you give yourself credit for."

"Believe it." His handsome face blurs as I stare at him through building tears. "You were the only person who helped me shoulder all this."

He flips our hands, brings my knuckles to his lips, and presses a chaste kiss there. "I'll make sure this gets delivered."

"Thank you."

He smiles sadly, grabs his keys, and walks out.

Now all I can do is hope my plan works.

I pick up my phone and go to Dawn's myBubble message from this morning, in desperate need of a distraction.

And...? How was it?

I contemplate her question. I told her how Jack showed up in Las Vegas for Dad's award ceremony. I told her about the kiss. I had to! I still feel the ghostly press of his mouth against mine. With quick fingers, I answer her honestly and hit Send.

I still feel it. Everywhere. ;)

I bite my lip, nervous to put my feelings out there in text. Typing them makes them real somehow. The text bubbles come and go, and I wait nervously for her reply.

Wow. So... you have plans to do it again?

Do I? All I've been able to think about lately is my exhibition. Since Jack showed up in my life, I've felt a little more like the person I was before—same but with modifications. And that... well, that's something I never thought I'd feel again. So...

. . .

I hope so.

I'm glad I'm alone and the only one to hear my ridiculous laughter after being so honest—not only with Dawn but also with myself.

I want to kiss Jack again.

I can't imagine ever wanting more, but a kiss?

Yeah.

A kiss I can do.

JACK

Holy. Fuck.

My pulse roars, my lungs pumping hard as I stare at my phone in my lap, under the table, at a meeting with Mr. TK Anderson, one of New York's most influential restaurateurs.

Sadie still feels my kiss.

Good, because I feel hers too.

And she wants to kiss me again.

Fuck yeah!

"Fuck *yeah!*"

"Jackson..." Tanner mutters and clears his throat.

I peer up, grinning. Really fucking smiling huge and my heart is punching my chest. "Yeah. I love the idea, Mr. Monroe." Can't. Stop. Smiling. "Fucking love it." I stab at my salmon and shove a bite into my grinning mouth. "Let's do it."

Mr. Monroe's frown tilts slightly on one side. "I appreciate your enthusiasm, Mr. Daniels." He looks at Tanner, whose eyes are wide—as if he's sitting next to a grenade he's not sure will go off or not. "I'm in."

Tanner gives me a *how the shit did you pull that off* look then nods. "All right, I'll draw up the contracts."

Mr. Monroe holds out his hand to me, and I shake it.

I can't help it. I'm floating, lighter than air, probably glowing. I laugh.

Mr. Monroe joins in while Tanner chuckles uncomfortably in his Armani suit.

"If you'll excuse me." I palm my phone. "I have a conference call."

"What—*Jackson*," Tanner hisses.

"We'll be in touch with those contracts, Mr. Monroe," I say over my shoulder as I head out of the restaurant to message Sadie back.

I'm already typing when my feet hit the sidewalk, and I hit Send.

Are you going to call him?

What would I say exactly? Hey, wanna fly across the country and kiss me until I can't feel my legs?

I groan and fall back against the brick wall of Level78, Monroe's most famous restaurant. "I'd be there in a heartbeat, baby," I say while typing.

Why not? Give it a try.

"Please give it a try," I mumble to myself as Tanner comes to stand in front of me, his cheeks slightly red from either embarrassment or anger. "What?"

He jerks away from me as if I slapped him. "*What?*" He motions to the restaurant. "That was one of our biggest potential clients."

"Not potential. He is a client. Or were you not paying attention in there when I sealed the deal?" I turn to walk down Third Street. With all this excited energy, I need to move.

Tanner jogs up beside me. "'Fuck yeah'? That's how you seal deals now? What the crap, Jackson? That was a huge risk!"

"But it worked." I check my phone and see Sadie's text bubbles still going strong. "Why are you pissed?"

"You haven't been yourself lately." He dodges a group of tourists. "You're detached. Distracted. You're going out of town every weekend."

"Jesus, Tan, since when did you become such a wife?"

"Shut up, I'm serious. What's going on with you?"

I stop in the middle of the sidewalk and turn toward Tanner. People swerve around us with muttered curses, but I don't give a flying shit. Nothing could get me down because... "I'm still madly in love with Sadie and I'm going to get her back."

He blinks then narrows his eyes at me. "That's it? All this for a chick?"

"Not *any* chick. Sadie. *My* Sadie." I thump my chest. "I'm going to get her back this weekend."

He tilts his head, looking more skeptical than I've ever seen him. "And then what? You're going to hit her over the head and drag her back to New York by her hair?"

"If that's what it takes." I'm kidding, of course. I would never. But I will stop at nothing to get her back.

My phone buzzes in my hand.

Maybe I will give it a try, IDK. After my exhibition I'll decide. My only focus is getting through the weekend. If I survive that, then I'll figure out what this thing is between me and Jack.

I flip my phone screen to shove it in Tanner's face. "She wants to give us a try!"

That's all the encouragement I need. I dial Andrea and continue walking toward the office.

"Jackson, what's up?"

"Andrea, book me a flight to San Diego on Friday."

Tanner curses. "You've got to be kidding me. We have to work on the Anderson campaign."

"I'll come back Saturday night. We can work Sunday."

Frustrated, he flips me off, drops back, and heads the opposite way.

He'll get over it.

This weekend, I'm getting Sadie back for good.

CHAPTER SEVENTEEN

JACK

The cab driver drops me off on the corner of Hawthorn and First Avenue at a storefront with a generic Art Studio sign. I grab the dozen cherry Blow Pops I managed to pick up from the mini-mart five minutes beforehand that I've secured together with a rubber band to make a bouquet. I straighten my tie, suck in a deep breath, and head for the door.

The welcoming room is lit with nothing but candlelight, and close to forty people are gathered. A small sign reads, "Please remain silent while waiting for entrance."

"Excuse me," I whisper as I squeeze through the crowd and make my way to the corner.

There's a mix of people in attendance—some I assume are classmates of Sadie's, coworkers, friends, and professors. I keep quiet and study the room and the black velvet wall that separates the welcoming room from what I assume is the exhibit on the other side.

My eyes take in the large stamped letters on the wall.

Insufficient Trauma

Sounds interesting.

The mood in the room is somber and a bit morose. Not at all surprising. Sadie's always had weird taste in art. A group of guys pushes in beside me, knocking into my arm and laughing before muttering a half-hearted apology. One of them eyes the candy bouquet in my hand and scoffs.

If it weren't for my love for Sadie and wanting to obey her wishes for silence, I'd ask him what the fuck his problem is. He and his two buddies whisper and laugh, earning glares from those around them. Including me.

Finally, the speakers above our heads crack to life and a voice speaks. Not any random voice. Sadie's.

"Welcome to *Insufficient Trauma*. What you're about to see is more than art. It's a window. A firsthand, front-row view of the truth. My truth. Please remain silent until you're outside the studio. Thank you."

I recognize Ricky as he unhooks a velvet rope, allowing us entrance, but Sadie isn't with him. The crowd moves forward through the small opening. I'm eager to see Sadie's art, to see Sadie, to surprise her and give her that kiss she admitted to wanting.

"Front-row view of her truth?" the guy next to me mutters, and his friends chuckle. "Been there."

"Yeah you have," the other says.

What the fuck is that supposed to mean?

I should ask, but it's my turn to head into the room and I'm too excited to see what Sadie's been hiding behind those sheets.

The interior room is much bigger but equally as dark. Except in here, there are paintings of varied sizes with a spotlight from above illuminating each in different variations of light. The room is silent, with nothing but barely-there whispers, and dim. The lighting works beautifully with the dark red, black, and contrasting light of Sadie's art.

The first painting is of a couple. The style is abstract, so the closer I get to it, the more it looks like random swipes of color on a canvas, but when I stand back, it's most definitely a couple, from behind, hand in hand. I would like to believe the guy is me, and the girl has Sadie's long, shiny dark hair, but the man in the painting isn't blond and has some tribal tattoo on his forearm that's barely noticeable in the moonlight. Most definitely *not* me.

It's art, Jack. You can't really be jealous of a painting.

Like hell I can't.

I force myself to keep from frowning and move on to the next painting. The style is the same, the swipes of color making up two faces, one male, one female, side by side and decidedly romantic. The picture after is bare feet in the sand. Pale-pink-painted toenails between larger feet as if she's sitting between his legs. I get the feeling that the images are telling a story.

"She's so good," someone whispers.

I'm submerged in the story, mesmerized, and the room around me disappears as I follow along, painting after painting, listening intently to the story Sadie's art tells. Strong hands around a tiny, fragile waist. A mixture of extreme close-ups and landscapes that show a secluded beach cove surrounded by tall cliffs with nothing but moonlight to illuminate the couple below. The progression of people moves on along the walls, five-foot-tall canvases mixed in with some as small as only six inches. Lips touching. Hands in hair, eyes closed.

And then, the story changes.

The brushstrokes become more violent. Angry slashes create an image of hands gripping bare skin.

My stomach clenches painfully and my heart punches my chest.

I can't move fast enough, scooting from image to image.

A hand knotted in dark hair.

Powerful hands, painted larger than natural size, groping breasts.

A female face pressed into the sand, mouth open. I can practically hear her scream.

A hand down the front of her jeans.

Groping. Raping her with his hands.

My thoughts register the sounds all around me. The gasps. The whimpers of sadness. The sniffles. The mumbled *what the fuck*s.

I can't look away from the paintings. My fists squeeze the candy bouquet so hard, the sticks snap in my grip.

A hand over a mouth. Masculine hand crushing her fragile face.

Sadie's face.

Saliva-soaked tongue licking at her mouth. Pushing through her lips.

My eyes burn.

A twisted body, naked from the waist down.

Towering shadow of giant man cast over her.

The sound like a dying animal bubbles up from my chest and I whirl around, searching for Sadie. Needing answers. But deep down, I know all the answers I need are plastered on the walls. My eyes burn and fury rages through my veins.

The click of a spotlight calls the room's attention to the far wall. What was once cast in darkness is now a stark contrast in white—with three final paintings.

Those same pink toenails hanging off an exam table, knees covered in a hospital gown.

My skin goes from hot to deathly cold, and my throat swells and fills with bile.

The next picture...

The bold word VERDICT slams against a bleeding heart, causing fissures to splinter through it. What looks to be a million different names in different sizes and angles litter the space around the heart. So many it's hard to make out any of them.

And the final painting is a jumble of messed up letters, utter confusion, except for those in red. I squint and push through the crowd of people to get close and read the red letters.

No Arrest: Insufficient Trauma
5 out of 1,000 Rapes Committed
Ends in Felony Conviction

"Insufficient trauma..." I spin around—or does the room spin around me? I'm not sure. I'm dizzy and sick and the Blow Pops slip from my hands. "Sadie. She was..." I can't say the word. But I should be able to, shouldn't I? If she suffered through it, I should be able to say it. "Raped."

SADIE

"We're getting close." Ricky calmly pulls my fingers away from my mouth. "Stop chewing your nails. It's gross."

I try to smile, which is hard to do, considering what must be happening on the other side of the wall. My throat swells when I consider what everyone out there must be thinking. Hopefully everyone who isn't involved will see the exhibition as artistic expression, but deep down, I know they're much smarter than that.

Ricky looks through the monitor then turns toward me, his expression pained and worried. "Are you ready?" When I don't move, he holds a hand out to me. "I won't leave your side."

I let Ricky help me to my feet. "I need you to..." I take a deep, shaky breath. "Promise you'll keep him away from me."

"Jesus..." He grips my hand. "You're fucking shaking." His light eyes sear into my soul when he promises, "There's no way I'll let him near you. I swear it."

I smile, he takes my hand, and we move to the door. My feet freeze.

Ricky looks at me. "It's not too late to change your mind."

My eyes fill with tears and I aim a shaky smile at him. "Yes, it is."

He unlocks the door, swings it open, and we emerge into the art studio on the opposite side of where my paintings are

displayed. The room is a jumble of murmurs as those in attendance bounce from painting to painting. My heart hammers and
fear floods my system.

Ricky's powerful arm wraps around my shoulders, pulling me
to his side, steadying me on my feet.

"Sadie?"

I jump at the sound of my name even though it's softly
spoken, and I exhale when I see my professor approach with
tears in his eyes.

"Professor Tull," I say, and I force my spine straight.

Ricky releases me but stays close enough that our arms
touch.

"Powerful exhibition. You were so vague about the content in
our meetings, I had no idea. Honestly, I'm..." He clears the
emotion from his throat, his lower lip quivering. "Speechless."
He meets my eyes. "You're very brave."

Brave.

And yet I feel as brittle as a dead leaf.

Angela, a girl from my class, approaches with wide eyes and
hugs me. "I didn't know."

I hug her back even though we aren't close. Females understand these things better than anyone else can, and that
somehow bonds us. People continue to approach, and soon I'm
surrounded by people congratulating me on my strength and
talent, giving me hugs of encouragement and praise. True to his
word, Ricky stays close, his gaze constantly scanning the room.

"*When?*"

I turn toward the booming voice over my left shoulder, and
shock drops my jaw seconds before I find my voice. "Jack?" Oh
no, oh no, oh no. I swallow back the thick emotion that swells in
my throat. "What are you doing here?"

His eyes are red-rimmed and glistening, and a bundle of Blow
Pops hangs loosely from his hand. Blow Pops, not flowers. I'd
smile if I weren't mortified for what he'd just seen. He's dressed

in a blue suit, and guilt weighs against my shoulders from the thought that he dressed up for something so ugly.

"Want me to get rid of him?" Ricky whispers.

The pain in Jack's eyes has me choking, my eyes tearing up. "No."

Jack steps closer, his gaze fixed on mine. "When?"

I hate that my story is hurting him. He was never supposed to find out. I swallow back a surge of nerves. "Ten months. Nineteen days. Twenty-three hours."

Jack's frown morphs into something deadly, a potent mix that crackles in the air—fury and devastation.

"I'm sorry," I say, my voice wavering.

Jack steps closer, his gaze moving over my face as if searching for injury. "I never should've left you alone." His voice cracks, and despite the angry slash of his brows and the flex of his jaw, a single tear falls from his eye. "If I would've stayed, you'd never have moved here and—"

"Don't." I grab his free hand and squeeze, tilting my head back to meet his eyes. "I've been down this road. There is one person responsible, but he is not you or me."

His jaw hardens, and he grits through clenched teeth, "*Who?*"

"You weren't supposed to see any of this." For this very reason, I protected him and my family from this dark and disgusting part of my life. Because I knew they would want revenge. I knew they'd stop at nothing until the man who'd hurt me paid in blood and pain. And I knew they'd drag me back into that cage that I'd finally gotten free of.

Whatever Jack sees in my eyes softens his expression and his Adam's apple bobs before he asks, "Can I hug you?" He looks from my face to my feet and back up again.

I nod, and he rushes into me as if he was pushing at an invisible wall I'd dropped without notice. His powerful arms envelop me, and I rest my cheek on his chest, feeling the urgent flutter of his heart. He's upset. As he should be. My goal with the exhibition was to raise awareness to an upsetting epidemic. To shake up the public's blind trust in our judicial system.

In fairness, I had two goals.

And when Ricky mumbles my name and jerks his chin across the room, I know I've accomplished both.

Fabian struts toward me with his two lackeys in tow. A ripple of satisfaction slides through me. I pull out of Jack's arms, and he gives Ricky a strange look when Ricky settles up close behind me. Jack, of course, has no idea who Fabian is.

Ricky knows exactly who he is and why he's here.

Fabian pushes his long hair off his face—hair I used to think was Southern California surfer boy cool. I can still feel it, sweaty and sandy and rubbing against my skin, and my stomach turns.

"Nice *art*, Sadie," he says as he steps up to me. He expects me to be afraid. Intimidated by his six-foot frame and unforgiving stare.

He's right. I am a little afraid. The memory of him holding me down while he groped and probed my body comes back. But overriding my fear is my overwhelming vindication.

"Who the fuck are you?" Jack barks.

Fabian ignores him and his buddies flank his sides, probably noticing that if push came to shove, they outnumber Jack and Ricky. "Bit of an exaggerated telling of our date, don't you think?"

Jack shoves Fabian back. "Who the fuck do you think you are?"

"Whoa, easy there." Fabian chuckles. He holds up both arms and his cold, dark eyes glitter with excitement as he inspects me. "Sadie here might remember things a little differently, but everything that happened that night she wanted—"

Jack seizes Fabian's arm and twists it to get a closer look at his dumb tattoo. When he looks up, he doesn't release Fabian's arm, and like a noxious gas, the room slowly fills with Jack's unbridled fury. Fabian winces and tries to pull his hand away, but Jack yanks him forward, bringing them nose to nose. "*You.*"

One of Fabian's friends grabs at Jack only to get shoved to the floor by Ricky.

Jack wrenches Fabian's arm, earning a squeal of pain from Fabian. "You're a fucking dead man." The air is stifling and crackles with violence.

"She wanted it!" Fabian tries to pull from Jack's grip only to cry out in agony after Jack twists him to the floor.

Ricky rears back and kicks Fabian in the ribs.

"No! Wait!" I scurry to the huddle and push between them. "Let him go."

Jack's bloodshot eyes come to mine, confusion on his face. "I can't do that."

"We're gonna fuck you up," Ricky says, and he kicks Fabian again. "And you?" He points at Fabian's friends, who have sunk back into the crowd. "If you're still here when we're done with him, you're next."

Jack grabs Fabian by his hair and attempts to yank him to his feet.

"Stop!"

Jack's head whips around, his jaw pulsing with rage. "I have to."

"No, you don't." I get closer and place my palm on his chest. "I'm asking you to let him go."

"How can you ask me to let him go?" Jack says. "He needs to pay for what he's done."

"What do you think all this was for?" I say.

Jack shakes his head. "You think a little humiliation is going to keep this dickbag from doing the same thing to someone else?"

"I don't know. But please, for me, let him go."

He grips Fabian's hair tighter and Fabian curses and swings at Jack, but Jack hardly registers the hit.

"The only thing that could make what he did to me worse is having the people I love get arrested because of him." I note Jack's lungs pumping and muscles quaking. "Please."

His eyes search mine, and finally he lifts Fabian to his feet—only to shove him barreling into the crowd and onto his ass. Fabian hops to his feet, yelling a string of profanities as he scrambles toward the door. One of the people in attendance sticks her foot out and trips him just shy of the exit, and he falls forward so hard, his chin smacks the concrete. The group chuckles as he storms out, noticeably without his friends. They must've scurried out before him.

I take a deep, fulfilling breath.

I did it.

I came here to say what I needed to say, to expose the truth, and to expose disgusting Fabian to a room full of people he'll probably never see again.

I wish I could say I had no regrets, but looking at the heart-break in Jack's face, I wonder if my attempt to expose the kind of man Fabian is, the kind of injustice that goes on our country every single day, was worth it.

CHAPTER EIGHTEEN

JACK

I'm fucking sick.

My head pounds, my body feels feverish, and my stomach threatens to unload what little I've managed to eat.

Sadie was sexually assaulted.

I had that fucker in my grip.

I let him go.

I fucking let him go!

"Thank you, everyone, for coming," Sadie says, calling me from my thoughts.

With that, she heads back through the single door at the rear of the studio and I follow her. I don't need to look to know Ricky is following us.

Once we get to the dressing room, she crashes into a chair and blows out a long breath, a tiny grin on her lips. "I'm so glad that's over."

"How can you smile at a time like this?"

"You mean, how is it possible to be excited about life and excited about my accomplishments and my future after I've been assaulted?"

I cringe, hearing the word from her lips. That anyone would hurt someone as kind, sweet, and beautiful as Sadie... well, there's a special place in hell for that motherfucker. If it weren't for the pleading in Sadie's eyes, I would've sent him there ten minutes ago.

"This, my exhibition, is my closure. I needed them to see what he did."

"He needs to pay." My deep grumble surprises even me. That slimy cockbag needs to pay, and I want in line for the delivery of justice for Sadie.

"You have to let it go."

"I don't have to do shit. And you need to go home, back to Las Vegas where you'll be safe and—"

She sits up and glares at me. "This is exactly why I didn't want you or my family here! I knew you guys would try to take over my life again!"

"By trying to keep you safe?"

"You have to let me handle things my way. You can't go around beating up everyone who hurts me."

"The fuck I can't," I say.

Her eyes come to mine, and there's an apology in her gaze. Maybe even a little guilt. "Jack..."

There's a knock on the door and it cracks open. Ricky and I stand in front of Sadie protectively when a woman peers in through the open door. "Excuse me, Ms. Slade?"

We nod, and the door opens wide.

A distinguished older lady in a pantsuit holds out her hand to Sadie. "I'm Suzanne Rothschild, curator for the Aldridge & Shultz Art Gallery in Los Angeles."

Sadie stands, clutching her chest with one hand and shaking with the other.

"I love what you've done here tonight. I'd like to talk to you about bringing your exhibition to LA."

Sadie's face pales. Instinct takes over and I find myself next to her, my arm around her lower back, making sure she stays on her feet. "That would be... amazing. Wow, thank you."

The anger and frustration drains from my system as I watch with pride while Sadie speaks with the curator, eloquently describing how the pain and injustice of her abuse fed her artistic drive. "What happened that night robbed me of my power. I felt vulnerable, like I'd lost control of my own life. Telling my story in this way seemed to be the only thing I could do to regain control. I took my power back."

Sadie doesn't need me to swoop in and save her. If I did, I'd be taking away her power, babying her. Fuck. Every man in her life, from her dad to her brother, myself included, we've been doing that to her for her entire life.

As Sadie goes on like a seasoned pro, discussing anti-mimesis and how it's important that art imitate life, I whisper to Ricky, "You knew about this?"

He answers with a cold stare that tells me everything I need to know.

"Why didn't you fuck him up?" I growl.

He glares at me as though he might throw a punch. "Because if I got arrested, she'd be alone. I promised her I'd never leave her alone."

I open my mouth to say something, but slam it shut when I realize he was there for her the best way he could be. The way she needed him to be. He didn't run off half-cocked and full of rage. He listened to what she needed and held back his instincts in order to be what she needed most.

His gaze settles on her as she talks animatedly, as if she hadn't been traumatized and destroyed. "She hasn't touched the sand since. Not that I blame her."

"How'd she meet him?" We continue our conversation but keep our eyes on Sadie.

"After you two broke up, she tried to move on. This fucking prick Fabian used to surf at our favorite surf spot. They met, he was relentless, she really wanted to move on, and..." He clears his throat.

I fill in the blanks. I was so caught up in the rat race I left her alone and completely unprepared for assholes like Fabian. I always treated Sadie with kid gloves because it's what she deserved. She had to assume that fucking cunt would treat her the same.

Sadie's right. The only person to blame is that scumbag who hurt her, yet I can't help but blame myself.

SADIE

I walk Mrs. Rothschild out to a cab and say goodbye shortly before ten o'clock at night. We'd hit it off and chatted about art, completely losing track of time.

When her cab's taillights disappear around the corner, I turn around to find Jack patiently waiting. My heart sputters and coughs before picking up a hurried pace. I can't believe he flew all the way here for my exhibition. Dressed in a suit and tie, he looks every bit the high-powered New York ad exec, and my mouth gets dry as I take him in. His open coat, slim hips, hands tucked into his pockets as he leans casually against the brick wall of the art studio. He looks like something out of a men's fashion magazine.

When I approach, he pushes off from the wall, and I say, "You didn't have to stick around."

He shrugs his wide shoulders and tilts his head. No smile, only thoughtful compassion in his eyes. "I wanted to."

"Ricky can take me home."

"I gave Ricky the night off." He licks his lips. Not in an overly sexy way. Still, it draws my attention to his mouth.

"You, uh..." I blink to break my focus on his lips. "You didn't have to do that."

"I already told you." He takes a couple steps closer but leaves a comfortable distance between us. "I wanted to. There are some things I need to say, and I didn't think we needed Ricky in on the conversation." His eyebrows pinch together and an urgency flashes in his eyes. "Unless you don't feel safe with me." He runs a rough hand through his hair. "Fuck... I didn't consider you might—"

"It's fine. As long as you're sure you feel safe being alone with me." Whoa, am I flirting?

"I like being alone with you." He tries to hide his smile and stutters a little.

He's always the picture of togetherness, and I forgot how easy it was to throw him off balance when I wanted to. Nice to see some things haven't changed. "I always feel safe with you, Jack."

He blows out a relieved breath. "Phew. Okay. Are you hungry? Want to grab a drink—shit, I forgot, you don't drink. I could use a drink." He laughs uncomfortably.

"After that night, I haven't trusted myself around alcohol again."

He frowns. "Fuck." The breeze tosses his silky blond hair and his jaw pulses a few times as if he's working something out using his molars.

I take pity on him. "We can go to my house, but Ricky will probably be there with a friend. How about your hotel?"

"Are you sure?" he asks slowly, openly staring at me.

"You're going to have to stop treating me like I'm breakable." After tonight, I feel powerful and a little more in control of my life. I go back into the studio to shut off the lights and grab my purse.

He follows me. "But you are. Everyone is."

I snag my purse. "I'm not as fragile as you think."

"I don't think I'm ready to accept that about you, especially after what I learned tonight."

I stop at the curb meet his gaze. "That's fair."

An Uber pulls up and Jack opens the back door, ushering me in, then slides in behind me.

After a few minutes, he breaks the silence. "I don't think I properly congratulated you on finishing your degree tonight. Congratulations, Sadie."

"Thank you." I feel shy and a little embarrassed about how long it took me. Thankfully it's dark, and I hope he can't see my blush.

"Don't do that. Don't belittle your accomplishment."

"What makes you think I am?"

He tilts his head and smirks adorably. "I may be a little rusty, but I can still read you, Sadie girl."

My stomach tumbles in a way it hasn't tumbled since... well, since the last time Jack and I saw each other on good terms.

After he stopped calling, I missed feeling loved and cherished by someone else. I agreed to go out with Fabian because he was nice and persistent. But I never once felt giddy around him —not before he forced himself on me and certainly not after.

I realized after that night that it wasn't feeling loved and cherished that gave me that falling feeling. It was being loved and cherished by Jack specifically.

We pull up to the Westin, and Jack helps me out of the car. Once I'm on the sidewalk, he quickly lets go of my hand. He seems afraid of touching me for too long without my permission. I can appreciate that, given all he's just learned, but with Jack, I'm never afraid.

The elevator ride is short, and when we get to his hotel room, he pulls his card key from his pocket. With his chin down, he closes his eyes. "I only want to talk. Please don't think my intentions are anything other than that."

Oh darn. Surprised by my thoughts—because being intimate with a man has been the furthest thing from my mind for a very long time—I chalk my response up to instinct. Like muscle memory, my body knows Jack's body as if it were my own.

He peers up at me, bashful and maybe even vulnerable. "Are you okay with coming inside?"

"Don't be silly." I place my hand on his and squeeze. "Of course I am."

He pushes the door open and flips on the lights. The room is what I'd expect from a five-star hotel in downtown San Diego—modern furniture, expensive-looking bedding, and a great view.

I place my Blow Pop bouquet on the dresser and grin. He remembered my love for the candy and bypassed the flowers. Jack offers me a drink from the mini-fridge. "I can't drink one of those. They're probably ten dollars each."

He shrugs and snags a Dr. Pepper, then hands it to me. "Dr. Pepper used to be your favorite."

I thank him, because it's still my favorite. He doesn't seem conflicted about splurging on the high-dollar beverage, but I can't stomach spending that kind of cash on a soda I could get from the mini-mart for a dollar, so the can goes unopened.

He drops his suit coat over the back of a chair, pulls off his tie, and releases the top button of his shirt before he snags a water bottle and sits on the foot of the bed, opposite where I'm seated at the table. "I have to apologize for the way things ended between us—"

"You don't—"

"I was caught up in getting ahead, and in the process, I failed you and I'm..." He runs a hand through his hair then focuses on me. "I'm so fucking sorry."

"You're not the one who should be apologizing." At his apparent confusion, I swallow and prepare to confess. "After everything happened with Fabian—"

"*Fuck that guy and his stupid fucking name,*" he growls, then grimaces with a muttered apology.

"I couldn't tell my parents, but I had to get out of San Diego, so I went home and..." I knot my fingers in my lap. "I was so upset. You have to understand."

His brows pinch and he tilts his head.

"I was crying. A lot." I suck in a breath. "My parents. Carey. I tried to hide from them, but the fear and humiliation would hit out of nowhere and they assumed it was because I missed you and was upset about our relationship ending."

I see the moment the information clicks. He tips his head to the side. "You told them I hurt you."

"No, I didn't, but..." *Please don't hate me.* "I didn't correct them."

He breaks eye contact and takes a few seconds to stare blindly over my shoulder before his gaze comes back to mine. "Okay." He nods.

I frown. "Okay? My entire family thinks you destroyed me, and I didn't correct them. How are you okay with that?"

He seems to think that over. "I'd take a bullet for you. If giving you what you need means vilifying me to your family, that's fine. Besides, I failed you. I deserved it."

"You did not fail me. We were too young to make the kind of promises we made to each other five years ago."

He fidgets with the bottle. "And now? How do you feel about making promises to each other now?"

I laugh uncomfortably. "So much has changed. We don't really know each other now."

He seems taken aback. "Of course we do. I'll admit a lot has changed for you in the last couple years. But me? I'm still me and I'm..." He chuckles, then sobers and fixes his gaze on mine. "I'm still hopelessly in love you."

My stomach plummets and my jaw follows suit.

He cracks a smile. "I can see you weren't expecting that."

I slam my mouth closed and slowly shake my head. "I wasn't."

"You can't be that surprised. I felt it the moment I set eyes on you at Tanner's wedding. It was like I'd gone so long without the missing piece of my soul, I'd forgotten it was even missing. But after seeing you again, the emptiness I feel without you is unbearable."

I swallow, unable to find words. Mainly because I don't know what to say. I'm attracted to Jack, I always have been. He was my first love, my first *everything*. I miss him touching me, but I'm not ready for sex again and I don't know if I ever will be. It's unfair to make any promises when I'm not sure I can be everything he needs.

"I don't mean to make things weird," he says, shifting uncomfortably. "And I'm sorry if this is too much too soon, but I have to be back in New York tomorrow and I can't leave the state without telling you how I feel."

"You realize how silly this sounds, right? We are on opposite sides of the country. History has proven our relationship can't handle distance. You have a great job in New York, and my exhibition will be on display here in Southern California for a while. We would never work, not like this."

"What if it doesn't have to be like this? What if you ran your exhibition by the curators in some New York galleries?"

"You want me to move to New York?"

"I want us to be together. No matter what that looks like, it's what I want."

"I can't see myself living in New York. Maybe you could move to San Diego?" The words are barely out of my mouth and he's shaking his head.

"It would be stupid to give up my job. I make great money."

I narrow my eyes on him. "There are more important things in life than money."

"Nothing is more important than food. We need it to live. And shelter. And transportation. All these things are paid for with money."

I slap my hands on my thighs. "Looks like you've got this all figured out, huh?" I stand. "I should get going. It's late."

"Wait!" He jumps up, and although his arms come out to touch me, he doesn't, and he drops them back to his sides. "Please think about it, okay? We deserve to give *us* another chance."

"As long as it doesn't inconvenience your life too much, is that right?"

"No. Dammit, I'm fucking this up." He looks around, his eyes going to the television. "Watch a movie with me. Please. I want to be close to you. I've missed you so much."

I cock a hip and lift a brow. "TV. That's it?"

"Yes. That's it. Just a movie, and I promise on my mother's grave I'll keep my hands to myself."

"Your mother's still alive."

He shrugs and grins that cocky smile I love. *Loved.* Past tense. "I promise on my mother's future grave."

"That's not even a thing."

He pops his lower lip in an exaggerated pout.

"Not the lip. Fine! I'll stay, but only for a half a movie." I kick off my heels and crawl onto the king-sized bed.

When my back is to the headboard and my legs are crossed at the ankles, he takes a similar position next to me and presses buttons on the remote. Warmth expands in my chest. It's been a long time since I've felt so safe. Maybe it's because my exhibition is finally over and all those memories I put on canvas are locked away in an art studio, in the dark and far away from my mind. Or maybe it's Jack. His presence brings me back to a simpler time when I knew exactly what I wanted and I knew what he wanted was me. And that was good enough for us. I try not to overanalyze the feeling and simply relax into it.

And shortly into *Top Gun*, I fall asleep.

CHAPTER NINETEEN

JACK

I wake to the sound of my alarm. My eyes dart open to see generic hotel furniture, and it takes me a bit to remember where I am. I blink, wondering why I'm so tired without being the least bit hungover. Then I remember.

Sadie.

The movie.

She fell asleep right after Maverick hit on Charlie at the bar. And once Sadie's eyes were closed, the movie held zero appeal. With a big fucking smile, I watched her sleep, as if I were some sort of sick, deranged psychopath. How long has it been since I had Sadie in my bed?

After Goose died, I folded the comforter over Sadie and fell asleep next to her.

With a grin, I roll onto my back then over, only to frown when I find the spot where she had been last night empty. And the comforter is folded over me. She left sometime in the night without saying goodbye?

I grab my phone and hit her number, rubbing my eyes and yawning. The call goes straight to voicemail. I check the time and decide if I shower quickly and forgo coffee or breakfast, I can leave early enough to swing by her place—ya know, to make sure she got home okay. And ask her why the hell she snuck out of my bed.

In record time, I'm showered, dressed in jeans and a T-shirt, and have my duffle slung over my shoulder as I wait for my Uber. Thankfully, it's less than a ten-minute drive to Hillcrest. With my driver waiting, I jog to her door and knock. No answer. I continue to bang on the door for another five minutes, then check to see Ricky's truck is gone.

"Dammit!" I stomp back to the car and pull out my phone as we make our way to the airport.

When she doesn't answer my call again, I open the myBubble app.

How was your exhibition?

I want to ask her if anyone special showed up and what she did after, but I can't. At this point, I just need to know Sadie is okay.

Her reply finally comes after I've been herded through security, and as I'm going up the elevator to the terminal, I read her response.

It was amazing. Better than I ever could've imagined. I wouldn't have changed a thing.

Okay, so Sadie is alive. Then why did she leave?

What made it amazing?

. . .

I hunt down my flight gate and have to apologize for bumping into travelers as I stare at my phone. Sadie responds, telling Dawn all about the curator from Los Angeles and the crowd. I notice she doesn't give away the content of her pieces or anything about that fuckwad Fabian. She also avoids any mention of me.

Not good.

I find my gate and drop into a seat, mumbling a string of curse words.

"Bad morning?"

I know that voice.

I lift my eyes to find the object of my obsession sitting across from me, and I smile so hard my cheeks hurt. *Sadie.* "You could say that."

She's wearing a tight blue sweater, her hair long and straight and falling over her shoulders, and a pair of black leggings. A backpack sits at her side. I spot her phone face down in her lap, and she's holding a coffee. She grins and takes a sip. "You feel like talking about it?"

I close the myBubble app before she can see it and shove my phone into my duffle before leaning forward with my elbows on my knees. "I fell asleep last night with a beautiful woman then woke up alone."

She sucks air through her teeth. "Ouch. That sucks."

"Tell me about it." I slump back in my seat, my heart beating a steady pace as the peace that comes from her presence and her smile washes over me. Legs wide and unable to swipe my grin off my face, I continue. "She didn't even say goodbye."

She shrugs. "Maybe that's because she wasn't ready to say goodbye. And maybe she had a bag to pack and a plane to catch."

I chuckle and resist the urge to pull her into my lap and kiss her breathless. I grip the armrests to keep from doing just that. "Are you saying what I think you're saying?"

She flashes her ticket, and I catch the only information I need.

8:20 a.m. to New York.

"How'd you know?"

Her face pinches. "You told me last night."

I shake my head. "No, I didn't."

She laughs. "Okay, fine. I texted *Andrea My Assistant* from your phone and asked which airline and what time the flight leaves."

"You did that this morning?"

"You should really password protect your phone."

My muscles tense when I consider what would've happened had she seen the myBubble app on my phone. Thankfully it's three swipes from the home screen and she's never been the snooping type. "I can't believe I didn't feel you get out of bed."

She shrugs and sips her coffee. "You were snoring like a baby."

"Do babies snore?"

"Of course."

We share a drawn-out moment of eye contact that's broken by the announcement that our flight is boarding. I ignore my seating assignment and stick close to Sadie, unable to stop looking at her.

"What?" she says as we shuffle down the jetway that leads to the plane.

"I can't believe you're actually here."

Her expression turns serious and maybe a little concerned. "I thought a lot about what you said last night, about how we owe us a chance to try again. With my exhibition over and no work until Wednesday, I figured why not treat myself to a couple days in New York?"

It's brave, and ballsy, and probably stupid, but I slip my hand in hers and squeeze. She flinches and blows out a tiny breath. I'm about to apologize and release her when she flashes a wavy grin and squeezes my hand back.

I allow Sadie to lead the way to the back of the plane and her assigned seat. The back of her seat is against the lavatory wall, so not only will it stink, but she also won't be able to recline. Literally the worst seat on the plane. A young guy wearing earphones and already asleep is on the aisle seat and a woman occupies the middle seat next to Sadie. Her seat belt already fastened and her nose buried in a book. When she sees Sadie, she hops up to allow her through.

"Hi there, what's your name?" I say to the other passenger.

She narrows her gaze. "Linda."

Linda is older, probably in her sixties. Should be an easy sell.

"I'd like to switch seats with you, Linda. If that's all right?"

She looks skeptical. When I wave the ticket in front of her, she doesn't even look at it. "Why?"

"Because I'm madly in love with this girl here," I say and watch Sadie's beautiful skin flush pink. "And I can't fathom being on the same plane and not close enough to hold her hand."

Linda grins but eyes my ticket.

"I think you'll be happy with it. You'll be able to put your seat back at least. So? What do you say, want to switch?"

She gathers her things. "Sure, I guess that's fine." I hand her the ticket and, after looking at it, she laughs. "First—"

"The stewardess should be able to help you find your seat."

"Is there a problem here?" a steward says as he studies us gathered in the aisle.

"Nope, no problem at all," I say, nodding to where my booty should be.

Linda's still staring at her ticket. I talk a little faster and get her moving, and thankfully, she eventually moves on up to first class. I drop into the middle seat with Sadie at the window. Literally the worst possible seat on the entire plane, but I don't care. I'm with my girl. I turn and smile at her, then rephrase in my head.

Woman. Most definitely a woman.

"Jack Daniels?" She leans in close, and the feel of her breath against my ear brings a soft moan from my throat. "Did you give up your first-class seat to sit back here with the peasants in coach?"

I sigh and my shoulders drop. "I was hoping you wouldn't notice. I get the feeling you already see me as some pretentious prick with more money than sense. I didn't want to reinforce your opinion of me."

"What you did was really sweet."

When she slips her hand in mine, I practically gasp like a fourteen-year-old virgin.

"So you can add that to the list of things I think about you," she says before turning to the window.

We take off and watch the Pacific Ocean fade behind us as we head to New York. This will be the first time she's ever come to New York with me. When I was in college, I always came to Vegas to see her, and I never did make it to San Diego. I want her to love New York enough to want to move there, live with me, and complete the life I've made for myself that has been missing something so vital.

Missing her.

SADIE

Our flight lands at JFK shortly after four thirty in the afternoon New York time. Jack and I spent the five-and-a-half-hour flight catching up on his life and mine. I mostly talked about school, Ricky, and the few friends I've had who had the sense to move on to different states. I touched briefly on the assault—enough to explain what my exhibition left out—and talking about it with Jack wasn't as hard as I'd thought it would be.

Although I still carry the mental scars of what Fabian did to me—the thought of allowing another man to touch me intimately is terrifying—I believe I've finally left behind the shame and stopped blaming myself.

Jack grabs my backpack and his duffle, and being in the last row in the plane means we're the last to get off. We hold hands through the airport. Mostly so we don't get separated in the hustle and bustle—or at least that's what we pretend. The fact is, being touched again by a strong and gentle hand feels amazing and it's easy for my skin to remember how good having Jack's hands on me felt.

We walk out of the airport and get a cab. Jack rambles off an address in a matter-of-fact way that reminds me he's probably done it a million times. There's no small talk, no typical Daniels charm in his interaction. This is the business side of Jack. New York Jack.

"You hungry?" he asks, a sweet smile pointed my way.

"Starving."

"Good. There's a place in my building that has the best pizza, and I know how much you love pizza."

"Sounds perfect."

I look out the window, soaking up as much of the New York scenery as I can. Tall buildings, crowded streets, lots of honking. The feel is very different from So Cal or even Las Vegas.

Jack makes a couple calls, asking about meetings and deadlines, getting caught up on work stuff, I guess. I tune him out and take in New York. I've never heard so many car horns. After a lot of stop-and-go, I'm grateful to feel the cab stop and hear the driver mutter the amount.

Jack swipes a card, hits a couple buttons, and then offers to help me out of the back seat. He grabs our bags from the trunk while I stare at a tall building made of glass, metal, and concrete. It's more modern than I would've expected, looking more like a business building than a residential one. The smell of garlic and dough calls my eyes to a cute pizza place at the base of the building.

"Come on," Jack says, motioning for me to follow him through the double doors.

"Welcome home, Mr. Daniels." The doorman wearing a black

suit and name tag greets Jack, then does a double-take on me. "Miss."

"Jonathan," Jack says with little feeling. "Good to be home."

Jack guides me to a bank of elevators, and I'm amazed at how comfortable he seems living in what seems to be more hotel than home.

"What do you think?" He leans proudly against the elevator wall.

"Fancy," I say with a smile.

I won't tell him the truth, but his demeanor changed since we got here. The silly, fun-loving Jack was apparently left behind on our plane. As far as the building goes, it seems cold, sterile. It lacks any personality or personal flare. I'm used to places covered in folk art and colors. This place doesn't seem like Jack at all. When he was young, his room was covered in sports posters, and his two guitars hung on the walls. This new Jack has more refined tastes, more culture, less... me.

He leads me down a long hallway with wood floors and modern wall sconces. Like a hotel, every door looks the same. We stop at 2533 and I commit the number to memory in the event that I might have to find it again on my own.

"How long have you lived here?" I ask as he unlocks the door and pushes it open.

"About a year." He flips on the lights.

The apartment is as bland as the rest of the building. Modern furniture, generic framed art on the walls, nothing with any kind of personality.

"Did it come furnished?"

Jack looks around as if he's trying to see his place through my eyes. "No. I bought all this, with the help of a decorator."

I follow him through the small living room, past a nook-style dining room, to a hallway that leads to the bedroom.

He drops our bags on his king-sized bed. "I only have one bedroom. I'm happy to take the couch if—"

"It's fine." I smile, hoping to relieve some of the nervous

energy buzzing between us. "That bed is plenty big for the both of us."

"Remember squeezing into your twin at your parents' house?"

"My dad refused to get me a queen." I laugh. "We had to spoon the entire night to fit."

"His plan to keep you alone in that bed backfired big time." His gaze darts down my body. "Meant I got to hold you closer through the night."

The nervous energy changes to tension, the kind that pulls at my belly and makes my body warm.

He blinks and clears his throat. "Food. I should get you fed. That airplane food is shit."

He heads toward the open doorway where I'm standing, and I take a second too long to move. He stops inches from me.

"I'm sorry, I..." I side step only to have his big hands catch my hips, keeping me in place. I stare at his shirt, afraid to see what emotion might be burning in his eyes. "Jack..."

Cautiously, his hands slide from my hips to my lower back, tugging my front flush with his. "Is this okay?"

Is it? I do a quick inventory of my feelings and find only comfort, safety, and heat. "Yes."

He presses his lips to the top of my head, and I hear his deep inhale. I tentatively rest my hands on his powerful back, falling deeper into the hug. A soft sigh falls from his lips as I rest my cheek against his chest. His heart hammers, matching the urgency of my own.

I don't know how long we stand like this—his body curled around mine while I hold him as tightly as I can. All I know is that I would stay like this, wrapped up in Jack, for as long as he'd allow it.

My stomach growls and he chuckles into my hair. "I need to get you fed, Sadie girl."

Now it's my turn to sigh, both at the tender way he says my old nickname and at my reluctance to pull away.

His lips press to my head again, a little firmer, lingering a little longer, then he pulls back enough to grab my hand. "Thank you for that."

"I was about to say the same to you."

The smile that stretches across his face is nothing short of brilliant, and I can't help but match it with one of my own. I didn't realize how much I missed Jack, and now that we're together, I wonder how I ever managed so long without him.

CHAPTER TWENTY

JACK

"Tanner had to walk all the way home in snow, wearing nothing but his shirt and boots, holding his dick and balls in his hands to keep them from freezing off." I'm telling Sadie about the last day of our junior year, when Tanner hooked up with a chick in the bathroom at a bar and she stole his pants to get his wallet.

Sadie laughs, and the sound swirls around me like an embrace. She sips on her water through a straw. The straw I've been cursing all night, because there's something beautiful about watching her lean forward and wrap her lips around it.

I'm a fucking pig.

"That sounds like something that would happen to Tanner," she says, leaning back in her seat. We polished off a large pepperoni pizza. She had two pieces, and I ate the rest. "His wife must be something special to put up with him on a daily basis."

I take a gulp of my Peroni. "She's something, all right."

She grimaces. "That doesn't sound good."

"Do you remember Amy Alcott from high school?"

"How could I forget? She stole the Tiffany necklace my parents got me for my sixteenth birthday, remember?"

"Oh shit, that's right!"

"Remember she swore it was hers? But I know I swiped it from my PE locker. I always took it off because I thought I would lose it. Bitch."

"Let's just say, Tanner's wife, Maribeth, reminds me very much of Amy Alcott."

She grins but says, "Yikes."

I grin back. "Yeah."

We fall into a stretch of silent eye contact. It's been happening more and more tonight, and I wonder if her thoughts are headed in the same direction mine are. It's as if our hormones have picked up right where they left off years ago.

She breaks the eye contact and scoots her water glass around on the table. "I uh, I'm going to hit the ladies' room. I'll be right back."

"Sure." I point her toward the bathroom and watch her sexy ass as she moves across the room before she disappears around a corner.

I know the polite thing to do would be to offer to do a little sightseeing. After all, it's not even six o'clock yet and she's never been to the city. But all I really want to do is take her home, strip her down, and pull her into my bed.

Shit. No, I can't do that. Not after what that fuck in San Diego did to her. I down the rest of my beer and wish I could break the bottle over that Fabian fuckers head then slice off his dick with the broken glass. Then I would gather the severed— the myBubble app pings with a new notification, dissolving all thoughts of a bloody revenge.

I look toward the bathrooms. What could she possibly be texting Dawn about from the john?

I pull out my phone and check the message under the table.

Have you ever hooked up with an ex-boyfriend, ya know, when you're not actually together?

. . .

"Holy shit," I mumble and text back.

Absolutely! Highly recommend.

Really?

"Umm, yeah," I say to myself while typing back.

Umm, yeah!

Why?

"Because your ex-boyfriend is sitting out here feeling like he might explode if he doesn't get his hands on you? Because he loves you? Because you need to be reminded of what it's like to be with someone who can make you feel good? And safe?" I can't say that, so I come up with how I think a female would respond.

To see if there's still something there. Chemistry. Compatibility. Love?

None of those were ever an issue for us in the past. ;)

A winky face? A slow grin tugs at my lips. "No, sweetheart, they sure as fuck were not, and they still won't be if you'd only let me prove it." I type back a speedy response.

I say go for it!

What if it ends up meaning more to me than it does to him? What if I fall for him again and he doesn't feel the same?

My chest throbs painfully that she'd think that's even a possibility. "Not a chance, Sadie girl."

What does your gut tell you?

When she doesn't respond right away, I check the bathrooms, nervous she'll walk out at any moment. My heart pounds when the text bubbles come back, and I wait not-so-fucking-patiently for her response.

My gut tells me to go for it.

"Yes!" I shout, earning a glare from the couple next to me. "I'm sorry." I type back.

There's your answer.

. . .

Having all the information I need, I tuck my phone into my pocket as Sadie comes out of the bathroom.

She slides into the booth across from me and scowls. "What?"

"What do you mean *what*?"

Her gaze roams my face, studying my attempt to smother a stupid grin. "Why do you look weird?"

"Me? Weird?"

She tilts her head adorably. "Yeah." She's smiling and so fucking cute. "You have that look."

"This look?" I point toward my face.

Her expression warms as we fall into our familiar old banter.

I lean my elbows on the table, holding her gaze. "Get used to it, because this is the look of a man who is not going to take even a second of his time with you for granted."

She leans into the table too, her hand propped under her chin. "You know, sometimes I think you've changed so much, but other times, when you say stuff like that, I think you haven't changed at all."

"I'm still me, with a few improvements."

"Improvements? I'll be the judge of that."

Is it just me or did her voice drop an octave? "What do you want?"

Her brows pinch together. "What do you mean?"

A flush of pink kisses her cheeks, telling me she knows exactly what I mean. When she shifts uncomfortably in her seat, I break the tension, fearing too much too soon might spook her. "To do? What do you want to do?"

Her eyes flare a little. It's subtle, but I catch it. "What, uh, what are my options?"

"I could take you sightseeing?"

She seems a little relieved but shrugs.

"A movie?"

"Out? Or... in?"

I'm not sure if she hesitated before the last word or if I imagined it, but either way, I like how she said it. With expectation and promise. "Your choice."

When it comes to taking things between us to the next level physically, after what happened to her, it has to be on her terms completely.

"It's been a long day of traveling"—she draws patterns on the table with her finger—"and I didn't get any sleep on the plane because the guy I was sitting next to *wouldn't* stop talking."

"Dick."

"I know, right." She smiles and meets my eyes without a hint of hesitation. "A movie in sounds great."

Yes, yes, *fuck* yes!

"Cool. I'll get the bill." I flag down our waitress and rather than give her a card and have to wait for her to bring it back, I throw down cash and hold out my hand to Sadie. "Let's go get comfortable and I'll even let you pick the movie."

She looks at me with a sparkle in her eyes. "*The Fault in our Stars.*"

"What?"

"It's a movie. You haven't seen it?"

I shake my head. If I know Sadie like I think I do, it's a romantic movie. The title implies fate and destiny and a meant-to-be kind of love. Sounds perfect for us.

She smirks. "Oh, this'll be fun."

SADIE

"I'm not crying." Jack swipes his eyes. "Stop staring at me."

I roll my lips between my teeth to keep from laughing because oh my God, he is totally crying. "You don't have to be ashamed. It's a sad movie."

"Why would you suggest this?" He sniffs. "It's fucking awful."

I snuggle deeper under the blanket to hide my grin.

Once we got back from having pizza I changed into sleeping shorts and a tank top and he kicked off his shoes but kept on his jeans and T-shirt. He assured me we would be able to find any movie we wanted on his gigantic big screen TV, and he was right. We rented *The Fault in Our Stars*, one of my all-time favorite movies that I've seen a million times. It helped when I was in desperate need of a good cry, but I'm desensitized to it now.

"It's romantic." I shrug.

His wide, bloodshot eyes swing toward me. "*Romantic?*"

"In a *Romeo and Juliet* kind of way."

"Fuck." He makes another pass at me with his eyes then pushes up from the couch. "This dark side of you. It's new."

"Life will do that to a person." I sit up taller to talk to him over the back of the couch as he fills a glass of water in the kitchen. "Sorry I'm not all unicorns and rainbows anymore."

He looks at me thoughtfully. "I'm sorry, I didn't mean—"

"It's cool. I get it."

He drains the glass of water and comes back to the couch. Rather than sitting on the opposite end where he spent the entire movie, he sits right next to me, his hip pressed to mine, his torso twisted to face me. "I didn't say I didn't *like* this new side of you."

I open my mouth to say something snarky, but the words die in my throat when his hand pushes hair off of my face and tucks it behind my ear. His gaze drops from my eyes to my lips.

"Are you going to kiss me?"

"I'd love to kiss you." His eyes search mine. "Would it be all right if I did?"

I swallow and slowly nod. I've wanted to kiss Jack all night, fantasized about what it would be like to feel his lips on mine again, but now that we're here, so close, a flutter of fear crawls up my throat.

This is Jack.

Safe. Sweet. Gentle Jack.

He leans in, bringing his lips so close, but stops before they touch mine. He studies me again, and whatever he sees makes him close the distance and press his lips to mine. His hands stay at his sides, only our mouths making contact. He lightly kisses the corners of my mouth, one then the other, teasing, testing, toying.

All too soon, he pulls back, his eyelids low, and checks with me again. "Okay?"

"Yes," I say, my voice deeper than normal. I shift my legs, and this time, I lean into him, tilting my head, pressing my mouth to his.

I watch his eyes flutter closed, feel his hands clench the blanket covering my legs, but he's still cautious and doesn't touch me.

I run through a checklist of how I'm feeling—steady pulse, clear airways, mind in the moment. I'm good.

Better than good.

I want more.

Tossing the blanket aside, I crawl onto Jack's lap, straddling his thighs and running my hands through his hair.

He gasps, "You sure?" seconds before I press my mouth to his.

I've always wondered what people meant when they said falling into the arms of someone you love feels like coming home. I get it now.

The familiar way our mouths fuse together, his comforting touch that grips my hips softly as he pulls me closer to fit our bodies together. As if no time had been lost between us, we kiss with an abandon I haven't felt in years. His silky hair slips through my fingers, reminding me of the way he used to moan when I'd rake my nails along his scalp.

"Still okay?" he whispers while he dodges my efforts to chase down his lips. He chuckles softly. "I'm going to assume your answer is yes, but I need to hear you say it."

I pull back enough to get his eyes. "Yes." I roll my hips against his and he drops his gaze to the point of friction between us. He sucks his bottom lip into his mouth. "I'm fine. I promise I'll let you know if things get uncomfortable."

His eyes are back on mine, full of compassion. "You promise? Because I'm going to do my best to go slow, but you know that has never been easy for me when I'm with you."

"Promise," I say against his lips then drag the tip of my tongue along the seam of his mouth. "Open."

The word is barely out of my mouth when he dives back into a deep kiss that sends chills all over my skin. Jack was always a fierce yet conscientious lover, more in tune with my body during the throes of passion than I ever was. He licks into my mouth with a gentle urgency that has me leaning in to pin him in place with my body.

His head falls back, his thick muscular neck open and begging for my mouth. I kiss down his jaw to his throat. The soft skin combined with the harsh scratch of his beard growth is delicious. The scent of his cologne is stronger here, and I lick up to his earlobe, breathing him in the entire way.

"You smell so good."

His hands clench against my hips and a flutter of panic reminds me to stay present. I can't get lost in his touch. Not yet. The last thing I want to do is scare him away by having a complete mental breakdown during our first make-out after all those years apart.

I am in charge.

I have control.

Jack is not Fabian.

We make out for a while, me repeating my mantra to stay calm when his hold gets too tight, and him practically shaking with the effort it takes for him to leave me in control of our progress and pace.

All the kissing makes me dizzy with want, but the fear of starting something I won't be able to finish is enough for me to hold back. I forgot how much I loved his kisses. I could do this all day.

But I don't want to.

Now that we're both warmed up and I'm feeling the whis-

pered desire for more, I figure why not try? Who knows if I'll
ever get these feelings again? With shaky fingers, I pull his hand
from my waist.

He releases me and pulls his head back, his eyes wide with
worry. "Too much?"

I shake my head and slide his hand under my shirt. His gaze
darts from his hand to my face. "Not enough."

Inch by painfully slow inch, I bring his hand up my bare
stomach, over my rib cage, and finally, I press his palm to my
naked breast. He doesn't move, I don't even think he's breathing,
as he watches his hand under my shirt.

"Remind me it doesn't always hurt to be touched here," I say,
feeling anxiety surge through my body in an unforgiving wave.
My pulse picks up and my breathing speeds, but I don't want
him to stop.

His fingers quake against my skin, his thumb putting forth
minimal pressure to cup me. "Can I see?"

Fabian shoved his hands roughly up my shirt. I wonder if
removing it all together might alleviate some of my fear, make
this experience different from the last.

Without words, I hook my fingers under the hem of my shirt
and pull it off over my head. I don't have a bra on, and as soon as
his eyes fix on my naked boobs, he lifts his torso off the couch
for a closer look. His barely-there touch still cups my breast, and
his other hand holds me steady at my hip. He licks his lips.
Once. Twice.

"It's okay."

He seems apologetic when he says, "Are you sure?" As if the
last thing he wants to do is give in to his baser instincts but he
knows it's a losing battle.

I arch my back, offering my chest, bringing my hard nipples
closer to his mouth. He leans in with a long, deep, gravelly moan
as he sucks the tip and swirls his tongue around it. His gaze
comes to mine to judge my response, and I smile because he
doesn't break his connection to ask.

"I'm still okay."

His eyelids flutter closed and he licks, sucks, and nibbles on my breasts until I'm moaning rocking against him. My hands tighten in his hair. His hard-on is thick and punching at his button fly, and I rub against it with long, firm rolls of my hips, making him growl against my sensitive chest.

"Don't stop," he says. When I don't, he mumbles, "God, I missed you." His words dissolve against my skin as he licks and kisses between my breasts, my collarbone, and my neck. "Let me take you to bed?"

My muscles lock up. His mouth holds still against my neck, but I know he can feel my hard swallow because he backs away, peering up at me with a cautious gaze.

"I'm not sure I'm ready for... that."

He nods, and his big hands run up and down my bare arms in soothing strokes. "Sex."

I cringe involuntarily then feel guilty about my reaction. "I'm sorr—"

His finger pressed to my lips silences my apology. "Don't." He lets his hand drop away from my face, and I cover my breasts with my arms, feeling bashful. "You have nothing to be sorry about."

I can't help but laugh. "I'm straddling your lap with my top off, Jack. I practically jumped you, and when you mention the word s-e-x, I act like you threw a live sewer roach in my face."

He studies me, taking in my more guarded position, but makes no move to lull me back to comfort. Instead, he rests his hands at his sides on the couch, and as much as I miss his touch, I appreciate the space.

"Why can't you say the word?" There's no condemnation in his tone, only curiosity.

"You say..." I struggle to get the word out. "Sex. I hear sexual assault. I know it makes no sense, but it's involuntary. I hate the word."

"Did he..." He seems to struggle to find the right words. "I couldn't tell from your paintings if he…" His lips curl back from his teeth.

"Are you asking about penetration?" I have to use medical terms or it'll dirty whatever we end up doing tonight. "He did, with his fingers." I clear my throat.

"*Fuck!*" He holds up his hand. "I'm sorry. I don't want to scare you. I'm just so pissed I didn't kill that asshole when I had the chance."

"If it makes you feel better, he didn't rape me in the traditional sense."

His eyes snap to mine. "Make me feel better? No. That doesn't make me feel better. What does make me feel better is knowing you feel safe enough with me to finally talk about it."

I stare off at nothing over his shoulder and consider that. I had tried so hard to hide it from my family, from anyone with ties to my family, and I would've continued to hide it from Jack if he hadn't crashed my exhibition. If he hadn't done that, we wouldn't be where we are. Because I would've kept the horrific nature of that night away from him for as long as I lived, and because of that, I never could've really been with him. I would've always been holding back a big part of myself.

"I do feel safe talking about it with you."

He wraps me up and crushes me to his chest, his face in my neck and his warm breath against my throat. "I don't care if we never make love." He must sense me rolling my eyes in disbelief because he continues. "I'm dead fucking serious. If all you're okay with is kissing and letting me hold you, I swear that's enough for me."

"Liar." I chuckle.

He growls, holds me tightly, and stands with me in his arms. I squeal at the abrupt change in position—and seriously, what kind of thigh strength does it take to lift both of us from a sitting position? I wrap my legs around his waist, and he carries me to his bed. If we hadn't just talked about my bedroom hang-ups, I may have panicked, but I put all my issues out on the table and he accepted them, accepted me, scars and all.

When he drops me on the bed and lies next to me, I have no concerns about his intentions with me.

"Tired?"

I shrug. "Not really."

"Want to watch another movie?"

I roll onto my side to face him. "I was kind of enjoying what we were doing on the couch."

A slow smile spreads across his handsome face. "Oh yeah?"

Nodding, I slink up and over his big body, mimicking our position on the couch, but this time he's lying flat on his back.

He puts his hands behind his head. Surprisingly—since I'm topless—he keeps his eyes on mine. "I'm all yours, Ms. Slade."

I run my hands from his firm, muscular stomach to his chest, down, then back up again. The next time my fingers follow the same path, I pull his shirt up and he shifts to help me tug it from his body and toss it on the floor. "I have an idea."

A low rumble vibrates in his throat as I kiss his neck and brush my bare torso against his. I have to agree—skin on skin, we feel so good.

So right.

Meant to be.

JACK

"Are you sure you're okay with this?" Sadie stands over me on the bed, wearing my shirt and checking her work.

I flex my hands against the restraint of my BOSS necktie and adrenaline races through me. "I think it's pretty obvious I'm more than okay with it." The tip of my hard-on is strangled by the waistband of my jeans. I tip my head and smirk playfully. "You think you could free up a couple buttons there before I lose circulation?"

Since she suggested tying my hands above my head, I've been

practically shaking with excitement for whatever she has planned. I hope she teases and plays with me all night. There's something so sexy about her using me to get back her power and feeling of control.

She straddles my thighs, her soft fingers going to my fly. She brushes against my erection while releasing the first few buttons. My hips thrust forward and Sadie flashes a sly grin. "Better?"

I'm biting my lip so hard it hurts, and I nod quickly.

"Good," she whispers as she drops forward to press her T-shirt-clad breasts to my bare torso.

I vacillate between asking her to take off the shirt and wanting her to keep it on because she wears it like a claim. My claim on her. Her claim on me.

Her lips find my neck, and she tortures me with her tongue, teeth, and those sweet fucking lips as she draws them down my chest. She sucks my nipples, and I groan when she scrapes her teeth against them. "You've gotten bigger."

I roll my hips. "Thank you."

She tickles my ribs. "Not that—Hey! Arms down."

"Sorry." I lick my lips. "You know I'm ticklish. They responded on their own. I won't move them again, I promise. Just please." A shudder of pleasure skips up my spine as she drops her sexy ass on my dick. "Don't stop."

Her long hair falls beautifully over her shoulders, and she walks her fingers down to my belly button, where she swirls the tips of her fingers around and lower. My lips part and I'm fucking panting.

"I like this side of you, Jack Daniels."

"Oh yeah?" It takes effort for me to catch a breath big enough to speak a complete sentence while she's teasing so close to where I want her most. "What side is that?"

"Tied up, on your back, and at my mercy."

"Always been at your mercy." And it's true. Our entire lives, she has owned every part of me. Up until I left for college and, without realizing I was doing it, I took back all those parts of myself and lived for me rather than us.

She dips down and kisses along my abdomen, taking what feels like hours on each spot that makes my hard-on kick before she moves to the next. My hands flex and release, a light sheen of sweat breaking out against my skin. The restraints burn against my wrists from my pulling against them, but I refuse to move my arms.

Time slows to a crawl as she tempts me with her mouth on my hips. I'm hypersensitive to the brush of her hair as it trails along my skin. She tugs at my jeans and I lift my hips to assist her as she pulls them down, along with my boxer briefs. But she stops at my thighs, locking my legs together as she looks at me. I want her to touch me there, but I refuse to ask. Tonight is all for her.

If I screw it up, I may never get a second chance.

Silence builds between us, the air thickening as tension builds. Her gaze slides along my body in what feels like a physical caress.

"Are you doing okay?" She eyes my wrists tied above my head.

"So good."

She grins at the rugged sound of my voice.

Touch me, please.

She must pick up on my mental communication because she rakes her nails down my rib cage to my belly and grips my dick in a firm hold.

"Oh fuck," I groan, and I fight against the orgasm that's begging to be released.

Her gaze darts to mine, and heat fires behind her blue-green eyes as she strokes me.

My mouth falls open. I wouldn't be surprised if my tongue falls out of my mouth as I pant to catch my breath and keep from passing out. "Sadie, baby—"

My words dissolve in a moan when she tightens her grip and twists.

I'm about to tell her to slow down, warn her that I'm seconds away from making a mess in her beautiful hand, when she dips down and licks the tip.

Every muscle in my body coils and my back arches off the bed. "Sadie, I'm gonna... if you, oh my..."

Her mouth wraps around me in a vicious suction that robs me of all rational thought. This is not how I wanted tonight to go. I wanted to spend hours making her feel good, reminding her what being made love to is supposed to feel like. Remind her of what we felt like together, but...

"*Oh shit.*" It's coming. I try to pull away from her, but like she did with my lips when we were kissing, she chases me down. I promised I'd keep my hands above my head so the only other thing I can do is—"I'm gonna come."

Her grip tightens. She takes me deeper, to the very back of her throat.

I've never finished in Sadie's mouth before. I always pulled out, thinking she wouldn't like it, and she never fought me on it.

Until now.

She licks me with more pressure. Sucks. Tugs.

I explode.

I swear my fucking vision blacks out. Stars dance in the darkness and my entire body bows off the bed. She stays between my legs, mouth sealed, fist tight as she moans and draws a similar sound out of me.

My arms itch to fall forward, grab her, and pull her to my chest so she can feel my racing heart. I keep them above my head. "I want to hold you."

She releases me from her mouth and crawls up my body. With a little work, she manages to untie my hands. The muscles in my shoulders ache when I bring my arms down and wrap them around her, pulling her tightly to my chest.

"You're sweaty," she says, pressing her cheek to my pec and throwing her arm over my waist.

"I don't think you realize the workout you put me through."

My voice is even hoarse. "Keeping my hands off you was impossible."

She smiles at me, lips pink and swollen. "But you did it."

I take her sweet lips in a slow, tender kiss. The saltiness of my release is fresh on her tongue. I should care, right? Tasting myself should gross me out, but it doesn't. If anything, I can already feel the stir of arousal as a second wave fills me. I suck on her lips and mumble against them, "Your mouth is magic, Sadie girl."

"I've never done that before."

"No? I mean, I know you've never swallowed with me, but—"

"There's only been you, Jack."

Relief wars with disgust, and to hide my reaction to her confession, I pull her back to my chest. I had a feeling her only sexual experience outside of me was what that rapist fuck put her through, and I hate that for her. With every part of my being, I hate that for her.

"What about you? I'm sure you've had plenty of women do that for you." Her voice sounds uneasy, as if she doesn't really want the answer to the question.

"Honestly? Not one."

Her head pops up, disbelief in her eyes.

I chuckle and run my fingers through her hair, tucking the silky strands behind her ear. "The most I've ever done with another woman is kiss, and in my defense, I was drunk and she kissed me."

"Really?"

"Yes. Of course. Sadie, even when I thought I was ready to let someone else in, I never could. You were the standard I held every woman against, and none of them came close. I would never lie to you about that." *But I lie to you about other things.* An ache forms in the back of my throat, guilt reminding me that the myBubble conversations need to stop.

I forget about all that for now as I watch a slow smile spread across her face. "So... you've never done... um..."

"You're the only woman I've ever made love to, had sex with, fucked—whatever you want to call it, the truth is still the same."

"Wow..." Her eyes get dreamy, and she drops back to my chest. "I'm happy to hear that."

I work my boxer briefs and jeans back up but leave the buttons open before I roll to my side and push up on one elbow. I trace her bare thigh with my fingertips, watching goose bumps trail my touch. "Will you let me make you feel good?"

Her muscles tense, drawing my eyes to hers. "I don't think I'm ready for that yet." She sounds so small, so vulnerable, and again I go back to wanting to crush that dickbag for taking her sexual freedom from her. "I need to be the one delivering for a while, if that's okay. I-I'm afraid if you touch me, I'll flashback to that night."

"However long it takes, I'm not going anywhere. And if you never get to a point where you're okay with me touching you, that's all right too. We'll work around it."

She blows out a breath and her shoulders relax. "Thank you."

I pull her into my arms and close my eyes, amazed that I have my Sadie back in my life, in my arms, and in my bed.

Not a single thing could ruin this.

CHAPTER TWENTY-ONE

JACK

I'm staring at the light on the waffle maker, waiting for it to change colors, with a big, stupid grin on my face. Not because I love waffles, but because the woman who does is sound asleep in my bed.

Sadie.

My Sadie.

She slept in my arms all night, her arm thrown over my gut, her leg interwoven with mine, and I fought sleep for as long as I could so I could lie there and enjoy it.

I would still be there if it weren't for my wanting to make her breakfast in bed. The desire to meet Sadie's needs before she's even aware of them overrides all desires to meet my own.

The light turns green and I open the iron to find the waffle not quite as crispy as I know she likes, so I fork it out, trash it, and pour another.

My phone pings with the myBubble notification, stealing my attention. I stare at the closed door to my room and smirk. She's messaging Dawn. This early?

I open the message and grin.

. . .

I did it and it was ahhh-mazing!

My heart gallops. It really was incredible. I was so nervous to touch her, so afraid that she'd be hesitant after what she'd been through, but she blew me away with her honesty. She was clear about what she needed from me, and I loved every bit of it.

I chew my lip, wondering how to respond. Then I type and send.

And? Feelings still there?

I'm afraid to know the answer, but I have to. Was last night just a trial run for her? Was I a safe guy to experiment with? Or is this leading where I hope it is?

I frown as her text bubbles come and go and start up again. She's thinking way too hard about this. Not good news for me.

When I smell smoke, I whirl around. My phone pings with her response as I throw open the waffle iron and curse at the charred breakfast. I toss it in the garbage and reach for my phone.

"Good morning," Sadie says from right behind me.

I shove my phone in my jeans pocket and try to act casual.

"What smells?"

"That, my beautiful girl, was your breakfast." I lean in, hesitate while I wait for her consent, then press my lips to hers. "Good morning."

Her bashful smile warms my chest while my phone with her answer burns in my pocket.

She peeks around me. "Waffles?"

I follow her line of sight. "That's the goal."

"Need some help?" She steps around me, and I barely resist the urge to slide my palms up her smooth thighs and under her shorts.

"Evidence would suggest that I do."

She busies herself at the waffle iron while I make her a cup of coffee the way she likes it—cream, four sugars. She's sucking on her bottom lip while pouring batter into the iron, and I'm reminded of her mouth on me last night.

"Ouch—fuck." Hot coffee stings my torso.

I'm setting her cup down to grab a paper towel when I feel the soft press of her fingers as she swipes the liquid that has dripped down and around my belly button. She sticks two fingers in her mouth and sucks the coffee from them with a hot flare in her eyes. After licking them clean, she dips those fingers into the front of my jeans. Her saliva-covered fingers brush the tip of my hard-on and I fall back against the countertop, my legs going completely weak. She steps close, licks her lips, and eyes my dick.

"Sadie girl, are you trying to tell me you don't want waffles for breakfast?"

"Why can't I have both?" Her eyes flash to mine. "Hands?"

I grip the countertop behind me and hold on for dear life as the vision of her dropping to her knees in front of me, in my kitchen, wearing my T-shirt, brings me to the brink of orgasm. She slides my jeans down to my knees and grips me in a tight fist.

Smoke rises from the waffle iron, but my thoughts are stuck on Sadie as she takes me slowly into her mouth. My knees buckle and I hold the countertop tighter as the warm sensation of her tongue drives me crazy. The smoke thickens and I feel as though I'm in a race to finish before the smoke alarm goes off and makes Sadie stop.

I want to tell her to stop teasing, to go faster and stroke harder, but I know she needs to be in control. I won't take that from her.

My heart races. My chest rises and falls faster and faster as I watch her. Then she does something I've noticed she hasn't done yet. Not during our kiss in my old truck in Vegas. Not at all last night on the couch or in my bed.

She closes her eyes.

And when she does, she moans deep in her throat and the vibration pulls my release to the surface.

"Sadie..."

I try to pull my hips back to free her mouth, but like last night, she chases me down, securing the suction that punches my hips forward. I watch her throat work as she helps me ride it out.

My arms shake with the effort it takes to remain standing as she pulls free and climbs up my body to standing. She flashes a brilliant smile, and I take her mouth. Hot, heavy, and maybe a little too hard. But when her hands slip into my hair and she tilts her head, opening for me, licking inside my mouth, and tasting my tongue, I decide she's okay with my eager kiss.

The screech of the smoke detector breaks us apart, but only long enough for me to unplug the waffle iron, toss it in the sink, and turn on the water. Then we're back on each other, our mouths fused together as smoke burns our noses.

"Let me taste you," I say against her lips.

She sucks in a quick breath. "Not yet."

I swore to myself I wouldn't push her, but when we're together like this, it's nearly impossible to hold back. Visions of her paintings flash behind my eyes, and I rest my forehead against her shoulder, catching my breath, pulling her tighter to me. "I'm sorry. I shouldn't—"

"Don't apologize for wanting me." She pulls back and I leave a few inches between us so that I can calm down. "How about we grab some fresh air?"

With the waffle iron soaked, breakfast in bed is out of the question. "I know a great place we could go for some real New York bagels."

"That sounds perfect." Her voice is as shaky as mine as we recover from the wave of arousal that nearly took us under.

I bend forward to pull up my jeans and there's a crack of something hitting the floor. By the time I realize what it was, she already has my phone in her hand. I snag it from her too quickly and her eyebrows pinch together.

I make a show of checking out the screen. "Thank God, I thought it cracked." I shove the device in my pocket and flash a reassuring smile. "It sounded like it cracked, didn't it?"

She doesn't look convinced but lets it go and grabs her coffee mug. "I need twenty minutes and then we can go."

"Yeah, sure. Of course. However much time you need." *Slow down, Jack! You sound guilty.* This is what happens when I'm forced to think fast, like, fifteen seconds after an orgasm. My brain isn't back online yet!

She disappears into the bedroom, and when I hear the bathroom door close, I scramble to get to my phone. I hit the myBubble app and open Sadie's last response. Dawn had asked her if she still had feelings for me. My eyes skim the response once. Twice. And a third time to make sure my eyes aren't deceiving me.

All of the feelings are there and MORE. I think I'm still in love with him.

I watch my bedroom door, hear the shower running, and smile so big it hurts.

"I love you too, Sadie girl. I'm never letting you go."

SADIE

"Is it me or is our waiter totally flirting with you?"

From my position on the patio of a little vegan café, I watch as Jack glares at our server from across the room.

"He wasn't flirting, he was just being nice." I'm lying. He was kind of flirting.

By the time we were both showered and ready to leave his apartment, it was closer to lunch than breakfast, and after pizza last night, I was craving something healthier than bagels. Jack swore this place was the best vegan restaurant in town, so here we are.

Jack's scowl swings to me. "Your eyes *are* gorgeous, but what was that he was saying about your hips?"

I shrug and fork another bite of kale into my mouth. "He said I have good hips."

"Yeah, that." He goes back to watching the man. "What the fuck was the point of telling you that other than to imply that he'd like to get his hands on them?"

"You're overreacting," I say, half entertained, half bored.

He leans over the table. "I've been coming here for three years and I've never heard that asshole so much as talk. He's totally flirting with you. In front of me."

I drop back in my seat and tilt my head. "You should be flattered then."

He lifts a brow. "Yeah? Like how you were flattered when the hostess at La Jolla was being *friendly* with me?" When a response doesn't come to me immediately, he laughs and shakes his head. "That's what I thought."

"Okay, that was different."

"Not even a little bit."

"She looked at your ass."

He rolls his eyes. "You don't think our waiter checked out your ass?"

"All I'm saying is—"

"*No fucking way*...Sadie?"

"Shit," Jack mumbles.

Tanner steps up to our table with the woman I recognize

from his wedding as his wife. She's a gorgeous brunette, clinging to his arm almost as tightly as her bright pink dress is clinging to her hourglass body. Whoa... and she's draped in enough gold to fund a small country.

"Tanner," I say, and I look between him and Jack, who looks less than pleased to see his friend. "It's good to see you."

"I had no idea you'd be in town." Even from behind his dark sunglasses, he's clearly scowling at Jack. "You lose your phone, bro?"

Jack looks guilty but meets Tanner with a glare of his own, lips thin. "It's Sunday."

Whatever is going on between them feels as if it has something to do with me. I set down my fork, suddenly full.

"I'm going to get a table," his wife says quietly.

"No need." Tanner grabs two chairs and whirls them around, pushing them up to our table that's hardly big enough for them both. "We'll join them."

"Out of all the places in New York." I grin and sip my tea. "What are the chances?" Because this run-in feels very intentional.

"Jack didn't tell you?" He chuckles. "We had an important meeting scheduled today." He nods toward a building made of glass and metal that practically touches the clouds. "I've been trying to get in touch with him all morning." He lifts his glasses and stares pointedly at me. "Now I see why he blew me off."

"*Tanner*," Jack warns.

I turn away to avoid the tension simmering between them. The skyscraper is exactly what I'd expect of a high-powered Manhattan advertising firm, but for some weird reason, it's difficult to picture Jack in that life. He was always smart, always driven, but he was too down to earth for the suit-and-tie, cut-throat lifestyle. At least, he used to be.

"We're about finished here," Jack says, waving his hand for the check.

"Sadie Slade." Tanner shakes his head. "Always such a distraction." His gaze swings between Jack and me, a shit-eating grin on his face.

Not enjoying the attention on me, I nod toward Tanner's wife as she clutches her designer handbag to her stomach and curls her lip at our dirty plates. "Aren't you going to introduce me?"

He throws an arm over his wife's shoulders. "Maribeth, this is Sadie, an old friend from high school."

She gives me her fakest smile. "Nice to meet you."

"You too." I contemplate telling her I was at her wedding, but figure she's not the type who would be interested in fraternizing with the help.

Our waiter brings our bill and hands it to Jack while grinning at me. I can practically hear Jack grinding his molars.

"Here." Jack shoves the check back at the guy with a wad of cash. "Keep the change." He pushes back his chair. "Hate to break up the party but—"

"So that's it?" Tanner says to Jack cryptically.

Jack takes my hand and pulls me to my feet. "See you at the office tomorrow."

When Jack moves away from the table, I follow, wanting to escape the tight air and Maribeth, who won't stop looking down her nose at me.

"It was nice to meet you," I say. Just because she's mean doesn't mean I have to be. "Bye, Tan."

We make it two steps before Maribeth turns her entire body toward us. "Oh, Jackson?"

He freezes and his jaw flexes.

"Have you talked to Anaya?"

He turns and glares at her. "Classy, Maribeth."

Tanner laughs and his wife joins in, shrugs, and says, "Just curious. She was hoping for a repeat."

Jack ignores her and tugs me through the restaurant with Tanner calling behind us, "Calm down, Jackson! It was a joke!" through his laughter.

Once we're outside and headed down the crowded Manhattan street, I lean into his side. "Now I see why you became uncomfortable when they sat down."

He shakes his head. "Tanner's not the guy he was in high school."

"I can see that."

"Maribeth gets off on causing problems and being a bitch, and when Tanner's with her, he's not much better."

"Who's Anaya?"

I practically stumble from the speed with which he stops and steps in front of me to meet my eyes.

"No one. Anaya is literally no one to me. She's Maribeth's friend who struggles with boundary issues, but I have never touched her. I'm not attracted to her at all in any way, but she isn't picking up the hints. It doesn't help that Tanner and Maribeth are always trying to push us together."

"She's the one who was hanging on you at the wedding." I put it together instantly—the way she threw herself at Jack and how he seemed not the least bit interested. "She's gorgeous. There's no way I believe you're not attracted to her in *any* way." I lift a brow, daring him to deny it.

He snags my hand, and we continue walking. "If you spent more than ten minutes with her, you'd understand."

I laugh and snuggle closer to him by wrapping my free arm around his. "You know, I never would've pictured you in this kind of life." I motion around in case he didn't understand my meaning.

"You mean a bustling city thriving with opportunity?"

"Exactly. Look at this place. It's packed with business professionals *on a Sunday*. After what Tanner said, I guess it's rare for you guys to take a day off?"

He seems to contemplate that before he answers. "The short answer is yes. If you slow down for even a second, there will be ten guys racing to take your place. You slow down, you die."

"Yikes. Seems to me the drive to stay afloat will kill you faster."

He shrugs. "I never really thought about it like that."

"You did when we were younger. I think you just forgot."

He pulls me out of the way of a messenger bike then guides me back when it's safe. "I'm curious, what kind of life did you imagine me living?"

That's easy. "I always imagined you'd live like our dads—working hard but making fun a priority too. I saw you as the kind of man who loves his job but loves his family more. Always goes for that one more kiss before leaving every morning. A man who works hard but plays just as hard. Takes weekends for barbeques, pool parties, movie nights with his wife, lots of dates."

He squeezes my hand as if to say he likes what he's hearing and wouldn't mind hearing more, but I refuse to embarrass myself more than I already have with my fantasy. "You act like that kind of life would be impossible here in New York."

I stop, and this time, it's me who commands his eyes. "Wouldn't it?"

He clears his throat, and I really hope he doesn't try to lie to me. After all, only minutes ago he was talking about why he can never slow down. He can't deny the lifestyle here is vastly different than the one he would have had back in Las Vegas.

"Maybe at first, but once I get into a position with seniori-ty..." He sees something in my expression that makes his words trail off.

We continue to walk, this time in silence. The sad truth is, Jack may love me, but he's not ready to give up all he's worked for in order to be with me. And he shouldn't have to. Which means I'd have to accept that his drive for success would always come before me. And I'd have to move to New York for us to be together.

We would go into our relationship with the best intentions,

but he'd work all the time and we'd never see each other. That's not the kind of life either of us deserve.

With a sadness that surprises me, I hold on to him a little tighter.

His professional success is his priority, and I will never accept being second to his job. We've both changed too much to make our relationship work.

CHAPTER TWENTY-TWO

JACK

"Wake up, sleepyhead." Lying next to a sleeping Sadie, I brush her hair off her face and watch her dark lashes flutter before her eyebrows drop in frustration. "Don't be like that, beautiful."

I'm holding back laughter because my girl has always hated waking up from naps. After we spent the day sightseeing—which mostly consisted of me dragging her to every well-known art gallery in the city (I'm a selfish dick, I know)—she was dead on her feet by the time we got back to my apartment. I suggested she take a nap and we'd spend the night in. (Selfish. Dick.) What can I say? I'm sick of sharing Sadie with New York. And I have the perfect night planned.

I check the clock. It's after seven o'clock. If I don't wake her up, she's likely to sleep 'til morning.

"Wake up," I say in a sing-song voice. "I know you're hungry."

She groans, rolls over, and pulls the comforter over her head.

"That's it. You asked for it, Sadie girl." I slip off the bed, stand at the foot, and grip the comforter and sheet before ripping them off her body. "Wake up!"

"Ughhh..." She flops to her back, her fists slamming into the mattress.

I grin.

Huge.

"I hate you."

I climb up over her body, making sure to hold myself away from her so she won't feel my weight on her. "Liar."

Her eyes eventually open, that heart-stopping blue-green gaze made even greener with sleep. "What's for dinner?"

"Demanding," I tease.

"I'm trying to decide if it's worth getting out of bed for."

"You don't have to get out of bed. I'll be happy to feed you right where you lay." God, why did that sound so dirty? The sexual tension between us has been stringing tighter and tighter, our innocent touches becoming less innocent with every brush of our skin.

She smirks, her thoughts obviously on track with mine. "I guess I'll get up."

I frown. Not the answer I hoped for, but I have all night to change her mind. "Great!" I hop off the bed. "Meet me in the living room when you're ready."

She moans and flops to her side.

I point at her from the doorway. "Don't you dare go back to sleep." A pillow flies at my head, but I expected it, so I dodge it easily. "Still so feisty."

She flips me off.

God, I love her.

With a smile, I head to the fridge and bust out the large plastic trays that were delivered thirty minutes ago. I ordered practically every item on the menu from Oko Sushi, wanting to make sure Sadie was satisfied with her options. I pull out the bottle of chilled sparkling apple cider I picked up while she was sleeping and bring it all to the floor picnic I set up.

The History of the Industrial Revolution is cued up on the television. I fill two champagne glasses, remove the plastic tops from our dinner, and when she doesn't come out, I take the opportunity to check my phone.

I open the myBubble app. Check the doorway. Type. Send.

Any updates?

I hear her phone ping in the bedroom and frown. This is so fucking wrong. Dawn needs to disappear. Back when I started pretending to be Dawn, I felt justified because I simply wanted to know if Sadie was all right, what had been going on in her life since we broke up. When she was refusing to take my calls, I had no other choice.

But now?

Fuck.

I close the app and shove my phone in my pocket—then it vibrates with a new message. *Don't look at it. Just ignore it.*

Oh, who am I kidding? I look at the screen with hungry eyes and an eager heart.

Nope. Still blissfully happy and in love.

This is why I still need to be Dawn! Why won't Sadie say those words to me? I've confessed my feelings for her, told her I still love her, that I'm in love with her, and she doesn't feel comfortable saying it back. I need to know why. I reply and hit Send.

You tell him yet?

· · ·

She doesn't respond right away, but I hear the bathroom door close. Seconds later, text bubbles appear.

No. I'm not sure I should.

"What the fuck?" I whisper. "Why not?"

Why not?

Text bubbles come and go, and I wait with bated breath for her response. Finally, after what feels like forever, her reply comes through.

Regardless of how we feel, we still have the same problems. We live on opposite sides of the country. We have different life goals. We couldn't overcome those things years ago. I can't imagine we'll be able to overcome them now.

"Bullshit." I type the word then backspace to delete it. My fingers hover over the keys, but when I hear the bathroom door open, I close the app and shove the phone into my pocket.

She drags her tired feet toward me, her eyes fixed on the feast. "Sushi?"

I clear my throat, feeling a little off-center after her last text to Dawn. "Yes. Best in town."

Her eyes slide to the television and she chuckles, the sound gravelly from sleep and so fucking sweet. "No way! *History of the Industrial Revolution?*"

"Thought I'd bring us back to our first date."

Back then, I'd picked the most boring movie I could find because I'd hoped the theater would be empty so we could sit in the dark, share popcorn, and talk. Or, ya know, make out a little. The night ended up being a disaster when my dad showed up and was the only other person in the theater. Thank God he fell asleep during the first ten minutes and we managed to sneak out.

She sits on the pillow across from me and lifts her cider. "It's perfect. Cheers."

We touch glasses, and I hit Play on the movie that, again, I'm hoping is too boring to watch. But my stomach already feels full and I haven't taken a single bite.

Full of defeat.

Full of doubt.

Full of fear that I may never be able to fix what's wrong with us.

SADIE

"You didn't have to eat it!" I don't know who has more tears falling from their eyes—me from laughing, or Jack from the donut-hole-sized wad of wasabi he ate.

His eyes are slammed shut, his fingers pinching his nose as he falls to his side and groans. "Yes, I did!" He tucks his knees into a fetal position. "You dared me!"

"You feel that burn, *Jackson* Daniels? That's your body punishing you for being prideful." I laugh when he flops onto his back, breathing heavily, his eyes still dripping with tears. "Was it worth it?"

He inhales, exhales, and shakes his head. "It felt like burning acid was poured in my nose and dissolving my brain."

I giggle, and he pushes up on his elbows. The look in his eyes has me scooting backward on my butt.

"This is all your fault, ya know."

"Don't you blame me for that. You accepted the dare!" I squeal and dart away from him as he crawls toward me.

"You knew I'd accept it." He's on all fours, prowling after me. "Have you ever known me to not accept a dare?"

"Now that you mention it..." I say playfully, because of course I knew he'd accept the dare. Jack has a biological propensity for needing to be the toughest guy in the room. It's in the Daniels' DNA. "You did eat that ant I dared you to eat in third grade."

He nods, his green eyes alight with humor and his signature playful sexiness I always loved. "I did."

"And when I dared you to TP Principal Gilbert's house in eighth grade, you did that too." I continue to scoot away from him as he inches forward.

"My point exactly."

My back hits his leather club chair. "You also wore my hot pink tank top to school our senior year when I dared you to do that."

He gets closer, and I'm stuck with nowhere to go. "I got hit on by three different girls that day, so I'd say that dare backfired."

"Maybe I dared them to hit on you."

He laughs, the sound deep and soothing as he breaches my personal space. Feeling cornered, I involuntarily suck in a breath so quiet I think he may not notice. He becomes unnaturally still and his playful smirk melts into a frown before he drops his gaze.

To break the awkwardness between us, I push up to bring my lips to his. Initiating the contact helps me bypass memories of that night on the beach. It helps remind me I'm in control. His soft lips mold to mine, and his mouth tastes of soy sauce and wasabi.

I smile against his lips. "Spicy."

He chuckles and pulls me closer. "Now it's settled. History has proven there's little I won't do for you, Sadie Slade."

"Only on a dare." The familiar sting of him leaving, getting caught up in his life and forgetting all about me flares.

"No." He cups my jaw, forks his fingers in my hair, and waits for me to nod my approval of his touch. "Not anymore." He presses a kiss to my lips. "From now on." He kisses the corner of my mouth. "I'll give you whatever you want." He kisses the other corner. "Ask and it's yours."

He continues to kiss my face. My eyelids, down my cheek to my earlobe, my neck. Every brush of his lips has my pulse pounding a little harder. He shifts his butt to get closer and pulls me onto his lap—not straddling him like last night but sitting sideways. I dip my chin to capture his lips, slip my tongue into his warm and welcoming mouth, and his other hand tangles in my hair along with the first one.

With his back against the couch, my hands clutching his T-shirt, we kiss until our lips are sore and swollen. He makes no move to push things further, seeming as content to lose himself in my mouth as I am in his. I study his closed eyes as we kiss, his dark lashes that don't seem right with his light hair, his perfect skin I know is as soft as it looks. He really is so pretty, and for the time being, he's all mine.

So what do I want to do tonight?

I take a quick inventory of my body. My tingling legs, racing heart, and the delicious ache between my legs. I almost break the kiss with surprise, and I'm grateful that I manage to hang on. It's been so long since I've felt turned on.

Leave it to Jack to bring me to the point of near orgasm with nothing more than kissing. He's so perfectly predictable, and I love it. With everything about him that has changed—his focus on success and expensive tastes—one thing that hasn't changed is the effect he has on me.

I'm not sure how far I can go, but I want to try to be touched again, and he's the only man I'd trust to do it.

Pulling back from his lips, I rest my forehead against his. My pulse roars and I try unsuccessfully to calm it. "Take me to bed."

With a tiny hitch in his breath, he asks, "Are you sure?"

I manage a smirk. "I dare you."

Quicker than I would've thought possible, considering our position on the floor, he scoops me into his arms and stands.

He whirls toward the bedroom door, his face scrunching up in disgust. "I think I stepped on an eel roll."

He shakes his foot, sending clumps of rice to the floor, then continues forward with me laughing in his arms. He slows when we enter the bedroom, the air growing heavy with anticipation and expectation. He sets me on the bed but doesn't follow me to the mattress. Instead, he stands there looking at me.

"I don't know if I can..." I swallow. "Make love yet."

God, he looks so handsome staring at me, his blond hair falling over his forehead, green eyes shining with affection and concern. His wide shoulders encased in gray cotton and his faded jeans that look as if they should've been trashed years ago hanging loosely on his narrow hips.

"You already have been making love to me, babe. Last night, this morning in the kitchen, holding my hand all day. Doesn't matter to me how you do it, but you should know you have been doing it."

"Come here."

He pulls his shirt off and crawls over me. He lifts his brows, and I nod for him to lower his weight between my legs. I expect phantom fingers to wrap around my lungs, but they don't. I expect his soft sheets to turn to coarse sand against my skin. But staring into his eyes, I only feel the warmth of his acceptance.

"I need you to speak up, okay? Be vocal. Let me know how you're feeling so I don't go too far."

"Right now, your weight feels good."

He dips his head and kisses my throat, up my jaw, and hovers over my lips maddeningly. I lift and press my lips to his, giving him permission to drop his chest to mine. He slips off to my side, giving me enough space so that I don't feel smothered as I get lost in the sensation of his kiss.

I grab his hand and slide it up my shirt, and he frees my breast from the confines of my bra. He toys with my hardened nipple, but not roughly. Gently. Coaxing me to brave more.

With a shove of my foot on the bed, I roll on top of him, sit up, and toss my shirt to the floor. He swallows hard and licks his lips as I unlatch my bra and it quickly follows the shirt. I forgot how arousing it is to be desired by him. To have his eyes communicate a want so extreme, he trembles. I grip his hands and pull them both to my breasts. He cups their weight, the pads of his thumbs brushing over my nipples, and soon I'm rocking against the thick hard-on held captive behind his jeans.

"This feels so good," I say, keeping my eyes fixed on his.

He hums his agreement. "You're so pretty."

I would think he was complimenting my body if it weren't for the fact that his gaze hasn't left mine.

The friction building between us, both at my breasts and between my thighs, brings to the surface a pulsing need that my rubbing against him can't satisfy. My hips still when I realize what it is I want, where the unbridled sexual need has taken me.

Sensing something's wrong, he drops his hands to my ribs. "What is it? Should we stop?"

"No. I think..." No, I don't think. I know. My throbbing insides and quaking thighs demand it. "I want you to touch me."

"Of course." He places his hands back on my breasts.

"Not there."

His eyelids, which had been at half-mast, are now fully alert. "Are you sure?"

Instead of answering, I roll to his side, lie next to him on my back, lift my hips, and push my sleeping shorts and panties down and off until I'm completely naked. And yet, I feel completely at ease. Being naked near Jack feels as natural as being alone in the nude. He's the only boy who has ever seen me like this. He knows every curve, every freckle and scar. Although time has passed, it seems my body hasn't forgotten him.

He props up on an elbow next to me, his gaze running the length of my body from hip to head. He licks his lips and finally rests his hand between my breasts at my sternum. "Your heart is racing."

"That's because I'm excited."

"Not scared?" He's giving me a chance to back out.

"A little, but only because I don't want to go back to that night in my head. I wouldn't be asking you to touch me if I didn't want you to."

He seems satisfied because he runs his hand down my torso, swirls the tips of his fingers around my belly button, then skates his fingertips from hip to hip and back again. The motion is soothing, calming. With each pass, my legs fall a little farther apart until they're wide and wanting.

"Tell me if it's too much," he says, his voice so heavy with want I almost can't make out what he said.

I agree to his request, and then finally, his fingers slip between my legs. I suck in a shuddered breath, and he watches my expression. He must be okay with whatever he sees because he doesn't stop. As he did with my torso, he does the same between my legs, teasing, tempting, winding me up so tightly that I'll be begging for release.

"Talk to me."

"I'm okay. Really." I arch my back and press against his hand, hoping to increase the pressure, but he backs off.

It's maddening. He's touching me enough to get me wound up, but I know he's in a holding pattern until I ask for more.

After minutes of this beautiful torture, I finally lose control and tell him what I want. "I need your fingers."

"You've got 'em, Sadie girl." He increases his pressure enough to prove a point, as if to say, "*See, here I am.*"

"Inside me." I arch my back again. "Please."

He hums in satisfaction and finally slips one long, powerful finger inside. Because my body is primed for what's next, his finger slips in easily, and before I'm able to ask, he joins it with another. "Still good?"

Incapable of words, I hold his wrist where he's at, forbidding him to remove his fingers, and nod. I keep my eyes on him, my breathing even despite the fact that it wants to speed up and send me spiraling—to ecstasy or the memories of that night on the beach, I don't know. My jaw clenches as I force my mind to stay in the present and focus on the way he makes me feel. The love that shines in his eyes as he watches me wrestle with demons that were violently gifted to me. I refuse to allow a lifetime of pure, untainted love between Jack and me to be dirtied by the acts of one hideous man.

Jack leans forward and brushes his soft lips against mine, where he whispers, "Breathe, baby."

Had I forgotten to breathe? I blow out the breath I'd been holding, and he rewards me with a tender kiss.

My muscles finally uncoil, and eventually he draws soft moans from me as he remembers exactly how I like to be touched. The weight of my eyelids feels like too much and they threaten to close. They flutter, then open, and he kisses them in turn.

"It's only you and me. You're safe. I promise."

His pace picks up, and soon I'm rocking my hips, helping him work me into a frenzy of need.

"That's right, take what you need from me." His voice is thick and heavy with desire, and I feel his erection at my hip.

I've moved beyond the worst of my fears. The rest should be easy, right? But what if it's not? What if I ruin everything we've managed to overcome by panicking and pushing him away?

JACK

The fact that I can keep a hard-on with the rage that courses through my veins is a testament to how much I love and am turned on by Sadie. Having her in my bed, completely naked and bared to me, my fingers buried deep in her silken wet heat, her breasts inches from my mouth—she's the ultimate fantasy. My forever dream girl. Yet watching her pull herself back from the brink of a panic attack has me envisioning busting open skulls. Sexy, right?

The only thing that's keeping me from throwing up my

dinner is her bravery. I watch her battle her demons. The darkness in her eyes comes over her and her muscles tense, and every time, she manages to push it back and work with me to give her the pleasure she deserves.

I know the physical part of our relationship will take time and patience, and she's said she may never get to a place where she's able to have sex again, but she's showing me tonight that she wants to reclaim that part of her life. She isn't going to give up what she wants without a fight.

I kiss her clenched jaw. "It's me, Sadie girl. Breathe." Her thighs release their death grip on my wrist and pick up the pace I'd set before her head sent her on lockdown. "That's it. You feel so good. I've missed this."

She nods quickly, but I can tell she's not ready to relax enough for talking. Maybe I can fix that with my mouth. Her nipples are hard and so damn close... I lean down and draw one between my lips, licking and tasting the sweet, supple skin. That seems to work. She moans and her knees fall wide. I pull my fingers from her body and her breath hitches. Bringing my soaked fingers to her chest, I rub them on her nipple, transferring the wetness there before sucking it off with a long groan of satisfaction.

"You taste the same. So fucking good." I put my fingers in my mouth and lick them clean while she watches with wide eyes. I smirk. "Can I taste more of you?"

With a shuddered breath, she nods.

"I'm gonna need to hear the words, love."

"Yes. I want you to taste me."

Not as specific as I hoped, but we're getting there. I slip down her body, drop to my knees on the side of the bed, then scoop my hands under her sexy ass to pull her to the edge. Her feet come to my shoulders and I grin. She remembers. I know her brain and her heart are working through some dark times, but one thing is for sure—our bodies are as familiar with the other as if we'd never been apart.

I run my hands along the outer part of her thighs, soothing her with my touch until I see her relax further. Her eyes are open, but they're not on me. She stares at the ceiling but seems to be seeing something other than the white plaster.

"Stay with me."

She blinks, and finally I get her eyes. I reassure her with a soft kiss to her inner thigh, then I slide down, kissing and caressing as she watches me until I finally get my first real taste. Her breath catches in her throat, but her muscles remain pliable and relaxed. I sink deeper, loving the different moans and sighs that fill my ears. Her head falls back on the bed. This time her eyes are closed, and I celebrate the enormous victory by giving in to my ravenous need and sucking on her tender flesh. Her back arches, her heels press against me, and her knees fall as wide as her flexibility will let them. Fingers sift through my hair and fist. Her hips roll. She's loving this. I close my eyes and lose myself to her taste, her touch, the satiny feel of her against my tongue.

Her muscles tense again, and I'm afraid her thoughts have taken her someplace dark. But when I peer up to check on her, she's lost in the throes of ravishment. Her lips are parted, hair tossed around her face, back arching off the bed, and the sweet sound of my name falls from her lips. My eyelids slide closed and I lose myself in her release. It fills my soul with feelings of possession and victory over what was done to her.

With a gentle pressure from her feet, she presses me back and I reluctantly give her up. I run my hands up and down her legs, bringing her back to earth. When she opens her eyes, I'm happy to see no regret, only a lazy contentedness for an internal battle won.

"You good?"

Her beautiful lips tilt up on the sides. "Not really. I'm ready for more."

If it weren't for the fact that I'm already on my knees, I may have dropped to them. "You serious?"

God, why am I smiling like a kid who got offered the most

decadent candy? *Because you did.* I clamber to my bedside table drawer so quickly it makes her laugh.

"Eager?"

I wish I could be the cool guy, the laid-back picture of composure, but I've never been able to pull that off with Sadie. Not at three and not at twenty-three.

I rip open a box of condoms and fumble one to the floor. I finally get my hands on it and feel my face get hot as she watches me make a fool out of myself. "Sexy, huh?"

She chuckles—the sound is throaty and so hot. "I've always loved that I could make you nervous."

I release my dick from the confinement of my jeans and slide on the condom. Am I shaking? "Can't deny that."

I climb on the bed, kicking off my jeans. When she holds out her arms for me to crawl between her legs, I hook one arm behind her and slide her up the bed to place her in the middle. She welcomes me into the cushion of her thighs, and when her arms wrap around me, I allow my weight to drop. We're pressed together, hearts pounding against the other, and like everything else, our bodies know exactly how we fit together.

"You're not saying yes to this for me, right?"

She looks more relaxed than I've ever seen her, and when she cups my face and says, "No, I'm one hundred percent doing this for me," I believe her.

I flex my hips, shifting forward, and bury myself inside her. Her heat envelops me, her eyes consume me, and I'm reminded what it feels like to be home.

For so long, I've been living for my next A grade, next promotion, bigger paycheck. I thought all those things would fill the emptiness I felt in my soul shortly after leaving Sadie. I was so stupid to think any of those things would fit in the space my soul had carved out for her. And now that I have her back, her legs locked behind my thighs, her hands sifting through my hair as she looks at me with all the trust in the world, the burn of tears gathers in my eyes.

I kiss her, hoping she won't notice. What kind of a pussy-ass bitch cries during sex? *This is so much more and you know it.*

If she notices my emotion, she ignores it and kisses me as if the key to her happiness lies within the depths of our love. I thrust in slowly and pull back at the same pace, my hips matching the rhythm set by our kiss. My elbows braced at her shoulders, I hold myself up to feel the tips of her breasts slide against me with every slip inside. Her nails scrape at my scalp— her demand for me to pick up the pace, deepen the depth, increase the pressure. I roll my hips in a firm circle, and her body tightens beneath me. Around me.

She's going to need more.

At the risk of being too rough, but feeling in my heart it's what she needs to send her over the edge, I pull almost all the way out then slam forward. When she moans my name, I repeat the action over and over until she's clawing at my back and waking the neighbors with her cry of release.

The second hers hits, mine quickly follows, and I chase her right over to drop into a free fall of explosive ecstasy. I kiss her hard, and she swallows my moan while I fight to keep from blacking out. My vision tunnels, I fight for my lungs to accept a full breath, and then I collapse on her for a second before rolling off and pulling her to my chest.

"We've always been amazing, but that?" I'm still catching my breath. "How did we get better?"

She sighs. The sound is so comforting and satisfying as she settles her cheek on my pec. "If I didn't know better, I'd think you'd been practicing."

I hold up my right hand, flex my fingers, and flip it over a few times. "This here is a poor substitute for you, Sadie girl."

She giggles sleepily. "I should hope so."

I close my eyes, basking in the glow of our shared release, her steady pulse, warm body, and the hope that after tonight, she won't be able to walk away from us.

CHAPTER TWENTY-THREE

SADIE

I wake to the scent of coffee and bacon. My body is sore in places that only remind me of Jack, and that realization makes me smile. Rolling to my side, I see the door open and take the opportunity to grab my phone and punch out a quick update to Dawn.

I don't know what I would've done this weekend without her to talk to about all of my resurfacing feelings for Jack. Having her to help me make decisions has been a godsend and makes me sad that she doesn't live in San Diego anymore.

When I open the app, I see I already have a message from her—sent at eight o'clock this morning, almost an hour ago.

How'd last night go?

I bite my lip to keep my smile under control, but it's pointless. I grin like an idiot and type back.

. . .

Oh, Dawn... I think I might be in trouble here. I don't think I'll be able to live without him after last night!

I hit Send and hear Jack fumble in the kitchen with a muttered, "Shit."

Still smiling, I wonder if he's out there cooking breakfast in nothing but a pair of boxer briefs or if maybe he decided to go commando in only his worn-out jeans. My curiosity gets the best of me, and I pull back the comforter, in search of my clothes. I check the floor and the bench at the foot of the bed. Huh... I spot a gray NYU T-shirt hanging over a chair, my underwear folded neatly beside it. Did he really hide my clothes so I'd be forced to wear his shirt? He really is the same ol' Jack.

With a yawn, I get dressed and get my phone to see I have a new myBubble message.

Then don't.

If only it were that easy. I close the app and toss my phone on the bed, then I follow my nose to the kitchen, where I'm met with the smooth landscape of Jack's incredibly toned back. He's absently stirring a steaming pan of scrambled eggs while looking at his phone in his other hand. He hasn't noticed me yet, so I allow my eyes to drop to his narrow waste. He went with the jeans. Excellent choice. I trace the upper swells of his ass and crack, which peek up above the sagging waistband. Such a pretty picture. And bonus, he's barefoot.

"Good morning—"

"Shit!" He startles, dropping his phone and flinging half-cooked eggs into the air.

"I'm sorry!" I laugh and bend over to retrieve his phone. "I didn't mean to scare you."

His eyes are wide on his phone in my hand. "I didn't know you were up."

I hand him back the device. "I can see that."

He grabs his phone, checks it—I assume to make sure it's not broken—then slips it into his back pocket. "Work stuff."

"What?"

"I was on my phone dealing with work stuff."

I shrug, because I don't really care. "Smells good."

He blinks a few times as if he'd forgotten what he was doing. "Yeah, you hungry?"

I tilt my head, studying his gorgeously built, yet rigid body. "Why are you being weird?"

"I'm not." He chuckles and turns to pull the eggs off the burner.

With a mighty heft, I hop up to sit on the counter next to him. "You totally are. It's because of last night, isn't it? Do you... regret—"

"What? No. Fuck no." He positions himself between my knees, his big palms sliding up my thighs as he brings his lips to mine. "Can I have a do-over?"

Lost in his emerald eyes, I nod. God, that smile!

"Mornin', Sadie girl." He kisses me softly, sweetly. "I loved last night. Making love to you again, holding you in my arms while you slept. I cursed the sun when it came up."

"You did?"

"I did." He brushes my hair off my face and frowns. "I can't believe you're leaving today."

I kiss him. I try to keep it sweet like he did, but I can't control myself around him. To be honest, I never could. I tilt my head and part my lips, inviting him to deepen the kiss. And just like I figured he would, he does. I lift my knees and lock my ankles at his ass, pulling him close when I notice how aroused he is between my legs. Hands grip and explore as we nip at each other's lips and grind against one another.

He pulls his lips away, resting his forehead against mine, our

panted breaths mixing. His smells of coffee and toothpaste.
"Don't go."

Stay in New York? Is it crazy to even consider it? I don't
work until Wednesday. There's really no reason why I can't milk
my trip another few days.

"What about your work?"

He kisses down my jaw to my neck. "I'll call in sick."

"Tanner will throw a fit. He seemed really angry that you
missed your meeting—"

"Fuck Tanner," he says against the sensitive skin where my
neck meets my shoulder. "He'll get over it."

I close my eyes and breathe in his clean, calming scent before
I whisper, "Okay."

He jerks his head back, his expression so hopeful I feel it in
my soul. "You're serious."

"I'll check the flights—*oh my gosh!*" I giggle as his arms wrap
around my middle, his face buries in my neck, and he squeezes
me so tight he might break a rib. But I don't care. I hug him
back just as hard.

"I'll pay whatever they charge to change your flight."

"You don't have to—"

He kisses me quick and hard. "No arguing."

"I wonder, did you and my dad go to the same school for
overprotective and bossy men?"

"I should be offended that you're comparing me to your dad."
He scoops eggs onto a plate then adds two strips of bacon and a
handful of fresh strawberries. "But I'm not because your dad is
the only man in the world who loves you as much as I do." He
hands me the plate. "OJ or coffee?"

I take the plate and my stomach flutters with happiness. He
loves me. "Coffee."

After one more kiss and a grab of my ass as I sit at the table,
we finally get to dive into the breakfast he prepared. I didn't
realize how hungry I was until I took the first bite of eggs. I
clean my plate embarrassingly fast and steal an extra piece of

bacon off his plate. We talk about our childhoods, laugh about our huge family back in Las Vegas, and with every story, I feel more and more convinced that we really are meant to be together.

"Could you ever see yourself moving home?" I sip my coffee while gauging his response.

His thoughtful expression surprises me. I expected an immediate no. He leans back in his chair, and his perfectly shaped pecs call my eyes, making him smirk. "If anyone had asked me that days ago, I would've said no. But now?"

"What?" I hear wistfulness in my voice as I await his answer to the question I'm really asking. Are you willing to leave New York?

"Yeah, I'd go home. Vegas was a great place to grow up. I think as far as raising a family, it'd be smart to do it there."

Me too.

He stands, clears our plates, and brings them to the kitchen. I follow with our empty coffee mugs and place them in the sink.

"Why don't you see about changing your flight while I jump in the shower? Do you need to use my computer?"

"No, I'll use my phone."

He picks up his wallet, which is sitting on the counter next to his keys and pulls out his credit card. "Use it."

I take it, rolling my eyes. "Fine."

He slips his wallet into his pocket and kisses my forehead before heading off to the shower. A surge of excitement blasts through my body and I dab, floss, and hit the quan in Jack's kitchen before pulling my crap together and hunting down my phone.

Where did I put it?

I head to the bedroom as the shower turns on and see Jack's discarded jeans on the bed. I grab my phone and head back to the living room to call the airline.

After a small wait, I get on a flight for Wednesday. It leaves early enough that, with the time change, I'll be able to work that night. After using Jack's credit card for the two-hundred-fifty-dollar charge, I end my call with a new flight number and two more days with Jack.

I feel so reckless, so adventurous. More importantly, I feel in control, which is something I haven't felt since that night on the beach.

Finally, I feel... free.

I go back into the bedroom to give him his card, but he's still in the shower, so I fish his wallet out of his jeans and place the card inside. Standing there, overflowing with excitement from my newfound independence, I fall back on the bed and punch out a quick text to Dawn on the myBubble app.

You are never going to believe what I did!

I hit Send.

Jack's phone vibrates in his jeans. Probably more work stuff. I make a mental list of the things I want to see during my last two days in New York. I've always wanted to go to the 9/11 Memorial.

When Dawn doesn't respond, I punch out another message.

I changed my flight! I'm staying two more days!

Jack's phone vibrates again.

Weird.

Can you believe it?

I stare at Jack's jeans and hit Send.

Vibrates.

What the hell?

I have no reason to feel sick, but the eggs and bacon are crawling up my esophagus, as if my body is aware of something my mind hasn't caught up to yet.

Dawn?

Send.

Vibrate.

I swallow the sickness in my mouth.

Are.

Vibrate.

You.

Vibrate.

Oh God, oh God... no.

There?

Vibrate.

Tears sting my eyes. With quaking fingers, I pull his phone from his pocket and flip it around to look at the lock screen.

· · ·

You have 7 new myBubble messages.

My breathing shudders when I try to take a breath, and tears stream down my face when I hit the notification bar and it opens the myBubble app. I don't have to read what the messages say—I've been living them for a *month*.

How could he do this to me?

Why?

The shower shuts off, and I panic. I close the app, shove the phone back in his jeans, and grab my bag. Grabbing the first pair of pants I can find, I slide them on, slip on my Vans without socks, and snag my wallet before I race out of the apartment.

I need a minute to think. I can't... fuck!

Jack was Dawn this entire time!

I told her things... oh my God!

I'm sobbing uncontrollably when I hit the elevators and slam my palm on the Lobby button. With blurry vision, I punch out a quick text to Jack.

Went for a quick walk for some Advil. Brb.

My initial reaction is to feel sick for lying, but how could I possibly feel bad after all the lies he told me? All the betrayal and deceit! Damn him!

I race through the stupid pretentious lobby and out onto the busy city streets. I have no idea where I'm going, but I need to keep moving, so I walk, wiping fresh tears from my cheeks.

I was right. He has changed. What I thought I saw in him, the things I thought I was still in love with, were nothing more than a mask of the old Jack. A façade he slips on whenever it suits him.

He had sex with me. Lied to get in my head, to get his hands on information I wasn't comfortable telling him. All so he could seduce me.

My feet freeze on the pavement when the realization hits me.

Just because he didn't take what he wanted by force doesn't make him any better than Fabian on the beach.

It might even make him worse.

I flag down a taxi and jump in the back, grateful the cabbie doesn't look back and see what a mess I am. "JFK please."

"Which airline?"

"Delta."

The cab lurches forward, and like the cabbie, I don't look back to see the mess I'm leaving behind.

JACK

"Sadie!" I call out of the open door in my bedroom as I tighten the towel wrapped around my waist. "Let's go see a show on Broadway tonight!" I'm fishing through my drawers for underwear and socks. "I heard *Mean Girls* is a good one!" I snag a pair of dark-washed jeans and a maroon shirt from my closet. "You always loved the movie!"

I keep my eye on the doorway, expecting her to come through any second and throw her body into mine. We'll tumble to the bed while she shows her excitement about my idea by kissing the shit out of me.

I'm fully dressed and still no Sadie. No breathless kiss.

I do up my fly, run a hand through my wet hair, and go into the living room in search of her. Empty. "Sadie!"

She's not in the kitchen. My place is so small, there's nowhere else she could be hiding.

Her bag is still on the floor in my room.

I pull my phone out of my jeans to call her and relax a little when I see I have a text. She went to get Advil. I text her back.

. . .

I have Advil here. Come back.

Another five minutes pass before she texts me back.

I stumbled into a little art studio. I'll be awhile.

My stomach roils with sickness that makes no fucking sense. Am I that addicted to Sadie that I can't stand the idea of her being right down the street without me? Naw... I text her back.

Where? I'll meet you.

I chew on my thumbnail, waiting for her response. After thirty minutes, I grab my keys and wallet and head out to find her. My legs move too slow, the elevator even slower, and when I pass Jonathan, I ask, "Did you see Sadie, the woman staying with me, leave about thirty minutes ago?"

"Yeah, she had her head down so I didn't talk to her. Figured she wasn't feeling social."

"She had a headache," I say more defensively than necessary. "Did you happen to see which way she went?"

He points to the left.

"Thanks." I head in that direction then stop and turn. "You wouldn't happen to know of an art studio down this way would you?"

"No, sir. None that I know of."

I point over my shoulder. "Is the closest convenience store on Tenth?"

"Yes."

"Huh." I turn in search of Sadie. She would've had to walk for nearly two miles in order to buy Advil if she headed in this direction.

I keep my phone in my palm, waiting for her to respond to my last text. Impatience quickens my pace and fuels my irrational fear. Fear that I can't put my finger on.

Using a map app on my phone, I search for art galleries, but there are none in the vicinity.

Sadie. Where are you? I'm getting worried. Please, text me back.

I wander the city blocks of my neighborhood for another hour. I'm drenched in sweat and about to call the police and file a missing person's report. *Think, Jack. Don't overreact.* I check the last five messages I sent, getting more and more frantic to hear from her. Why wouldn't she text me back? This is starting to feel like the days when she ignored my calls. The only way I could get her to talk to me back then was by being Dawn.

I stare at the myBubble app on my phone. It's worth a shot.

Wiping sweat from my brow with my forearm, I open the app. There are a bunch of new messages from Sadie from this morning. How did I miss these? They're marked as read. Probably when I fumbled with my phone in the kitchen after she almost caught me. I read through the messages, hearing her excited voice in each message. This must've been when she changed her flight.

I type out a quick text.

Two more days? I'm sure jack is excited to keep you a little longer. What did he say?

With heavy feet, I step back to a concrete wall and slide down to sit my ass on the dingy sidewalk, waiting for a response. I don't know how long I go between staring at my screen and keeping my eyes on every brunette who passes me, but I get no response. Not even text bubbles.

"Her phone died." That makes sense. "Maybe she went back to my apartment!" I call the lobby. "Jonathan, did Sadie come back?"

"No, sir. I haven't seen her."

"Can you send someone up to my apartment to check for me?"

"Of course, sir."

"Knock first!"

"Always, sir."

"Call me back and let me know."

I hang up and lean my head back against the building. What the hell is going on? Where could she have gone? This feels like a dream.

I close my eyes. "Please let me wake up and find myself back in bed with her. Please..." I crack an eyelid to find I'm still on my ass with people shuffling around my outstretched legs.

One guy passing by tosses a quarter into my lap.

"I'm not homeless!" I pick it up and throw it at his retreating back.

My phone vibrates and tumbles to the ground in my race to answer it. "Hello? Jonathan? Was she there?"

"Sorry that took so long. Paola was on her break, so I had to wait—"

"Did you find her?"

"No. Your place was empty, sir."

"Dammit!" I hit End and pull up the keypad to dial 9-1-1. My finger hovers over the keys. Sadie's been gone for almost three hours. I rehearse the call in my head.

"Yes, my girlfriend took off to buy Advil three hours ago. Last I heard, she was at an art studio. Can I file a missing person's report?"

Even I hear how ridiculous that sounds. They're not going to do shit for me.

I flip my phone around and check my text messages and the myBubble app for the millionth time. Nothing. "Where are you, Sadie?"

Then I remember. The location feature. Her phone should tell me where she is!

I open the myBubble app and search for that fucking feature. They've practically hidden it, but eventually I find it and hit it.

The result appears immediately.

Last known location New York, NY.

"Well that's fucking helpful."

I close the app, and even though it's hot and I feel dizzy with worry, I make the long trek home, hopeful I'll run into Sadie somewhere along the way and learn all this is one big misunderstanding.

CHAPTER TWENTY-FOUR

SADIE

I keep my head down as I head to baggage claim, and I stare blindly at the rotating belt for a good ten minutes before I remember I don't have any luggage. If my shame wasn't enough to make me dread my walk outside to the curbside pickup, the slot machines singing all around me are a blaring reminder of what I'm about to face.

Or rather... who.

The moment my feet hit the sidewalk, I feel his glare.

He's leaning against the passenger side of his truck, his massive tattooed arms crossed. His laid-back body language would seem chill to anyone else, but I know the UFL baseball cap pulled down low shadows eyes that are tight and zeroed in on me. When he sees me approach, he pushes off his truck and greets me with a quick hug and a mumbled, "Princess."

I don't respond because I have nothing to say. He can see my red, splotchy face and bloodshot eyes. His jaw tics, but he doesn't say anything when he opens the passenger side door, and he's still quiet when we pull away from the Las Vegas airport.

Is it possible I lucked out and he won't ask? Seems too good to be true, but I hold out hope.

"Your mom tried calling you," he says, disappointment dripping from his deep voice. "She's worried sick."

"My phone died." Jack called, texted, and used Dawn's identity to message me until finally, and blissfully, my battery died.

He's silent. I stare out my window because I don't need to see him to know he's working his jaw, mulling over how to approach the subject while trying to maintain his cool. Something he's never been very good at.

As I study the Strip cityscape in the distance, I'm reminded of all the memories I have with Jack in this town, and I mourn the death of the boy he used to be. The boy I fell in love with. To think he's changed so much, that he would manipulate and lie to me to get close, makes me want to empty my already empty stomach.

"You ready to talk?"

"Shit," I mumble, and stare forward. I knew this was coming, but I had hoped it would come later and preferably from my mom. "I don't know what to say."

That's the truth. I rehearsed a handful of lies to tell my parents, but they all made me feel repulsed. I'm so sick of lies.

"I bought you a nine-hundred-dollar one-way ticket from New York."

Calling my dad wasn't my first choice, but because I didn't have the credit card used for my new ticket from New York to San Diego, I couldn't touch my reservation. In order to get home, I needed a new ticket, and I couldn't afford one. I knew Ricky couldn't either, so my parents were my only hope of getting out without Jack's help. Of course, my dad insisted I fly into Las Vegas. I know he cares, but his overprotectiveness is suffocating.

He points flippantly at my shoulder. "You show up wearing an NYU T-shirt? I'm figuring shit out by myself, and I'm sure my imagination is ten times worse than the truth, so start talking."

I laugh humorlessly because I'm tired and hungry and I am so stupid. "I doubt that," I say mostly to myself, but when his head snaps around, I know he heard me.

His knuckles turn white on the steering wheel.

"Calm down, Dad—"

"What did he do?" Not a question, a demand.

There's no avoiding this, so I tell him the truth. "He's changed, that's all."

"He's changed? That's the bullshit you're going with, he's changed?"

I hear the countdown ticker in my head as my dad threatens to blow up.

"Tell me..."

In three... two... one.

"*What he did!* This guy made you cry for an entire summer! Why do you continue to—you know what?" He grabs his phone, hits a contact, and the ringing comes through the Bluetooth speakers.

I'm sure he's calling my mother. She's the only person who has ever been able talk some sense into him.

A man's voice answers. "'Lo?"

"Where the fuck is your son!"

"Dad!" He called Jack's dad!

"Stand down, asshole!" Blake sounds as though he's getting angry as well.

"I've got Sadie with me. We're on our way over."

"Why?" Blake's anger morphs to concern. "What's going on?"

"Be there in five." Dad hits the End button.

I clench my fists at my sides. Who the hell does he think he is? "We are not going to Blake and Layla's."

Now it's his turn to chuckle, but the sound is far from funny. "The hell we aren't."

I slap my hands on my thighs. "This is why I never tell you anything! Look at you!"

"You're my daughter! It's my job—"

"I'm an adult, and it's not your job. Not unless I ask for your help! You have to stop interfering!"

"I can't do that!"

"And that right there is why I can never talk to you!"

He looks offended. "You talk to me."

"No, I don't!" My temples throb, my nose burns, I feel like I'm getting sick, and I'm so tired. "You said I cried about Jack for an entire summer. I didn't."

"Bullshit! I heard you. I saw you. You were miserable."

"Not because of Jack."

"What are you saying?"

My shoulders slump in defeat and I hear the words I'd hoped I would never have to say pour from my lips. "Everyone assumed I was upset about Jack. I just didn't correct you."

He does a double take. "Not... Sadie, you were a mess. You cried in the shower where you thought no one could hear you. What were you so upset about?"

I can't tell him. I shake my head, and he makes a frustrated growling sound.

When we pull up to Jack's parents' house, Blake meets us in the driveway. His big body looks even bigger in a shirt that looks a size too small, specifically on his biceps. My dad shuts off the truck and jumps out to meet Blake in the driveway. Two giant men, lifetime friends, facing off over their kids off-and-on love affair. God, my life could be a movie.

Before my dad gets a word out, Blake holds up his palm. "I just got off the phone with Jack." His eyes, the same emerald-green as his son's, dart to mine, and worry and confusion color his handsome features. "He's worried sick."

I shrug casually, but I feel anything but casual when I respond. "That's not my fucking problem, Uncle Blake."

His eyes widen. My dad's do the same.

Blake must see something in my expression because he eventually nods, respecting my wishes not to share.

My dad, on the other hand, does not. "What the fuck did that asshole do?"

I find it interesting that Blake doesn't defend Jack like he usually would. Does he know something? Did Jack figure out that I found the myBubble app on his phone? Or does Blake know his prick son well enough to know he's a scheming, lying dickhead?

"Tell your boy to stay away from Sadie, you hear me?" my dad says as he climbs back behind the wheel.

Blake doesn't say anything. He stands there watching us pull out of his driveway, his hands on his hips and disappointment in his eyes.

"How many secrets you keeping, princess?" Dad sounds calmer, less angry, and more tender.

"You don't want to know."

JACK

"What the hell did you do to Sadie?"

My dad's growling voice should be making me tense and uneasy, but I feel nothing but relief. Sadie walked out of my apartment seven fucking hours ago. I ended up calling the police four hours ago, and although I couldn't file a missing person's report, once I explained that she was new in the city and possibly lost, they released an all-points bulletin to keep their eyes peeled for a girl matching Sadie's description.

I paced my apartment for hours, walked the streets until my feet were sore, and I finally received some peace when I got a call from my dad shouting in my ear, "Why the hell is a pissed off Jonah Slade calling me asking about you?" I knew right away Sadie had been in touch with her dad, which meant she was still alive. I further calmed down when my dad explained that Jonah was on his way over with Sadie.

She's home. In Vegas. Safe with her family.

Thank God.

Rushing in on the heels of my relief was a big fat *what the fuck?*

She took off, lied to me, and decided to fly home to Las Vegas without her things? Without telling me? I can see why Jonah would be furious. He probably thinks I beat her or worse—

"She looked really upset, Jack."

Forced from my thoughts, exhausted, and half crazy, I blink and refocus on my conversation with my dad. "You saw her?"

"Yeah. I've never seen her like this. Looked like she'd been crying for days."

I run a hand through my hair and rack my brain. "Someone must've scared her. Why wouldn't she tell me?"

"Not *someone*. You."

"Dad, I'm telling you, things were great with us. We had an amazing weekend together. She even changed her flight to stay longer." I know because in trying to track her down, I called and found out that while I was in the shower, she *did* change her flight. So what happened between that phone call and when I got out of the shower to find her gone?

"I told her you were worried sick. You know what she said?" He doesn't give me a chance to respond. "She said, 'That's not my fucking problem, Uncle Blake.' So you tell me, you still think you and her are cool?"

"She said that?"

"Think, son. Think really hard. The woman I saw in that truck this afternoon was destroyed. How could you do that without knowing what you did?"

"I love her. I want to spend the rest of my life with her. I would never intentionally do anything to hurt her."

"Intentionally."

"What?"

"Is it possible you did something unintentionally? Secrets you might be keeping? Naked photos of an ex lying around—"

"No. Nothing like that." Except... myBubble. I close my eyes and think back to when I picked up my phone to text her. The myBubble messages she had sent Dawn were marked as read. I assumed I had opened her messages accidentally, but what if...? Oh God...

Before I'm even able to fully think through what could've happened, I know.

Sadie knows I'm Dawn.

"Oh Jesus."

"Fuck." My dad's curse is fierce. "What did you do?"

I drop my head into my hand and groan. "Fuck, fuck, *fuck!*"

Of course she found out I'm Dawn. It's the only thing that would've sent her running away with nothing more than the clothes on her back. I should've told her. I should've stopped pretending to be Dawn as soon as Sadie started answering my calls. What must she think of me? And she found out the morning after we had sex!

"Dad, this is bad. She'll never forgive me."

"Are you sure about that? I mean, this is Sadie we're talking about. She's a sweet girl, understanding and forgiving."

"She wasn't answering my calls—I didn't know what else to do!" I'm back to pacing my apartment. My legs have the irrational urge to run to her, to fall at her feet and apologize, but I don't deserve her forgiveness. She must feel so betrayed. "There's a new social media app my company is representing. I pretended to be one of Sadie's old college friends and... I..." Dammit, I can't even say it!

"You pretended to be one of her old college friends?" Judgment laces my father's voice.

"It was supposed to be temporary, but she was talking to me, ya know? *Really* talking to me. I couldn't walk away from that."

"That's some fucked up shit, Jackson."

"You think I don't know that?"

"I think you don't, or why else would you do it! What a stupid idea!"

"What do I do? She'll never forgive me."

"You want the truth?"

I stare out at the city, thinking back to how worried I was about Sadie. The thought of her wandering the streets lost and scared tore me up inside. This? Knowing the woman I love discovered my big, ugly secret? That I helped her in some small way to heal from the cruelty that was done to her only to break her in a different way? Bile burns my throat.

"Explain and apologize."

"That's it? That's all you suggest I do?"

"It's what she deserves. As far as getting her back? I'm sorry, I think you may've sunk the ship if you know what I mean."

"No, I'm not letting her go, not again. I made that mistake once. I'll call her, text her, and if she doesn't answer, I'll fly to Vegas and—"

"Don't do that. After what I saw today? She needs time. Give her that."

Time? But... "I already went years without her. I just got her back."

"Yep, and you fucked that up. Respect her space. If she's open to hearing you out, she'll let you know."

"I feel sick."

"Seems appropriate."

"Dad, if you see her, will you... I mean, I don't know, just... make sure she's okay? She's been through some shit and I'm afraid this might..." Might what? "I don't know. I'm worried about her."

"I'll drop in and see how she's doing, but I'll be honest, when she sees me, I think she sees you. Sadie has her father's death scowl."

"I need to figure out how to make this up to her."

"Good luck with that, son."

When I hang up, I fall face-first into my bed. Sadie's scent envelops me in a warm embrace, possibly the only embrace I'll ever receive from her again.

I try to sleep, but sleep won't take. I toss and turn for twelve hours until I finally give up and burn myself out at the gym, punishing my body for what I did to Sadie's heart.

———

Sadie, it's Jack. But you already knew that didn't you? Please, answer your phone. Let me explain.

The response to the myBubble message I sent is immediate.

This account has been deactivated.

CHAPTER TWENTY-FIVE

Three Weeks Later

SADIE

"All set?"

I pat my pockets, touch my purse—am I wearing a shirt? Yep. "All set."

Ricky snags my keys from my hand. "You're scaring me, so I'm driving."

I follow him out the door, laughing. "Why am I scaring you —wait! My bag!" I whirl around to grab it only to have him snag my elbow and pull me toward my car.

"It's in the trunk."

"Oh, that's right. Thank you."

He opens the passenger side door, smirking. "You're the one who put it in there."

"I knew that."

He slams the door with a muttered, "Sure, you did."

I watch him grab today's mail from the box, then come around to the driver's side, get in, and toss a stack of junk mail and bills into my lap. "We're all gassed up, so we shouldn't have to stop unless you get hungry or have to pee."

"It's only a couple hours. I think I'll be okay."

He fires up the engine, and I gather the mail to toss it into the backseat—when one envelope catches my eye. I pull it away from the rest, anger stirring my already nervous belly. Even without a return address, I know who the letter is from. The handwriting is a dead giveaway, and it's the fourth one I've gotten in as many days. I roll down my window, tear the letter in half, then gather the two sides and tear them again before tossing it out the window in a shower of paper confetti.

"Let me guess..." Ricky says as he side-eyes me cautiously.

I toss the rest of the mail into the backseat. "He'll give up eventually."

"You sure about that?"

"When he finds another gullible idiot to smokescreen, yeah."

He doesn't argue, but turns up "Take on Me" by Ah-Ha and bobs his head to the beat. "Next stop, Los Angeles!"

His excitement is enough to wash out all thoughts of Jack and his incessant phone calls and text messages. After a week, I blocked him. That's when the letters started, and those are easy enough to ignore. The second they arrive they make a quick trip to the trash can and I don't think of them again until the next one comes a few days later. Receive. Toss. Repeat.

As I leave San Diego in my rearview mirror, I look forward to my exhibition opening this weekend in LA. Ricky and I are headed up early so I can give input on display layout. Mrs. Rothschild said there are reporters interested in interviewing me. I can't believe this is my life.

And to think I considered giving this up to be with Jack?

Lesson learned.

Never again.

JACK

Sadie looks more beautiful than I've ever seen her.

Even from my spot across the street, tucked away in the shadows, her beauty is as clear as ever, seen through the glass of the Aldridge & Shultz Art Gallery. But I didn't come to Los Angeles to ruin her weekend. I promised myself that no matter how badly I wanted to reach for her, speak to her, I wouldn't. She deserves this—a night where all attention is on her because of her bravery and talent.

Am I stalking her? Yes.

I'm not proud, but I had to see her. Almost a month has passed since she left New York, and I've been sick without her. She refuses to hear me out. I'm pretty sure she's blocked me on her phone, and I haven't heard a word back from the half dozen letters I've written. I'm running out of ideas. How much longer can she blow me off?

Forever.

For now, I'll settle for the glimpses I get of her as she moves gracefully through the crowd of art enthusiasts who've come for her opening. Ricky stays close by her side, and I look away when he places his hand at her lower back to whisper something in her ear that makes her smile. I scratch at two weeks' of beard growth as irritation makes me itchy. He's been a good friend to her. She deserves as much, and so much more.

When I peer back up, I find Sadie talking to a man in a nice suit. She's looking at him how she used to look at me—with a teasing grin and laughter in her eyes.

It won't be long before she moves on to someone new. Someone better for her than I am. Someone who won't deceive her to satisfy his own selfish needs.

I ask myself the question I've been avoiding since she left.

I'm on the verge of losing Sadie forever.

What the fuck do I plan to do about that?

CHAPTER TWENTY-SIX

Two Weeks Later

SADIE

I'm floating.

Not really floating, but I may as well be. With my sketch-book pressed to my chest, I glide down the sidewalk toward the Magic Bean, practically skipping.

My exhibition in Los Angeles was a huge success. So much so that I'm getting commissioned work for custom pieces. And the price people are willing to pay? Well, I've quit my job and am working as a full-time artist.

Currently, I'm working on a series of three paintings for a famous movie producer in LA. He requested an urban theme of my choice, and he jumped on the idea of people in their natural environment, art illustrating the human condition.

Which is why I'm headed to my favorite spot in Hillcrest for people watching and inspiration. I order my coffee and spot my favorite table on the patio. I'm about to set my things on the table when I spot something on the chair.

My pulse speeds.

A cherry Blow Pop.

I pick it up and look around, afraid of who might have left the candy in my favorite seat.

There's no one. Could this have been a coincidence? I suppose anything's possible. I chalk it up to a weird cosmic joke and sit down to sketch.

———

"Where'd you get that?" I point at the white stick currently poking out from the corner of Ricky's mouth. "Is that cherry?"

Three days have passed since I found the Blow Pop on my seat at the coffee shop, and I've found one every day since. One on the hood of my car and one on our doorstep. But I hadn't seen one yet today. I thought maybe the cherry Blow Pop shower was over until I came downstairs to take a break from an eight-hour painting session only to stumble upon what seems to be another one.

He pops the thing from his mouth, the inside of his lips and his tongue red. "I found it in our mailbox." He shrugs. "Figured it was a gift from the postman."

I haven't told Ricky about Jack's latest attempt to get my attention. Not only because I hope not acknowledging his attempts will make them eventually stop, but also because it's a little creepy. I'll let Ricky believe it was the mailman even though everything in me knows these spontaneous candy deliveries are from Jack.

"I forgot how good these things are." He crunches the tangy hard candy.

"They'll give you cavities." I grab a Dr. Pepper from the fridge, and my phone vibrates in my pocket

He looks pointedly from me to the can in my hand. "Right."

I push the paint-splattered hair that had fallen from my ponytail off my forehead and check the caller ID. "My mom. Third time she's called today and it's only ten o'clock in the morning."

"Sadie," he says, pulling the lollipop from his mouth, "all the press your paintings are getting in LA, you knew this day would come."

I nod, because he's right. With the handful of interviews and articles, I knew information about my exhibition would eventually get back to my parents. The phone stops ringing and I slump in relief at being off the hook, even if for only a few hours.

"Get it over with." He chomps the Blow Pop's bubble gum then flicks the stick into the garbage. "Like a Band-Aid."

"I don't want to."

He scoots up next to me and wraps an arm around my shoulder. "I know you don't, but it's time. Think about what they're going through."

"That's the problem, I don't want to think about what they must be thinking." I sit in my shame at having to explain to them what happened to me and why I didn't tell them about it. Will they understand?

"Call her back," he says, setting my phone in front of me.

"You're right."

He winks. "I'm always right."

With my heart in my throat and dread creeping up my spine, I hit the button to call her back and press the phone to my ear.

My mom answers after one ring. "Sadie?" The tension and panic in her voice confirms my fears.

"Hey, Mom."

"Gia read about your work in some art magazine she gets..."

Our family friends Gia and her husband, Rex, love contemporary art and keep a finger on the pulse of the market.

"Rex was so proud of you, he brought it to the gym to brag and your dad..." She chokes up. "Sadie... we didn't know."

"I know. I'm sorry, there's a lot I didn't tell you guys, but..." I look up into Ricky's warm, supportive eyes. "I'm ready to tell you now."

My alarm goes off before the sun is up. I roll out of bed, brush my teeth, throw on my bathing suit, and stare at the six feet of foam and fiberglass hanging on my wall.

Conquering the conversation with my parents about what happened to me that night at the beach took days and a lot of tears. They didn't respond the way I thought, and their love and support washed in, pushing away the shame my secrets brought. They accepted that I'd had to handle the aftermath of that night in my own way in order to regain control over all I'd felt I'd lost. I felt a piece of myself return, one that I thought I'd never get back.

Empowered by independence, I managed to heal another part of me that had been wounded that night.

"It's time," I say softly, and before I can talk myself out of it, I grab my surfboard.

Ricky's in the kitchen, wearing nothing but a pair of board shorts and a mean case of bedhead. Coffee mug in hand, he freezes when he sees me descending the stairs, and when we make eye contact, a slow smile spreads along his lips. "No fucking way."

"I'm ready." I lean the board against the counter and grab my own cup of coffee. I'll need the liquid energy to make up for what I've lost in muscle. When I turn around, I find Ricky texting someone. "What are you doing?"

He's still grinning. "Getting the crew to meet us down there."

"I don't think my getting back into the water requires an audience."

He finishes typing, hits Send, and dumps his coffee in a to-go cup. "Not an audience—a support team. In case you think about changing your mind."

"I won't." I sip my coffee as excitement charges my blood. "I really think I'm ready."

"I hope you're right." He kisses my forehead. "Now come on, let's go before you pussy out."

When we step outside, the sky lightening with the rising sun,

I spot the familiar white stick with the red-and-white wrapper on my doorstep. Before I can think too hard on it, I kick it into the shrubs and forget I ever saw it.

————

Another Saturday at the coffee shop.

I'm embarrassed to admit I didn't come last weekend because I feared I'd find more than another Blow Pop. I was afraid that instead of finding candy waiting for me, I'd find the one person I vowed I'd never acknowledge again.

I breathe a sigh of relief when I get to my table and see a couple sitting there. Usually I'd balk at having to sit somewhere else—that table has the perfect angle so I can see people inside, on the patio, and passing by. But not today. Today, I'm happy to find another seat.

I grab my coffee and take a spot in the corner with my back to the wall. I pull out my pencils, open to a fresh page, and sit back and wait for inspiration to strike.

"Sadie?" The barista, Maddie, approaches me with her hand in the front pocket of her apron.

Did I leave my change behind? "Yes?"

She pulls her hand free. "This was left here for you."

When she moves her hand to reveal a cherry Blow Pop, I want to scream. Instead, I snap at her, "By who?"

She bites her fingernails. "I-I'm not supposed to say."

Is he here? Watching me? Or is he sending these fucking things here with instructions?

I shouldn't snap at the poor girl—don't kill the messenger and all—so I try to relax when I say, "I don't want it." I hand the thing back to her. "And if he leaves any more for you to give me, please throw them away."

She nods, and, with her head down, scurries back behind the counter.

My blood heats, my face matching the temperature of my

flaming insides. I gather my things, leave my coffee behind, and head out in search of a new favorite coffee shop.

JACK

I know I'm taking a huge risk, but nothing else is working.

My calls go straight to voicemail and Sadie hasn't read a single text I've sent since the day she left me. I've sent letters, pouring out my heart, I've left at least one hundred Blow Pops, and it's all been for nothing. She hasn't responded to any of my efforts.

I'm losing hope, but I'm not ready to give up on her. On us. Not yet.

Which is what brought me across the country, to her front door, at almost one o'clock in the morning.

I lift my Bluetooth speaker above my head and hit Play on my phone. Leaning back against my reasonably priced rental car, I direct my efforts toward the single window of Sadie's bedroom.

She may have been able to ignore the Blow Pops, but she can't snub REO Speedwagon. I convinced her to date me with "Can't Fight This Feeling," and I'm banking on the magic that worked back then to work again. As the words to "Keep on Loving You" pour from the speaker, and hopefully straight to her heart, I slide up the volume to full blast.

"If you think I'll give up and leave, you're wrong!" I wait for her light to flick on or to see her face in the window. "I can do this all night!"

Maybe I should also knock? There's no way she can't hear the music. Still, no movement from anywhere in the house.

So I do what I must, and I belt the words at the top of my lungs, totally off key and obnoxious sounding.

I'm well into the chorus when the front door flies open with such force it freezes the words in my mouth. But it's not Sadie staring at me—it's Ricky. His hair is a complete mess, and he's

shirtless but wearing something from the waist down. I don't
know what though, because I refuse to look.

He glares at me through puffy eyes. "What the *fuck,* Jack?"

A bit of my desperation simmers and I feel like a dick as I
pause the song. I set the speaker aside and climb the stairs to
meet him, peering over his shoulder into the dark condo. "I need
to talk to Sadie."

"No shit," he says dryly. "And here I thought this whole John
Cusack thing was for me."

"Sadie's a sucker for eighties' references," I mumble, feeling
really dumb and looking hella desperate. "Can you please tell her
I'm here?"

He stares at me, props his shoulder against the doorframe,
and crosses his arms. "No."

"No?" He can't tell me *no.*

"Sorry to be the one to tell you this, but you're too late."

I'm already shaking my head. "What does that mean?"

He sighs, hard and heavy, then shrugs his big, stupid shoulders. "We didn't mean to fall in love."

My eyes snap to his and narrow. "What did you say?"

"We'd been best friends for so long. The attraction was
always there—I mean, how could it not be—"

"*You?*"

"But we never acted on it because we didn't want to ruin the
friendship."

"You're gay!" I laugh, hoping he does the same because this
has got to be one big fucking joke.

Only he doesn't laugh. He stares, expressionless. Protective.

I step back, needing the distance in order to keep from
knocking his perfect white teeth from his skull. My pulse pounds
between my ears and my skin flushes with heat.

"She was upset when she came back from New York. I
comforted her like I always do when cowards break her heart."

I swallow hard. "I don't want to hear any more."

"I've loved her for years—"

"Stop talking."

"And she loves me too."

I turn and stumble down the stairs. "That's enough."

"You sure?" he calls to me. "You came here to say something, so say it. Get it all out, then move the fuck on."

I pause on the sidewalk, my mind spinning, my heart breaking. Because truth be told, Sadie deserves a guy like Ricky. He was her security when I abandoned her the first time. When that monster robbed from her body, Ricky was there for her too. When I deceived her, he was there for her then. I've always taken Sadie's love, but never earned it. Ricky has more than earned it, but never taken it.

Until now.

Turning back to face the man who fairly won the only woman I've ever loved, I say the only thing I can. "Take care of her."

"I always have."

Ouch. He's right, but damn, that hurt.

"Can you..." I shove my hands in my pockets, my hands fisting against the urge to kill Ricky. If I didn't know how much it would hurt Sadie, I would already have my hands around his neck. "Tell Sadie I'm sorry and that I'll always love her?"

"I'll try to remember that. Go home, Jack." His words are punctuated by the soft click of the door, followed by the lock.

I pull the cherry Blow Pop from my back pocket and throw it as hard as I can across the street, then I head back to the airport to see about the first flight to New York.

CHAPTER TWENTY-SEVEN

JACK

Eight weeks.

It took eight weeks to unravel a life that took me five years to build. And no, I'm not being dramatic.

First, Sadie's moved on. I never thought I'd see our end. I couldn't fathom a world where *Jack and Sadie* weren't a thing. Now it's Ricky and Sadie, which sounds wrong and... stupid.

Second, I came to the conclusion that I hate New York. After hearing that Ricky and Sadie were together, I stumbled, drunk and exhausted, off the plane at JFK, and it was as if everything I used to love about the city felt like a dream. Where the crowded bustle of the city use to invigorate me, it now left me irritated and claustrophobic. All the restaurants I enjoyed now seemed pretentious and pompous. The food is stupid expensive. I pay a fortune for a tiny apartment I hate. I despise that I have to drag groceries up an elevator, and I have a goddamn doorman. Seriously, who the fuck do I think I am?

I went from loving my life and all the opportunity the city had to offer to absolutely despising myself and what I had become.

Oh, and third, I was "let go" from Riot Advertising. That's how they put it. "Jackson, I'm sorry, but we have to let you go." I guess they thought that particular verbiage sounded less brutal. They're wrong. And to add insult to injury, they had Tanner fire me.

Why did they fire me?

I've called in sick and blown off important meetings in order to take long weekends out of town for personal reasons. A.k.a. stalking Sadie. But the final nail in the coffin of my career was a complaint filed with the myBubble people. Yep. Sadie. She let them know she was catfished by yours truly. How fucking humiliating.

Thankfully, Tanner already knew—it was his dumb idea after all. He managed to convince the company to send me packing with a decent severance package.

So, jobless but with a hefty balance in my bank account, I was able to make some changes.

"Do you have any more questions, Mr. Daniels?" Victoria Lockman, my realtor, hands me the keys to my new house. "You sure you don't want me to walk through it with you?"

"No. Thanks for helping me find something so quickly," I say as I gaze at my new home. The barn-red siding is missing in places, the roof needs to be replaced, the landscape is over-grown, and weeds are growing from cracks in the driveway. I look beyond the house's flaws to the cliffs ahead and the great Pacific Ocean that yawns out before me. "This is perfect."

"Encinitas is a great choice. Thirty minutes to downtown, hour and a half to Los Angeles. Location, location, location!" she says in a sing-song voice. "If you have any questions, you know where to find me." She slips her slender body, encased in a tight pencil skirt and blouse, into her 'Benz and throws me a finger wave as she drives away.

I grab my suitcase, which has enough to get me by until the movers show up on Thursday with my things and drag it up the driveway to the carport entry. The key sticks in the rusted keyhole and takes some shimmying to unlock. The scent of dust mixed with humid air makes it clear that the place hasn't been opened in weeks. I leave my suitcase by the door and take in the open living space, happy to see it's accurate to the photos Victoria emailed me. The gas stove and refrigerator are at least twenty years old but are the newest things in the house. The sixties-era wood paneling on two walls and painted white brick on the other would be difficult to stomach if it weren't for the long wall of windows and sliding glass doors on the west-facing wall. I unlock and open them to let in the ocean breeze and clear out the cobwebs.

Stepping out onto the back deck, which is weak with wood rot, I shove my hands in my pockets and make peace with my new reality.

———

The small beach town of Encinitas is the polar opposite of New York—smiling faces, people who hold doors for strangers, and every storefront with a water bowl and treat for people walking their dogs.

I wonder if I should get a dog. Make life less lonely.

With every day that passes, big city life seeps from my pores —along with hard-earned sweat. I've ripped paneling off the walls, stripped linoleum floors, and removed most of the decaying wood from the deck. My back aches from the labor, and the old cot I found at the secondhand store in town doesn't help. As uncomfortable as it is, I'll miss sleeping in the living room, the ocean breeze pouring over my face, when my furniture from New York gets delivered this afternoon.

Finishing my jog a couple miles up and back down the coast, I wipe sweat from my forehead and slow to a walk. Two vehicles are parked in front of my house, and they aren't delivery trucks. I check my watch. Just after ten o'clock in the morning.

I recognize the cars and mumble, "You've gotta be kidding

me." I consider turning around and running to San Clemente, but two big bodies circle around the hood of one of the trucks and one of them waves. I've been spotted. "Too late."

I hang my head and approach, wondering what the fuck my dad and uncle are doing here. They walk to the end of the driveway to meet me, both grinning as though they know something they shouldn't.

"Let me guess," I say as I approach. "Mom."

My uncle Braeden throws his good arm around me and pulls me in for a back-thumping hug. His bad arm, maimed from his time as a Marine, stays close to his side. "Nephew, I love what you've done with the place."

I chuckle and hug him back. "It's dumpster-chic."

The moment he releases me, my dad gives me a similar greeting. He studies the piles of old flooring, vintage wallpaper, and deck wood I have accumulating in the driveway. "You've been busy."

"I have." Ripping the shit out of this old house has been the only thing that keeps my thoughts off Sadie. I cross my arms, feeling a little vulnerable and a lot transparent. My family has to know my sudden move to the left coast isn't at all like me. "What brings you by?"

"That." Braeden directs my attention to the vehicle parked next to my dad's Rubicon. "Thought you could use it."

I lean around and spot my old 4-Runner. "You brought me my truck?"

My dad nods. "'Bout time you took this ol' hunk of shit back. Sick of watching it collect dust."

My gut clenches as all the memories of Sadie and me in the truck wash over me, but I hide it well. Or at least I hope I do.

"Had the engine tuned up, new tires," my dad says while keeping his eyes on the truck rather than me.

"Raven do the work?" I barely choke out the words, but I already know the answer. Sadie's mom is the best mechanic in Las Vegas—hell, in the entire southwest.

He shifts uncomfortably and I brace myself because I already know the answer. My dad would never use a mechanic other than Sadie's mom. "Yep. She wanted to do more, ya know, little things on the inside, but..." He clears his throat. "Figured you'd want to keep it the way it was when you drove it."

"Thanks, Dad." The memory of Sadie and her family, my second family, hurts—fuck, it hurts—knowing things are forever changed between us. They have Ricky, so they won't miss me. Especially Jonah and Carey. "I can't believe you guys did this."

"Figure you'll need a vehicle to get you to and from your job." Braeden's eyebrows are raised.

"I'm working on it. I have an interview next week. Riot actually gave me a great recommendation."

"Oh, one more thing." Braeden reaches into the back seat of my dad's truck and pulls out a guitar case.

My chest expands and fills with a comfortable fullness as I take the instrument. "My guitar?"

My uncle lifts his chin, his expression serious. "How long has it been since you played?"

"Years. I'm not even sure I remember how."

My dad claps me on the shoulder and squeezes. "It'll come back to you. So you want to show us around?" He tilts his head toward the house. "Put us to work?"

"How long you guys staying in town?"

Braeden stares at the ground as my dad sniffs and studies the house. "As long as you need, son."

When he finally looks at me, I try to ignore the pity in his eyes. My mom sent them here because she's worried about me, and now that they've seen me, I'm confirming their fears.

I'm a lovesick, heartbroken, pathetic shmuck who moved all the way across the country to be closer to a girl who wants nothing to do with me.

She's moved on.

I never will.

SADIE

"Third day this week," Ricky says as he slides my board into the back of his pickup truck. "I'd say it's official." He quirks a handsome smile my way. "You're back."

I scrunch up my sand-covered toes on the blacktop of the Pacific Beach parking lot, feeling a slight flicker of unease that dissipates quickly. I rewrap my towel around my waist, unable to fight my grin. "I am definitely back."

He runs a hand through his wet hair to shake out some of the water. "Livin' the dream. I don't know a single person who wouldn't kill to have your life."

He's right. Since *Insufficient Trauma* spent three weeks at Aldridge & Shultz, I've been getting commission requests on top of commission requests. I made a website and posted some of my available pieces and nearly sold out. Between painting and surfing again, I hardly have time to consider the part of my heart that went missing the day I stormed out of Jack's apartment.

"Hungry?" Ricky's midway through a surfer change, attracting the eyes of several bikini-clad girls as they pass by, but he doesn't seem to notice them as he waits for me to answer.

"Sure." I do some under-towel-maneuvering to change out of my bikini and into cut-off shorts and a tank top.

"Burritos it is." He tosses his wet things into the bed of his truck, and I do the same with mine.

It's a short drive to the burrito shack. I suck in a fortifying breath before heading through the door that Ricky holds open for me. This is where I took Jack after our disastrous breakfast in La Jolla. It was the first time I saw a glimpse of the boy I'd fallen in love with. I still can't believe that even then, he was getting into my head by pretending to be Dawn.

We order, and I pay because Ricky is still working in catering at the resort. We settle in to eat in silence.

He finishes before me, and he studies me, making me think the companionable silence is coming to an end. "You miss him."

I force down my bite, sip my Dr. Pepper, and shake my head. "Not at all actually."

"I wasn't asking." His light eyes shine against his sun-kissed skin.

I push away my burrito wrapper. "I don't." I surprise myself with how convincing I sound.

"You're lying."

"What do you want me to say? Do I miss him?" I search the posters and old surfboards hanging from the walls. "He lied to me, like, a lot. How could I possibly miss someone who deceived me in such a personal way?" *Please, tell me, because I do miss him and I don't want to.*

He shrugs and shakes up the crushed ice in his Styrofoam cup. "Desperate people in love do stupid shit."

This is the first time he's spoken about Jack since Jack showed up, banging down the door at one in the morning. Ricky told Jack we were together, we were in love, and that Jack needed to move on. It's been twelve weeks and the letters and Blow Pops eventually stopped.

Jack finally gave up.

I should be relieved.

Right?

"What are you saying, that I should forgive him for lying to me? For pretending to be someone else so he could convince me to sleep with him?" Saying it is pissing me off again. How could he do that to me?

Ricky chuckles and grins. "Give me a break. You already knew you wanted to sleep with him when you asked 'Dawn' if you should. Besides, no one could talk you into doing anything you didn't want to do." He reaches across the table and his warm hand envelops mine. "I know what it's like to love you. I can't imagine not having you in my life."

I blow out a breath. "He chose to lie and deceive me. That's on him. I'm not taking the responsibility for this."

He pats my hand before releasing it to lean back in his chair.

"Life is way too short to hold a grudge."

"I am not holding a grudge!"

He shrugs. "You are."

"Ricky! He lied to me."

"He loves you. He will never be okay without you, and I'm getting the vibe that you'll never be okay without him either."

"I can't forgive him for what he did."

"Haven't you ever done something stupid for love?"

I shake my head. "No. I certainly wouldn't lie to someone I love. I wouldn't pretend to be someone I'm not with someone I love."

He raises his eyebrows as if to say I'm full of shit.

"What?" I throw up my hands. "I wouldn't."

"Have you never been so in love that it made you crazy and unpredictable?" He sinks casually back into his seat. "Do things out of character just to get closer to them?"

"You're implying I should forgive him."

"Am I?"

"Stop answering me with questions."

He shrugs, grabs his garbage, and slides out of his seat. "I'll be right back. I want to show you something."

"*So* not the same thing," I whisper to myself while Ricky heads out to his truck.

I watch him open the passenger side door and lean in. He grabs a big Ziploc bag from his glove box and comes back inside.

He holds eye contact when he drops the bag in front of me. "Read them."

I glare at the offending envelopes. "You kept Jack's letters?"

"The ones I could find, yes."

"You stole my mail!"

He nods, quickly and confidently. "I did."

Why doesn't he sound sorry?

I stand so quickly my chair rocks back on two legs. "What is it with the men in my life trying to control—"

"That's what you think I'm trying to do? Control you?" He

sounds angrier than I've ever heard him, and his lips become a thin white line. He steps closer and stabs a finger at the letters. "I'm trying to keep you from making the biggest mistake of your life. Read the fucking letters. You owe it to yourself and to the relationship you guys had to at least hear him out."

With my hands propped on my hips, I shake my head.

"What are you afraid of?" He studies my face, and his expression softens along with his voice. "Sadie, what are you afraid of?"

I take in a shaky breath and tears sting my eyes.

When I don't answer, he drops his shoulders in defeat. "If you can't be honest with me, at least be honest with yourself—"

"I'm afraid of loving him again."

He jerks back as if surprised by my response. "Why?"

I run my teeth over my lower lip. "He left me once and forgot about me. I left him in New York and I will forget about him."

He leans to the side to get my eyes. "Will you?"

Tears stream down my cheeks, the answer loud and clear without a single word.

He smiles sadly. "Read the letters. If you still want to try to forget him after you hear him out, then so be it."

CHAPTER TWENTY-EIGHT

JACK

Six months and two days since Sadie left me.

I tell myself I need to stop measuring time using the day she left, but I can't help it. Four months and two days since I started my new life in California. Three months and twelve days since I started working at Nitro Advertising, a small firm based out of Encinitas. I make less than what I made in New York, but aside from my mortgage, my expenses are low. I have no car payment, and I'm doing the remodeling myself. My life is simple. I have plenty of time to breathe, which I no longer have to remind myself to do.

Unless...

Unless I'm thinking of Sadie.

I stopped driving down to Hillcrest to watch her draw once she stopped showing up at her favorite coffee shop. I can't say that didn't hurt like a bitch. Now I can't find her. The last couple times I drove by her house, her car wasn't there. She could've moved to another state and I'd never know.

So I did the only thing I could. After months of being miserable, I tried moving on. I met a nice woman at work who invited me out for drinks.

But I couldn't do it.

I'm not ready.

Maybe someday I will be.

Maybe not.

After an easy day of working on branding for a local vodka company, I grab a bag of Chuy's famous mahi-mahi tacos and head home to watch the sunset with a few beers on my newly stained deck.

I wave to my neighbor, the Admiral, an eighty-year-old retired naval officer. He still wears the cap from his dress whites, yellowed from time, as he waters his lawn with a hose every night. I've offered to put in some underground sprinklers for him, but he told me if he didn't keep moving, he'd die.

I can relate.

I move through life one task at a time, being productive but not really living. Sadie's absence left me in a life without any flavor, and I can't begin to imagine how I went five years in New York without her.

I'm so busy thinking about the parallels between my life and the Admiral's that I don't notice right away the red Honda parked in front of my house. Or the beautiful brunette sitting on the car's hood.

My truck slows to a crawl then stops abruptly when I realize who's at my house. "No fucking way."

Sadie.

My pulse jumps, speeds, and makes me a little clumsy as I pull into my driveway, hopping the curb. "What is she doing here? How did she know where I live?"

My fingers shake when I shut off the engine, and the blood leaves my head when I slip from my 4-Runner and see her making her way toward me. The ocean breeze plays with her floral sundress. Her tan shoulders look soft under the warm light of the setting sun. Her flip-flops slapping against the concrete is all I can hear over the roar of my pulse. My lips part and I sway on my feet at the sight of her. She pushes strands of her long, dark hair off her mostly makeup-free face and stops a couple feet in front of me.

"Hey." *Yep, that's all I got.*

I'm stunned. What is she doing here? And how rude that she would show up here, looking so fucking beautiful I feel it in my lungs. I suck in a shaky breath and remind myself to keep the in and out of the oxygen thing going so I don't pass out.

"You *dick!*" She slams her fists against my chest, knocking me back a step. "How could you do this to me?"

I open my mouth to defend myself, but having no defense, I close my lips.

She hauls off and knocks my chest again. "You promised you'd never hurt me!" She hits my chest, and I fall back against my truck. Her eyes fill with tears, her cheeks flush with anger, and she sucks in a shaky breath. "Not you, Jack!"

Her pain-laced words bruise worse than her hits. When she slams into me again, I grab her wrists and hold them to my pounding chest. She collapses against me, and I notice then she has a wad of paper clutched in her fist.

"Why?" she mutters, her shoulders jumping with soul-deep sobs that rip from her throat and tear through my soul.

I wrap my arms around her and hold her while she falls apart in my arms. "I'm so fucking sorry." My eyes swell will tears, and I blink to keep them hidden while she soaks my tee with hers. "I'm so dumb. I know I hurt you."

I bury my nose in her hair and tell her how sorry I am until my voice cracks and my throat is raw. She takes a shuddered breath and pulls back and out of my embrace. I resist the urge to pull her against me again. With shaky hands, she wipes her cheeks and blows out a breath, fixing her reddened eyes on mine.

Not an appropriate time to smile, but I never thought I'd have her eyes on me again.

She squints a little as if she's unsure of my response, then her gaze slips over my shoulder. "I like your house."

"Um." I'm standing here like a dumbfuck. *Speak words, idiot!* "I... thanks."

She chews her lip, her eyes darting from her car to me. "I should've called first. I shouldn't have come—"

"No!"

Her shoulders jump in surprise.

"I'm sorry. I just mean—" Breathe. In. Out. In. "I'm glad you're here."

"I didn't mean to come." A stray tear still sits on her cheek, and I lick my lips, wishing I could kiss it away. She looks at the fist with the balled-up paper sticking from each end. "I read what you wrote and..."

I follow her gaze back to her fist as it opens slowly. I recognize my handwriting. "My letters."

She clears her throat. "We need to talk." She drags out each word as if she's speaking to someone with only one functioning brain cell.

Say yes! Say yes! "Yes."

Her blue-green eyes widen as if she's cueing me to make a move. I snap out of it enough to register that my car door is still open.

"Right, so..." I turn around on autopilot because my brain is shitting itself, grab the bag of tacos, and close the door. "Come in?"

She nods. I think. I don't honestly register anything except that she's following me inside.

"I'm sorry about the mess." I motion for her to walk in ahead of me. "If I would've known, I would've tidied up before work."

She takes a look around, probably noticing the dated appliances and familiar living room furniture from my tiny apartment dwarfed in the gaping space. "Work?"

I set the tacos on the kitchen counter. "Yeah, it's a small firm." I assume she's surprised I've been at work because of my

T-shirt, shorts, and leather flip-flips. "Southern Californian companies are a lot more relaxed with their dress codes."

When I turn around she's standing at the windows, the ocean in front of her, but her eyes are on the cot with the rumpled blanket and pillow. I open my mouth to explain, but I can't bring myself to utter the words. Instead, I get to the point. "You read my letters."

She blinks up at me, and I swear I see regret in her eyes, but it disappears before I can study it too closely. "I did. Not all of them."

Oh God, I poured my heart out in those letters. I should be embarrassed about some of the things I wrote, but I'm not because... "I meant every word."

She unfolds the one in her hand. "You're claiming temporary insanity?"

"Yes, it's the only way I could think to describe how I felt when you wouldn't talk to me. I needed you, needed to hear your voice, and when you ignored me, I..." I grimace at how fucked up I sound. "I'm crazy when it comes to you, always have been."

"You lied to me." Her voice hardens. "And all those trips to San Diego for work, all lies."

"Yes. I lied." My confessions looked better on paper than they sound out loud. I can't blame her for wanting nothing to do with me.

Her gaze darts to the far end of the room, the corner where my guitar is propped. "You're playing again?"

"A little."

"I don't, uh..." She blinks rapidly. "I don't remember seeing it at your apartment."

"A lot has changed since New York."

She seems to stare right through me when she asks, "Has it?"

I suck in a fortifying breath. "I lost you, Sadie. And losing the best part of myself changed me."

She breathes through what seems like a wave of emotion, and once she seems settled, she says, "I talked to my parents."

I suppose that's how she found out about my move.

"They, uh..." She clears her throat. "They found out about my exhibition in Los Angeles. I guess Rex brought them an article and... anyway. They had a lot of questions."

"How'd they take it?"

"Pretty good. I mean, after I got a bloody and detailed rundown of how Fabian was going to die."

I cringe, imagining. "Your dad is terrifying."

"My dad? Oh no, that was from my mom." She gazes out the window. "My dad shut down actually, got scary quiet for a long time. We had a long talk though, and he'll be okay. Your view is amazing."

Her subject change doesn't go unnoticed. "It's one of the reasons I bought the house."

"It's not what I would've expected."

I step closer to her, but not close enough to touch. "No?"

"I would've expected you to go for something flashier."

I nod but don't defend myself. The New York me absolutely would've gone for something flashier, something that people would look at with envy. A house that took the focus off what a piece of trash I was becoming.

"I can see why you choose to sleep out here." She tips her chin toward the cot. "Waking up every morning to the waves."

"It's not the view that keeps me out here," I say, unable to take my eyes off the gentle curve of her jaw, the fluttering pulse at her neck. "I can't sleep in my bed without thinking of you."

Her gaze slides to mine with such feeling that I'm knocked off center, thrown. Dizzy.

"I lied to my parents," she says.

I blink, focus, and try to follow.

"I love them so much, I lied to avoid hurting them by telling them what happened to me."

"No one would fault you for that."

"But I also lied because I was selfish. I knew if they found out about what Fabian did to me, they'd want me to move home.

And worse, I was afraid they'd think I was careless for being alone with someone I hardly knew."

"Bullshit. It wasn't your fault—"

"I know, I do. My point is, they didn't react in any of the ways I thought they would. I lied because I thought I knew what was best for everyone. I was wrong."

What the hell do I say to that? "You had no way of knowing how'd they respond."

"I didn't even give them the chance to do or say the right thing, to support me. I made them guilty without any proof." She tucks her hair behind her ear and licks her soft, pink lips. "The summer after what that asshole did to me? I let my family believe it was *you* who hurt me."

I nod, because I already know that. As much as I hate it, I'll take their anger if it means protecting Sadie.

"Using Dawn, you betrayed me."

"Yes." I swallow hard.

"You lied to me because I wouldn't let you in."

"I did. It's a pathetic excuse."

"Because you worried about me. Because you loved me."

"Yes." My throat swells more with every word she speaks, and I stand as still as a statue, fearing any move I make might shut her down.

"I understand now why you did it."

"It was wrong, I know. I should've told you sooner. I planned to, I did—"

"I want to forgive you, but..."

But. That last word knocks the breath from my lungs.

She steps closer, and my breath stalls when she cups my jaw. I lean into her touch. Her thumb brushes along my jaw and she smiles sadly. "I'm sorry, Jack."

I turn my cheek into her touch, my eyes sliding closed. "For what?" The words crack as they leave my lips.

Her hand slides from my face, down my arm to my hand,

where she puts the letter in my palm and closes my fingers around it. "I don't know if I can do this."

I don't need to read the letter she gave me. Every word is emblazoned on my heart. I shove the wrinkly page into my pocket.

I drop my chin, my eyelids close, and the first tear slips free. I don't wipe it away, but instead nod and give her the freedom to walk away. "I broke us. I know I don't deserve you, but if you need me, I'll *always* be here for you. I know you've moved on, but I never will."

Her brows pinch together. "Did you move here for me?"

"Yes. And I'd do it again a million times over. I regret that I didn't do it years ago." God, I sound pathetic. "You must think I'm a stalker."

"I'm afraid."

My gaze jerks to hers. "Of me?"

"I'm afraid of what I feel. Terrified of letting you in at the risk of being hurt again."

I close the distance between us but don't touch her. "You have every reason to be terrified. I'm far from a perfect man. I'm going to fuck things up over and over again. I'll say the wrong things and smother you with my overprotectiveness. I'll hold on to you too tightly."

"But...?"

"No buts. Just the truth. I'm never going to lie to you again."

Her expression grows serious. "Does my butt look big in this dress?"

"You've never looked more beautiful than you do right now. I haven't looked at your butt because I'm not able to stop staring at your eyes, lips, and hair."

"What do you really think of my art?"

"You're insanely talented. I hate that you have a painting of a good-looking guy with a huge dick in your living room. Your exhibition was intense and disturbing, but the world needs more artists like you who don't shy away from the ugly truths of life."

She tucks her chin in as if surprised by my response, but I wasn't kidding. I will never lie to her again. "Did you feel guilty pretending to be Dawn?"

"Yes. But the happiness I felt that I was finally talking to you overshadowed my shame."

"Do you love me, Jack?"

That one's easy. "With every single part of my being, I am in love with you. There hasn't been a single second of my life that I can remember when I wasn't in love with you."

"And you'll promise to love me and never lie to me again?"

I study her expression, the shine in her eyes as she leans toward me. "What are you saying?"

"If it's not obvious, I guess I'll have to spell it out for you. I'm scared, but I'm more scared of living a life that doesn't include you." She bites her lip then releases it to press hers to mine. My brain zaps and short-circuits. "I love you too."

My mouth gapes as the feel of her lips lingers on mine. "What about..." *Words!* "Ricky."

She grins. "Oh, yeah, I guess I need to apologize for that. He lied. We were never together."

"Why not?"

Her eyebrows drop and she backs up a step. I clench my hands to keep from grabbing her and pulling her close.

"You want me with Ricky?" she asks.

"No!" *What are you saying? Shut up!* I run a hand through my hair. "Sorry, I-I want you to be happy."

"I think..." She seems shy and hesitant when she says, "I'd be happiest with you."

SADIE

I don't know whether to guide Jack to the couch or try to catch him before he passes out. His face is white, his lips parted, and he's looking at me but not seeing me. I handed him my heart and I'm afraid he's going to drop it at my feet.

I didn't know what to expect when I got the bright idea to ambush him at his house. My plan was to hear him out, but when I saw him, all those old feelings rushed back and I knew I didn't need to hear his reasons. Ricky was right—we do stupid things for love. I couldn't deny my feelings for a second longer.

I've been in love with Jack my entire life. I foolishly convinced myself that if I didn't see him or talk to him, I'd fall out of love with him. When he was in New York, when I refused to take his calls after Tanner's wedding, and when I had to sit on my hands in my bed to keep from looking out the window when he pulled a *Say Anything* at my doorstep, I really believed that not seeing him would dull my feelings. All it really did was trick my heart into remission.

When he sways on his feet, I grip his biceps to steady him, but he's a big man. If he goes down, there's nothing I can do to stop him. "Are you okay? I think you should sit."

He's not looking at me but at my hands fisting the sleeves of his T-shirt. His skin is tanner than it was when I last saw him, his muscles a little bigger. His gaze moves slowly from my hand, up my arm, to my shoulder, and then slips to the side to focus on my lips. His eyes flare then darken.

"Jack, I—"

My words die as his lips mold gently to mine, so I'm left with only my body to communicate. I grip his shirt tighter, pull him closer, push up on my tiptoes, and return his kiss. His mouth opens for a breath and I sink deeper, arch my back, and give myself over to the swell of emotion between us.

He rips his mouth from mine, his breath coming in heavy bursts as he rests his forehead against mine. "Tell me this is real."

"It's real."

The corners of his lips twitch. "Are you saying you're mine?"

I clutch his forearm resting at my hip and bring his hand to my heart, pressing his palm against my breastbone. I pull back enough to get his eyes, and with the focus of an obsessed man, he peers through to my soul. "I have *always* been yours. Even when I thought I didn't want to be."

His six-foot-something frame folds around me, his arms over my shoulders, hands tangled in my hair, lips at my temple, where he groans. "I don't deserve you."

With my arms wrapped around his middle, my face buried in his neck, I shrug. "That's probably true."

He chuckles, but when he releases me and focuses on my mouth, his laughter dies. The way he kisses me sears through me, further branding him on my soul. We've always been like this, and life has never been okay when we're apart. Standing with the backdrop of the setting sun over the ocean, we kiss until we're trembling. Arms holding, hands gripping hard in a desperate need to never let go. Whispered words of apology coupled with confessions of love encapsulate us in a space where our separation becomes distant and our future falls out before us.

"Did you eat dinner?" he says while peppering kisses along my jaw.

My eyes are closed, my chin tilted toward the ceiling as I lose myself to his touch. "You're thinking of food right now?"

He dips lower, his lips sliding along my collarbone, tongue gliding and tasting as he makes his way to my opposite shoulder. "No. I'm thinking of *you* right now. What I have in mind is going to last far into the dinner hour. I want to make sure you don't get hungry."

I gasp at the way he nips my neck while he speaks, as if eating me is an option. *Yes, please.* "I'd love a tour of your house."

He freezes with my earlobe between his teeth.

"Start in the bedroom."

"Oh yeah?" I feel his smile against my skin as he catches my meaning. "Then where?"

"Hmmm..." His mouth is heaven against my throat. "The bathroom."

He moans against my skin, his grip on me growing tighter.

"The kitchen."

"Yes," he says breathlessly.

"And then, when it's nice and dark, the deck."

I laugh when he scoops me into his arms and carries me toward the hallway and into his bedroom.

He lays me on the bed and crawls over me, his body fitting perfectly between my open legs. Holding his weight over me with powerful arms, he dips to kiss me and whispers, "So this is the bedroom."

And without another word, we lose ourselves in another kiss.

His hips roll in firm, rhythmic waves, and I'm grateful I wore a dress. The only barriers between us are my panties and his shorts, and the heat created between us becomes unbearable. He must feel it too, because he reaches behind his neck and pulls off his shirt. He slips the spaghetti straps down my arms to reveal my strapless bra. I sit up, and reading my mind, he unclasps the hooks with one hand, freeing my breasts to his ravenous gaze.

I drop back to the bed, and he drops his weight to my side. His mouth finds my nipple while his hand pushes up my dress to find my thighs open and waiting.

"I never thought I'd feel you again," he says. My back arches off the bed as his breath ghosts over my breast, left damp from his kiss. He caresses my inner thigh, his palms roughened with calluses that weren't there the last time we were together. "I'm never letting you go."

"Don't stop touching me." It seems like such a silly thing to say, but I can't think of a better way to express my need. When his hands are on me, I feel safe, cherished, and like I'm the only woman he's ever seen.

"Never." He teases me from the outside of my panties. "So wet."

He knows what I want, he always does, and I don't have to beg, because he never makes me wait or suffer longer than I can bear. He tugs my panties down and I lift my butt so he can slide them off my legs, then I kick them to the floor. I'm not surprised that he doesn't remove my dress. He's always liked when I looked rumpled—shirt shoved up, shorts to my ankles, bra pulled down just enough to free my boobs.

Shifting his body to the foot of the bed, he presses my thighs open until I feel the twinge of stretching muscles in my hips. He holds me there and lowers his mouth to me. He starts off slow, with close-mouthed kisses that tease, until I'm pressing against his hold. He picks up on my cues and gives me more. Long swipes of his tongue gradually grow deeper until I'm gasping and lifting my hips to meet his mouth.

I'm so close, so damn close, when he stops.

"What are you doing?" My hands grip his bedding to keep from grabbing his head to make him finish the job.

He chuckles, the sound so low and promising it sends goose bumps up my body as he climbs above me. His shorts and boxers are off and he has his hard-on clenched in his fist. "I want us to finish together."

I run my hands over taut muscles to link my fingers around the back of his neck. "Yes."

He sucks in a breath. "There's only one problem."

His words are a splash of cold water. "What?"

"No condom."

"Oh." I gaze down at his erection, his big hand wrapped around it, and the view supercharges my arousal.

He narrows his eyes. "I know I've given you no reason to trust me, but I would never put your health in danger, Sadie."

"I believe you." And I do.

"Yeah?"

I nod. "I'm on the pill."

He frowns, and although he doesn't speak, I can see the question in his eyes. I bring my legs up and lock them around his back.

His entire body trembles. "You sure?"

"I'm sure."

And with that, Jack sinks inside me, filling my body the way his love fills my soul.

JACK

Being wrapped up in Sadie feels like a dream—her legs locked around me, her hands in my hair, and her tongue in my mouth. And her heat, with no barrier between us... *fuck*. This is the closest to heaven I'll ever be.

Our lovemaking has always been tender. When we were younger, I never wanted her to feel anything less than worshipped. I never took her as hard as my imagination fantasized, and that was fine with me. I'd take what I could get and die a happy man.

But something has changed in Sadie.

As I move inside her and revel in the sensations that skate up my spine, her body language is restless. Her hips lift off the bed, meeting me thrust for thrust. Her nails dig into my back hard enough to leave marks. She sucks my bottom lip, and when my pace stays steady, she bites.

I grin at her, really fucking enjoying this side of her. I slip one hand under her ass and scoot her up the bed until her back is against the headboard. I don't have a clue what I'm doing—all I know is that I want to take her harder up against something solid. She trembles and her eyes gleam as I shift my position enough to grab the headboard with both hands. I punch my hips forward and she moans. The sound goes straight between my legs.

She looks so beautiful propped up in front of me, her hair a mess around her face, those eyes crystal clear and focused on me, her lips dark pink and parted. I lean in and suck them while I pin her in place with my hips.

Keeping a close eye on her responses, I quicken my pace, and she encourages me with deep kisses and the bite of her nails. My orgasm coils at the base of my spine, and the logical side of my head tells me to slow down, draw it out, but Sadie is as desperate for release as I am. So I push a hand in her hair, grab tight, tilt her head back, and kiss her until she explodes around me.

In a rush of heat, I follow her right over the edge. I pump my hips, emptying myself inside her, joining our bodies in the most intimate way for the first time. I don't have a single fucking regret.

We're both breathing heavily. I pull her close and roll to my back, taking her with me to rest against my chest. Our hearts pound against each other, finding comfort in the other.

"What are you thinking about?" I ask.

"Trying to remember if I forgot a pill this week," she says, but there's a smile in her voice.

"From what I've heard, it's a lot harder to make a baby than they led us to believe in high school." As feeling flows back to my extremities, I trace patterns against the soft skin of her back.

"But it's possible."

"It's always possible."

"I didn't think your heart could beat any faster than it was, but..." She presses her cheek to my chest, and I feel her grin against my bare skin.

"Don't mistake that for panic. Talking about having babies with you makes me excited. For a lot of reasons." Now it's me who's grinning. If our relationship goes where I hope it's headed, I'm going to enjoy every second of the baby-making process. Which reminds me... "There's something we should talk about."

At the seriousness in my voice, she props herself up to look me in the eyes, her expression matching my tone. "What's wrong?"

Her bright eyes, pink-stained cheeks, swollen lips—I have to catch my breath, because looking at her steals the air from my lungs. "Marry me."

The tension in her face dissolves. "What?"

"You heard me." I cup her face and bring our lips together.

"Marry me, Sadie. Don't make me live one more day without you."

"You want me?"

"Fuck yeah!"

"Like, forever?"

Jesus, has she lost her mind? I sit up, bringing her with me so we're face to face on the bed. I lean over, hit the light, and open my side table, searching for something... anything... *ah-ha!*

I turn back toward her with a rubber band that I used to keep all my electrical cords together when I moved. She's naked with a pillow clutched to her chest, and I pull her left hand into mine to slip the too-big, tan elastic around her ring finger.

"Since I was aware you existed, I have been in love with you." Her eyes fill with tears as I speak, and satisfaction fills my chest. "I was so young, and I didn't realize that I had to become a man who deserved your love." I loop the band around her finger again. "Since I was a toddler, I felt like you were mine. I never considered the possibility that I could lose you. And then I did." I make another pass around her finger. "I had a lot of growing up to do. I realized that even though we were made to be together, that doesn't mean I don't have to earn your love." With a final loop, the band is tight enough to stay put but not cut off her circulation. "Like this rubber band is a never-ending circle..."

She giggles tearfully.

"No end and no beginning, so will be my love for you, forever if you'll let me." I bring her hand to my lips and kiss her ring finger. "Marry me, Sadie. It doesn't have to be next month or even next year. We'll take things as slow as you need. Just please say you'll be mine."

She sniffs, thumbs her temporary ring, then grins at me.

"*So?*" I scrunch up my face with my heart in my stomach. "Is that a yes?"

She launches at me, knocking me back on the bed. Crawling on me, she kisses me.

I turn my head, breaking the kiss. "I'm gonna need to hear you say it—"

"Yes, okay! Yes. Yes. Yes!" She punctuates each word with a kiss. "I will marry you."

I roll her over and kiss her until time fades around us and all that exists in the world is our racing hearts and eager bodies.

Life is so fucking unreal. I woke up this morning having to remind myself again that Sadie was out of reach and had moved on with someone else, only to fall asleep tonight with Sadie in my arms as my fiancé.

Like a needy animal, I'm hard and rubbing against her again. Self-control is a whisper in the back of my head as she reaches between us, grasping my erection. A hiss of pleasure escapes through my teeth.

"What's next on the tour?" she asks seductively.

"Um..." I bite my lip as she strokes me, hard and demanding. Fuck, it feels so good. "I think the, uh..."

"Bathroom?"

"I have a shower." I sound so stupid, but *ohh my...* "Fuck, don't stop."

"Take me to the shower, Jack." She licks her lips.

As if thrown from the bed by an unseen force, I'm up and pulling Sadie with me. She laughs, shimmies her dress to the floor, and steps out of it as I drag her toward the master bathroom. I reach in the shower, hit on the hot water, and when I turn around, I'm slammed back against the wall by Sadie. Her smile is all sex and promises as she slides down my body to her knees at my feet.

"This is a really nice bathroom." She fists me tightly.

My hips jerk forward. "Thank... you." I swallow a lump of lust at the visual of her eyes cast up toward me with a glint of excitement.

"Do you plan to do some remodeling in here?" She licks me from base to tip.

I groan and my head falls back to the wall. She stops touching me and lifts her brow.

"What are you doing?" *Don't stop!*

"Remodel. If I'm going to be your wife, I want to hear what your plans are."

"While you're—" I gasp when she puts her mouth on me. "Um, I, uh... tile. Tile floors, and—*oh yeah.*"

She backs off again.

"Tile! And... and..."

She grins and takes me in her mouth again.

"And the shower, I'm tiling the shower. Sink. New, um... faucets, but... towels and..." At this point I'm just naming shit that goes in a bathroom. I think at one point I was throwing out random colors, any color. My head spins, and I grip her hair. "Coming."

She digs her fingers into my ass cheeks, holding me in place while the surge of my release comes from what feels like my toes to her throat. Wave after wave of euphoria washes over me until I'm left drained and dizzy. But when her naked body slides up my torso and she fuses her mouth to mine, awareness hits me like an electrical shock. I lift her in my arms, bring her in the shower, and love her with my hands, my mouth, and my body until the water runs cold and we're a slumped heap on the shower floor.

Life with Sadie.

Loving Sadie.

From this day forward, nothing will come before her ever again.

CHAPTER TWENTY-NINE

SADIE

I wake to the feeling of Jack attempting to stretch out on the cot, and his contented groan rumbles against my back. The marine layer on the coast is thick this morning and gives me the sensation of sleeping in a cloud. With the cool breeze on my face and his warm body pressed against my back, I've never been more comfortable.

His arm snakes around my waist and I feel him smile at my ear, where he whispers, "So yeah, that's my house."

I laugh, the sound throatier than usual after a long night of making love and breaks filled with long conversations. "You're a great tour guide."

He kisses the back of my head. "I'd be happy to give you another one if you're up for it."

"Is there anything else to see?"

"Oh, baby, there's always gonna be more to see."

My giggle turns into a yawn that crawls up my throat. "Maybe later. How long did we sleep for?"

"Couple hours?"

A fish taco wrapper is kicked about by the wind and dances around the deck. After sex on the kitchen counter, we were starving. Wrapped in sheets, we pulled the cot outside and ate under the stars. No ridiculously expensive restaurant, only us under the moon with nothing between us but bedsheets. This is the Jack I remember and the kind of romance he knows I love.

With a lot of maneuvering, and some grunting, I manage to turn around and face him. We interweave our legs, and my arms are smooshed between us in order to fit. He has one arm folded under his head and the other holding me close. I study his face, the day's worth of blond scruff shadowing his strong jawline and high cheekbones. Green eyes glint from behind puffy, sleep-deprived eyelids, and his full lips quirk in that confident half-smile that has managed to make me feel warm all over since I was a girl.

"Jesus, Sadie." He pushes hair off my face with a gentle touch. "You are so fucking beautiful. I've never been able to believe you'd choose me. Not then. Not now." His eyebrows pinch together and his smile falls. "I don't think I'll ever believe it."

I wiggle my left hand free and hold up my finger wrapped loosely in the tan rubber band he gave me when he proposed. The most romantic proposal in history—at least, it was to me. "Believe it. There's no turning back." My heart thumps harder when that smile returns and he kisses my ring finger. "Moving forward. What's the plan?"

He presses my left hand to his bare chest and holds it there. "I'm going to get up, take a shower, and go to work. You should probably go home and pack your things. I'll bring home dinner."

"So the plan is I'm moving in here with you?"

"Yes." He looks at me as if I've lost my good sense. "What else would we do?"

"What if I don't want to move up here?" His home is beautiful, but I just forgave him twelve hours ago. Jumping into living together feels like more than I can handle. Besides, we're a partnership, not a dictatorship. "I guess this is the part where I gently remind you about your possessive tendencies."

He groans and rubs his eyes. "Yes. You're right." He scans the surrounding view and deck as if to take in all he'd be giving up. "I'll move in with you."

I try to hold back a laugh. "That's basically the same thing. And what about your commute to work?"

"It's doable." He hasn't taken his eyes off mine as he allows me full access to his thoughts and subtle reactions.

Wow. I think he really would give up his beach house to move into my tiny condo and room with Ricky and me. My heart expands further, filling with more love for Jack.

I kiss the tip of his nose. "I don't think moving in with me is the answer. Besides, this house is incredible. I want to live here."

"Thank, God." His shoulders lose all their tension. "Go pack your stuff—"

"Not today, Jack."

His jaw flexes and I can see he's fighting the urge to argue. I appreciate his effort and kiss him to communicate that.

Our mouths fuse together before his tongue slides against my lower lip and he whispers, "Whatever you want, babe."

Babe. I wondered if I'd ever hear him call me that again.

He nips at my mouth. "How long you gonna make me sleep in a bed without you?"

"Oh, I'll be spending most of my time here. Just not officially right away."

Ricky only let me move in with him after what happened at the beach. I'm sure he'll be relieved to see me go so he can have his place to himself again.

"I'll need space to paint."

"Not a problem."

"Like, a lot of space."

"Take however much space you need. Take a bedroom."

A bedroom? "I don't remember seeing another bedroom during the tour."

My face flushes at the memory of us moving from room to room, our naked bodies tangled in every imaginable position. Last night was different than any time we'd made love before, as we gave each other permission to stop holding back. Just thinking about it has my toes curling beneath the sheets.

"Tour's not over," he says in a low voice, his hips pressing his hardening length against my hip.

My body heats and my pulse flutters in the most intimate of places. I kiss his chest and he tilts his head back, giving me full access to his thick throat. He tastes of the salty ocean air and I inch my way to his mouth—

He presses his finger to my lips. "Hold that thought."

I ask why with my eyes because he still holds my lips.

"I have to go to work. I'm going to be a husband, I need to take my responsibilities seriously."

I grin at his cute teasing and twist away from him with a grumbled, "Party pooper."

We manage to get ourselves off the cot without major injury, and he wraps me in the big sheet before wrapping the smaller blanket around his waist.

His broad back is tan and smooth and I gasp at the red marks stripping his shoulders and ribs. "Jack, I'm so sorry."

He peeks over his shoulder at me, sees where my gaze is set, and rotates a little more to check out the damage. "Fuck, that's hot." He grins, his narrowed eyes filled with playful mirth. "When did you become such a hellcat in bed?"

My face feels as if it's going to burst into flames. "Last night, I guess?"

He cups my cheeks and kisses the heated skin. "*Do not* be embarrassed. Wearing your marks is an honor. Knowing I'm the one who made you feel free enough to do it, well..." He nips at my lower lip with a soft growl. "I'm never going to make it to work, am I?"

I shove him playfully. "Go!"

His face lights up, and he snags my hand. "First, let me show you something."

He checks the time as we pass the kitchen and seems satisfied that it's only ten after six in the morning. He drags me down the hallway toward two more doors. It was dark last night, and although I assumed the house had more than one bedroom, I didn't get a chance to see either of them.

He throws open the door to one then the other. "Take your pick."

I turn from the two rooms to him, smiling. "Really?"

"Of course." He nods toward the room with the big picture windows and ocean view. "I thought you might want to use this one as a studio. You can open the windows and get a nice breeze, not to mention the view."

"Jack..." I'm speechless. No more painting two feet from my bed.

He guides me to the doorway of the other room. This one doesn't have an ocean view, but it has windows that look out into a courtyard filled with hibiscus, lilac, and pigmy palms.

His arms come around me from behind. "Both rooms need a makeover, but I thought this one would make the perfect nursery. Maybe you could paint one of your murals on that wall?"

When I don't respond right away, his muscles tense at my back.

"Or not." He sounds nervous. Vulnerable. "Too much too soon?"

I turn in his arms and wrap myself around his middle. "It's perfect." I tell myself not to cry, yet tears form in my eyes. "I love it. I love you."

He folds himself around me. "You had me sweating there for a minute." He chuckles uncomfortably.

I pull back to get his eyes. "Did you buy this house for us?"

He licks his lips and shifts on his feet before he shrugs. "I bought this house for the life I wanted with you. I knew you had moved on, but I wasn't ready to. If I couldn't be with you, I wanted to be as close to you as I could get. I figured even if I had to do it alone, I wanted to live out the life I promised you."

"That's so sad."

He shrugs. "It's what I felt I deserved. And living here, imagining you painting in one room, our baby asleep in the other, the fantasy was better than the reality of not having you at all."

"I'm so sorry it took me so long to come around."

"Please, don't apologize. No matter what the future brings, you'll always be the best part of me. I'm done living without you."

JACK

The sun is low in the sky and I'm anxious as fuck.

When Sadie left this morning, she said she'd come back tonight. I went to work and threw myself into the latest project, hoping staying busy would make time move faster. I felt as if I'd worked a fifteen-hour day by the time I raced out of the office at five o'clock.

I came straight home and pulled out a couple steaks to grill up for dinner. At nearly seven o'clock, Sadie is still not here. I've called and texted with no response, the feeling all too familiar.

With clammy hands, I strum my guitar. I've been playing this song since I was a kid, and the notes flow effortlessly, thoughtlessly, as I try not to lose my fucking shit, thinking I've lost Sadie again.

My fingers move through the acoustic version of "Sweet Child of Mine" by Guns N' Roses on repeat. The only accompaniment is the waves beating on the rocks below. I check my phone on the table beside me. No new texts. No calls. Sickness swirls in my gut.

I'm about to drive to her place and make sure she hasn't changed her mind when I hear the slam of a car door in my driveway. Quicker than I thought I was capable of, I'm up and through the house. I swing the door open and blow out a long, shaky breath when I see Sadie's car—but she's not alone. Ricky gets out of a pickup truck that has pulled in behind her.

My feet move of their own volition. Some primal need to touch her pushes me to her. She has her eyes on Ricky, but he has his eyes on me when I wrap around her from behind.

"Oh, hey." She hugs me as best she can, embracing the arms that surround her as she falls back against my chest. "Why are you shaking?"

I nuzzle her neck, press a kiss below her ear, and whisper, "You came back." Those three words sound so pathetic, but I can't help how I feel.

She turns in my arms and peers up at me, her eyebrows pinched with concern. "Did you think I wouldn't?"

"You didn't answer your phone."

"I was waiting for Ricky to get home to help me grab my easel and a couple pieces I'm working on. I lost track of time while getting organized, and my phone died."

Ricky steps up beside us, his smile non-threatening, but it's hard to banish the images of him and Sadie together.

I try like hell to hold back a snarl when I say, "Ricky."

He must hear the lingering anger in my voice because he throws his head back and laughs. Sadie chuckles along with him.

Me? I'm the only one not laughing.

When he finally calms, Ricky offers his hand. "No hard feelings, bro."

Gritting my teeth, I shake his hand and tell myself I'm doing it for Sadie.

He pulls me in for a back-smacking hug. "You can thank me later."

"Thank you?" I pull away from him. "For what? Lying to me? Keeping me up at night imagining you with my girl?"

He turns his attention to Sadie, his brows lifted high.

She blushes. "Ricky saved all your letters and convinced me to read them."

I watch the handsome fucker smirk proudly.

"Ricky knew what I needed before I did."

"I really want to hate you," I say to him. "You've been there for Sadie, and I hate that you know her better than I do. No man has ever known her better than me."

He shrugs, not seeming intimidated in the least.

I step to him and hug him. His muscles go rigid. "Thanks, bro." When I back away, I grab Sadie's hand. "You have dinner plans?"

"No." He motions toward his truck. "No plans beyond dropping Sadie's art stuff off."

"Then let's get this stuff unloaded and throw some steaks on the grill."

Sadie squeezes my hand and leans into my arm.

"Let's do it," he says, motioning to his truck.

I kiss her knuckles. "I'm so fucking happy you're here."

"I can't believe you thought I wasn't going to show."

I square off with her, facing her head-on and dipping my chin to get her eyes. "I guess I'm still a little messed up from the last time I lost you. Eventually those fears will fade. But mark my words, Sadie girl, this is it." I grab her hand and thumb the rubber band she still wears on her ring finger. "I will never give you a reason to run again."

"You better not." Her words carry a threat even though they're said through a smile.

"Yo, Daniels!" Ricky calls from the tailgate of his truck. "You got her! Stop flirting and get your ass over here and help me!"

"Yeah, you got me," she says and slaps my ass. "Go help him."

I tackle her against her car and growl into her neck. "I love you."

After a quick, hungry kiss, I leave her out of breath and flushed to help move her life into mine.

———

That night, with Sadie's clothes in my closet, her toiletries in my bathroom, and her ass in my lap, we stare at the dark ocean with only the moon for light. I've never felt so content. My pulse moves at a steady pace, oxygen flowing in and out of my lungs with purpose but without a thought, and my life is back on track.

The best part of me has returned.

EPILOGUE

Seven Months Later

JACK

Our relationship hasn't been easy since Sadie officially moved in. We've had to work through all the ways I've hurt her in the past, but she never makes me grovel for long. And after every road-block we overcome, we're left closer than before.

There have been long nights when I've had to wake her from a nightmare and hold her as she shudders and catches her breath. She still refuses to go to the beach at night.

I couldn't stand the thought of Fabian roaming free, so I hired an investigator and a lawyer to do a little digging, looking for other victims who might be willing to come forward. If that dickhead so much as coughs on a woman without her consent, we'll pounce on a class action lawsuit. In time, I tell her, we'll nail that fucker to the wall and make the charges stick.

Until then, we live our life together and suck every ounce of joy from it.

"Stop touching my meat, asshole!" Jonah elbows my dad away from the roast they're prepping for our new and improved oven.

Having a house full of family is part of that joy. Mostly.

My dad shoulder bumps Jonah back. "You wish I'd touch your meat, you dirty fuck."

These two behemoths make our kitchen look dollhouse-sized.

"Dad, don't be so stingy." Sadie's at the cutting board, putting together a salad, when she flashes me a playful smirk. "If Uncle Blake wants to help you with your meat, let him."

"Thank you, sweetheart." The smile my dad aims at Sadie dissolves when he turns back toward Jonah. "Did you hear that, you shithead?"

"Suck it, Daniels." Jonah opens the oven.

"Don't put it in! Not yet!"

"That's what she said!" Sadie chimes from her spot across the shrinking kitchen.

My dad chuckles, and Jonah scowls at his daughter.

"Uh oh, he's going for it," she says through her laughter. "He's sliding it in!"

Jonah closes the oven door and turns on her. "I'm not sure I like the way these Daniels men are rubbing off on you."

I raise my hand. "Guilty. Rubbing off on Sadie is one of my favorite things to do."

My dad and Sadie respond in unison.

"Jack!"

"Oh shit..."

Jonah slowly turns his glare on me. "Future son-in-law or not, I'm not afraid to make you disappear."

"You wouldn't dare. Not on Christmas Eve." I'm laughing while preparing another round of margaritas for my mom and Raven, who are enjoying the view from the deck.

"Yeah, Vajonah." My dad snags some sliced cucumber off Sadie's cutting board. "It's Christmas Eve. You should've let me put my special seasoning on that roast."

"I've seen what your special seasoning is capable of." Jonah stares pointedly at me. "I want none of that near my food."

My dad freezes. "Don't talk shit about my seasoning."

"Thanks, Dad. Nice to see you're defending your seasoning and not your son." I grab the drinks.

Sadie leans over to give me a kiss and whispers, "I love you and your seasoning."

I fucking adore this woman.

I kiss her back then carry margaritas and beers through the living room, where Carey is flopped on our couch, his legs hanging off one end, his phone pressed to his face. "Why don't you put the phone down and hang with your family?"

He smirks at me. "No can do, brosky." He flips his phone around and flashes me a picture of a half-naked woman who seems ten years older than his eighteen years. "Got a female interested in meeting up tonight."

"Where'd you meet a woman? You've been here for a day."

He hefts his big body—all long legs and wide shoulders—off the couch. He shrugs. "She works by the pool at our hotel."

"Be careful or your dick will fall off before you hit twenty-one." I slide the glass door open with my foot.

"He's right, son," Jonah calls from the kitchen. "Ask Blake. He lost his to a nasty case of crabs. Ate his shit right off."

My dad laughs. "You lying prick—"

I slide the door closed before I have to hear those two go back and forth for another round. A person on the outside would never know they like each other by the way they talk to one another.

Raven and my mom are mid-conversation when I set their drinks on the patio table.

"Thank you, honey," my mom says and turns back to Raven. "Summer would be the perfect time of year to get married."

"Or winter in Vegas," Raven says.

Sadie steps outside, and I'm struck for the billionth time by her beauty. Her long hair in a loose braid that stands out against her bright red sweater—and those jeans. Good God, I've been fighting a hard-on all afternoon from staring at her ass in that denim. But her beauty comes second only to her heart. I'm the luckiest man on earth to call her mine.

She steps up next to me. "They're at it again?"

I snag my beer. "Non-stop since they got here."

Sadie squeezes my hand. "Let them have their fun."

"Winter as in next year?" My mom pouts. "That's so far away."

I lean close to Sadie's ear. With her hair pulled back, it's easy to get to the bare skin of her neck. I kiss her there because I can't resist. "You know, if you wanted to release all wedding plans to our moms, they could plan it and all we'd have to do is show up at the right time and place."

She grins. "Wouldn't that be nice? I don't know if it's because of all the years I spent in catering or what, but I have no desire to plan a wedding."

"We could elope."

Her smile grows bigger. "Now you're talkin'—"

"Elope?" My mom's voice rises an octave. "You *did not* just say elope."

"Mom, calm down—"

"No way they'd elope," Raven says. Her unique blue-green eyes, which match her daughter's perfectly, sear through me. "Right, Jack?"

I clear my throat. "We might."

"What?" they screech in sync.

"Mom," Sadie says, "you have to understand—"

"Ricky's here!" Carey yells through the open sliding glass door.

Thank God.

Ricky comes out to the deck dressed in a tight-fitting Henley and dark jeans. His white smile flashes at my mom and Raven, erasing all thoughts of weddings and probably replacing them with thoughts of the cougar kind.

"Merry Christmas, ladies," Ricky says, his voice seeping charm.

They both squeal and jump up to hug him and offer him the seat between them. Sadie giggles, and I shake my head as our moms act like sixteen-year-old girls around Ricky.

Eventually he makes eye contact with me and nods once, telling me everything I need to know.

Perfect.

SADIE

"Everyone come inside for a minute."

I hear Jack make the announcement to everyone on the deck.

After a delicious meal of my dad's famous roast (minus Blake's seasoning), scalloped potatoes, creamed spinach, fresh salad, and enough rolls to build a raft, Jack and I cleaned dishes while our family digested outside.

I was drying the final platter when Jack smirked and said, "I'll be right back," before he disappeared through the front door.

Our parents, Carey, and Ricky file in from outside and take seats in the living room. They all grunt and groan, complaining about how full they are, and even though I've grown up spending holidays with Jack's family, this particular holiday feels all the sweeter now that we're engaged.

"Sadie, get over here." Jack is standing in the living room, and he holds his hand out to me with a mischievous grin. "Come here."

I put down the dishtowel and move toward him. "You look like you've been up to no good."

He kisses my temple, and in a dark voice heavy with meaning, he growls, "You have no idea."

I suppress a shiver.

Clearing his throat to shake off any lingering lust, he hooks his arm over my shoulders and addresses our family and Ricky. "I have an early Christmas present—"

"Yes!" Jack's dad jumps from the couch, his fist pumping the air. "You're pregnant! Fuck. Yes."

Jack frowns. "Dad—"

"She's not pregnant, asshole." My dad's scowl pierces through Blake, but he doesn't seem to notice or care. "They're not married."

My mom and Layla snort-giggle simultaneously.

"Mr. Slade, you do know people have sex before they're married," Ricky says.

My dad shoves a big finger at my best friend. "Shut. Up."

"Uh, yeah," Raven says through a grin. "He knows."

Jack shifts uncomfortably next to me. "Can I please talk?"

"If we're going to keep talking about my sister's sex life," Carey says and stands from the couch, "I've got places to be."

"Sit." Jonah stares at Carey until the guy throws up his hands and sits. "And your sister doesn't have a sex life."

"More than a river in Egypt—*ouch!*" Blake rubs the shoulder Layla smacked. "No hitting!"

Layla nods to Jack. "Ignore them. Go on."

Jack huffs out a frustrated breath. "Right, so... I have an early Christmas present for Sadie."

He darts into the hallway, probably headed for one of the bedrooms where I assume he's hidden my gift.

Like a Rolodex, my mind sifts through the different things Jack would give me for our first Christmas as an engaged couple.

Diamond ring.

Diamond bracelet.

Diamond earrings.

Expensive watch.

All beautiful things any woman would love to get from the man they love, but I've always appreciated the simpler things—something Jack knew well about me when we were in high school but seemed to forget. Don't get me wrong, he's getting better, but I still have to remind him that thousand-dollar dates don't mean as much to me as the ones that come from the heart, regardless of cost.

I prepare my fake response, assuming it must be something flashy if he's decided to give it to me in front of my family. *Oh my gosh, I love it!* or *Jack, you shouldn't have!*

Then I hear the pitter-patter of paws on the hardwood. My thoughts dissolve the instant Jack comes around the corner with a leash in his hand.

Attached to the end of the leash?

My hand flies to my mouth and I scream. Yep, full-blown scream.

The room erupts in a series of "Awww"s and I drop to my knees as Jack leads the little brown-and-white beauty straight into my arms.

Tears spring to my eyes as I cuddle the tiny puppy. "Jack!" I sob. "A puppy?"

He drops to his knees next to me, his watery gaze sliding between me and the sweet angel currently licking my face. "Merry Christmas, Sadie girl."

I collapse into Jack's arms, the puppy blurry in my tear-stained vision. "He's perfect."

"She's a girl, babe." He chuckles, but the sound is tainted with emotion. "She's a boxer, and she's eight weeks old."

"I love her!"

Jack's lips touch my ear. "She'll protect you when I'm not around. At home, on walks, even at night if you want to walk on the beach."

I cough on an ugly cry. To think I assumed he'd give me some meaningless expensive gift. He gave me the gift of security and companionship when he's not around. The idea of having a powerful protector with me when Jack isn't brings a fresh round of tears. Happy tears. Emotion born of love and security.

It takes minutes before I'm able to calm down enough to look around the room, remembering we aren't alone. I swipe my cheeks. "I feel so stupid. I wasn't expecting a puppy."

"She's sweet, isn't she?" Ricky squats next to me to pet her. "Jack had me keep her last night and bring her up today."

"What's her name?" Carey says, petting her.

Jack shrugs and looks at me. "She's your dog."

I scoop her under her tiny armpits and hold her up. She has a white patch on her chest and snout, her nose still pink against her black mask. "She's the color of honey. Are you Honey?"

Her ears perk up, and Jack pets her tiny head. "She likes it."

I nuzzle the puppy. "Thank you, Jack."

"I love you, babe." He kisses me softly. "Merry Christmas, beautiful."

JACK

"She's finally asleep." Sadie tiptoes across the room, leaving Honey on her dog bed. "Hurry, take off your pants." She drops her sleeping shorts and panties to her ankles, and I stare stupidly while she rips off her shirt. "Jack!"

"Huh?" I can't pull my gaze from her breasts, round and heavy and tipped with dark, plump nipples.

"What are you waiting for?" She rips the comforter off me to reveal my pajama pants now tented with a growing erection. My jaw falls open when she crawls over me on all fours to snag the remote from my hand and turn off the television. "We don't know how much time we have."

"Uhh..."

She tugs on the elastic of my pants, freeing my erection. I suck in a breath when she takes me in her hand, literally jerking me to life.

"Don't stop." With my heel to the bed, I push up and roll over so Sadie is beneath me.

Her thighs fall open in eager invitation. "If we're quiet, we probably have an hour, maybe more."

"An hour?" I lick the seam of her lips. "I've been teased by your tits in that sweater and your ass in those jeans all night, babe. No way I'll last an hour." I grip my dick over her hand, running the tip through her wetness.

She gasps. "Maybe I'll need an hour."

"Nope." Back and forth, I tease her, pressing, pulling away, swirling my tip where she needs it most. "I'll light you up in five minutes tops."

She nods and moans. "Yes."

I continue working between her legs and kiss her long and hard. "How do you want it?"

I feel her racing pulse against my skin. Her quickened breath ghosts against my lips, her eyelids heavy.

"Rough," she whispers.

"You got it." I groan and sink my tongue between her lips while punching my hips forward, burying myself in one thrust.

Her nails mark my back, her thighs wrapping around my hips. I rock into her, milking gentle cries from her lips as she begs for more. Every sound she makes spurs me on, fuels my muscles, and increases my pace. I hook her leg with one arm, opening her wider, taking her deeper, losing myself completely to every gasp and shuddered breath between us.

I kiss her neck, lick along her collarbone, and bite her lip. "You like it like this?"

Her answer comes as a guttural moan.

A smirk twinges the corners of my lips. "Hold on."

I roll to my back. With a sexy-as-fuck toss of her hair, she sits astride me, towering over me, back arched and hands braced on my abs. With every day that passes, I swear she couldn't get more beautiful, yet she does.

My Sadie.

I cup her breasts possessively as she rolls her hips. Her pelvis tilts, searching for the sweetest contact, and when she finds it, her lips fall open in silent pleasure.

"Ride me."

I don't have to ask twice. As if getting the permission she'd been waiting for, her rhythm speeds up. My toes curl and the muscles in my abdomen flex so hard they ache as she swirls her hips and takes me hard.

"Jack," she whispers through staccato breath.

"Right here," is all I can get out before I'm thrusting up, meeting her pound for pound.

Tension coils at my spine, my orgasm at a boil and on the brink. Grasping. Chasing. Reaching. She bites my lip, slams down on me, and explodes. Her release squeezes, tugs, sucks my own to the surface. With her name on my lips, I bow off the bed and fill her while she's still riding out her release. Drawing pleasure while giving it, mixing in the most intimate way, in my orgasm-fogged brain, I hear a tiny mewl.

I decide whatever it is can wait, but cold air hits my dick as Sadie jumps off of me. "Oh, poor baby. Did we wake you?"

I rub my eyes, hoping to get some vision back after that brain-numbing orgasm. "Maybe we need to get a kennel and put Honey in one of the spare rooms—or not."

Sadie's already under the covers with her head on my shoulder and the puppy between us. "No way. Look, she fits perfectly right here."

I roll to my side, stare into her eyes, and pet the pup. "She won't always."

My woman pouts.

I sift my fingers through her hair. "Can't say no to you, babe."

She closes her eyes, a soft smile playing on her kiss-swollen lips as I continue to play with her hair. "Thank you." A yawn escapes. "I love you, Jack."

Those three little words sink deep into my soul. With my entire life in my arms, I kiss her forehead and remind her for the millionth time... "You'll always be the best part of me, Sadie girl."

WHERE IT ALL BEGAN

FIGHTING FOR FLIGHT (FIGHTING SERIES #1)

What happens when in order to win, you're forced to lose?

The only daughter of an infamous Las Vegas pimp, Raven Morretti grew up an outsider. Liberated from the neglectful home of her prostitute mother, she finds solace as a mechanic. With few friends, she's content with the simple life. Flying under the radar is all she knows and more than she expects.

Until she catches the eye of local celebrity, UFL playboy, Jonah Slade.

Weeks away from his title fight, Jonah is determined to stay focused on everything he's trained so hard to achieve. Undefeated in the octagon, he's at the height of his career. But resisting Raven's effortless allure and uncomplicated nature is a fight he can't win.

Jonah trades in his bad-boy reputation and puts his heart on the line. But when her father contacts her, setting in motion the ugly truth of her destiny, Jonah must choose. In a high-stakes gamble where love and freedom hang in the balance, a war is waged where the price of losing is a fate worse than death.

Will the hotheaded Jonah be able to restrain his inner fighter to save the woman he loves?

Or will Raven be forced into a life she's been desperate to avoid?

Read More

FIGHTING TO FORGIVE (FIGHTING SERIES #2)

When everything you avoid, turns out to be exactly what you need.

Easy and predictable, just the way he likes it, Blake Daniels flies through life the way he burns through women: on his terms, no regrets.

With his fighting career in full swing, he's on the threshold of title contention. But when his training is compromised by injury, the stakes grow impossibly higher. The rage that fuels his punches also chips away at his focus, and he risks losing everything he cares about.

He won't let that happen. Not again.

Layla's through with men. After a marriage that never should've happened, she hopes to reclaim the pieces of the woman she lost years ago.

Emotional abuse has left her insecure and terrified. A master at faking what she's not feeling, she masks her self-doubt in false confidence.

She'll never let another man hurt her. Not again.

Chased by shadows of the past, Blake and Layla know what they don't want, but their hearts have a different plan. As a web of lies and betrayal threatens to destroy them, they're forced to make a choice.

Is love enough to heal even the deepest wounds?

Or will they be left Fighting to Forgive?

Read More

ALSO BY JB SALSBURY

THE FIGHTING SERIES

Fighting for Flight

Fighting to Forgive

Fighting to Forget

Fighting the Fall

A Father's Fight

Fighting for Forever

Fighting Fate

Fighting for Honor

The Final Fight

Uncaged: A Fighting for Flight Short

THE MERCY SERIES

Ghostgirl

Saint

STANDALONE NOVELS

Split

Wrecked

LOVE, HATE, & ROCK-N-ROLL SERIES

Playing by Heart

Skipped a Beat

ACKNOWLEDGMENTS

To the crew of people who help bring my books from my brain to the page.

Piper Regan, thank you for your nitpicky critter skills and your elephant brain. I couldn't do this without your insight and memory.

Joy Editing, thank you for your eagle eye and for making me come across as way more grammatically correct than I really is. ;)

Thank you to Rebecca Shea and Ginger Scott for all the Write Clubs that helped me pull out of life and dive into productive writing seshes with you.

Thank you to Rose at Read by Rose for her amazing proofread.

A big huge thank you to all the bloggers who have supported and continue to support my work. I do not know what I would do without you.

Thank you to every Fighting Girl who begged for Jack and Sadie's book to be written. You (Tom Cruise sign language) complete me. I love you all so much and wouldn't be able to do what I love for a living if it weren't for you.

Last but never least, to my wonderful husband and daughters

who inspire me daily. You are my world and the reason I believe in love.